GLENN TRUST

SOLE SURVIVOR

GLENN TRUST

SOLE
SURVIVOR

VINCI
BOOKS

By Glenn Trust

Sole Justice

Sole Survivor
Road to Justice
Target Down
The Ghost
Dark Winter
Shadow Man

For the survivors.

Vinci Books

vinci-books.com

Published by Vinci Books Ltd in 2025

1

Copyright © Glenn Trust 2019

The author has asserted their moral right to be identified as the author of this work in accordance with the Copyright, Designs and Patents Act 1988.
This work is a work of fiction. Names, characters, places and incidents are the product of the author's imagination or are used fictitiously. Any resemblance to actual persons, living or dead, places and incidents is entirely coincidental.
All rights reserved. No part of this publication may be copied, reproduced, distributed, stored in any retrieval system, or transmitted in any form or by any means, including photocopying, recording, or other electronic or mechanical methods, nor used as a source for any form of machine learning including AI datasets, without the prior written permission of the publisher.
The publisher and the author have made every effort to obtain permissions for any third party material used in this book and to comply with copyright law. Any queries in this respect should be brought to the attention of the publisher and any omissions will be corrected in future editions.
A CIP catalogue record for this book is available from the British Library.
Paperback ISBN: 9781036704346

Printed and bound in Great Britain by Clays Ltd, Elcograf S.p.A.

ONE

Universal Law

He was alone now, on the move. He liked it that way. Moving meant he didn't have to think. Thinking was bad. Thinking made him remember, and he didn't want to remember.

Death. That was a thing he didn't want to remember. It was a thing to forget.

Thinking about it brought the questions, and there were too many of those. One lived, and one died. Why? That was the big question.

He shook his head. No, it wasn't a question at all. It was a fact, clear and immutable.

One lived, and one died. Why? For the sake of some unfathomable, inscrutable order in the universe ... Karma ... what goes around comes around ... God's will? It was irrelevant.

When it was your turn ... when it happened ... it happened, and that was it. Done.

There was no way to run from it. It was like gravity, holding everyone down. There was no way to escape it. You might just as well try to step out of a window and fly. Gravity wins out every time and cracks your skull open like a melon.

It was a universal law. It held things together and kept them from flying out into space. Maybe a few skulls were cracked, but by God, there was order in the universe.

That was death, a universal law, cold, heartless, unfathomable. One lived, and one died. There was no *why* to it. John Sole nodded as he drank, finally accepting the truth of it.

Somewhere, planets careened into each other in great cosmic explosions, wiping out entire worlds of people. They had no choice in the matter. The universe was an asshole. It didn't matter why.

A voice crept into his mind. It was the voice he had been trying to drink into silence.

Who are you kidding, John? You know the truth. Death doesn't always *just happen*. Sometimes, there is a reason. He looked into the bar mirror and lifted the glass to his lips. Admit it, John. Sometimes, you're the reason.

He nodded. Right, sometimes there is a reason.

Tired eyes stared back at him. God, he looked old. That was a law too. Everything got old. John Sole had gotten old.

He scratched the salt and pepper stubble covering his cheeks and chin. How long had it been? A month? A year? An eternity.

The face in the mirror was haggard. The dark, short-cropped hair had grayed around the temples. Deep wrinkles, etched around the eyes and forehead, marked the memories he carried—would always carry. He turned the glass up, drained it to the bottom and shook his head, but the memories remained.

TWO

Just Ask Felipe

Sometime earlier...

Dust blew into the truck's cab coating their faces, settling into every wrinkle, crevice and bodily orifice. The sweat rolling down from their brow left dirty smudges in the fine grit before dripping off their jaws.

Outside, the temperature soared above one hundred and ten degrees. Inside, the old box van's air conditioner had long since given up the ghost.

The two men in the truck found relief by dousing their shirts with water from one of the many gallon jugs they carried and opening the windows so that the hot air blowing in evaporated the water from their clothing. The cooling effect was temporary, but it provided a respite from the oppressive heat. When their clothes dried, they repeated the process.

They bounced along on a routine trip across the Sonoran Desert of Northern Mexico. At Cuitaca, they left Highway 2 and proceeded north across the desert, staying away from the border crossings at Nogales, Naco, and Agua Prieta. The backcountry dirt tracks and trails they followed had been there for centuries but were now largely forgotten. In some places, crews had been brought in to improve the dirt road with picks and shovels. It was an expensive process, but the truck's owner could afford it.

The men in the truck saw that there had been improvements since their last trip a month ago. They joked that Bebé must have money to burn, to send men with shovels and picks out into the desert, a hundred kilometers from anywhere, to patch a hole in a road that no one else used. In truth, Bebé had more than money. He had lives to burn, the lives of those who relied on him for their sustenance.

After bumping for hours across the desert, they approached the border with the United States. The driver eased the truck down a low bank into a dry wash and parked in the scant shade provided by a cluster of ocotillo plants.

The first part of the job was complete. Now came the hard part, to wait in the truck under the desert sun.

"Aiyee. it is hot today." The man behind the wheel, Ernesto pulled a soiled handkerchief from his shirt pocket and wiped his face, streaking the dust that had collected there and leaving dark circles of dirt under his eyes and around his nose.

He was a veteran of many such trips. Before working for Bebé, he had driven trucks from one end of Mexico to the other. For years, he made the border crossing at Nogales regularly while employed by a small company that shipped avocados.

"You have too many years for this, old man." His companion, Felipe, saw no need to wipe at the dust on his face only to have it replaced again soon enough.

"This is true," Ernesto said, nodding. "A few more trips like this and I will ask Bebé for the pension he promised. I have done enough. I am tired, and my old woman wants me home more."

"You think there is really a pension for us?" Felipe was young, in his twenties. His job was to provide security for the truck and its cargo, at least until it crossed the border.

Armed with a semi-automatic pistol tucked into his trousers and a Remington 750 semi-automatic carbine resting butt-down on the floor between his knees, he gazed out the window. A jackrabbit huddled a few feet away under the same ocotillo. It stared back at Felipe but was not disturbed enough to leave the shade for the blistering sun.

"Sure, sure." Ernesto nodded. "Bebé has always kept his word. For me, he is a man of honor." He smiled. "And who else in Mexico pays as well as he does."

"True," Felipe said, too young to be interested in pensions. He pointed at the jackrabbit. "I could shoot that jackrabbit."

"Why would you do that?"

"For something to do," Felipe replied with a shrug. "We could build a fire later and eat it for supper."

"Have you ever eaten jackrabbit?" Ernesto pulled his upper denture out and shook his head laughing. "Too tough and stringy."

"That's disgusting, old man! Put your teeth back in."

Ernesto complied, chuckling. "Wait until your time comes. You are a young rooster now, but one day …" He nodded as he settled the denture onto his gums. "I'm fortunate to work for Bebé and have enough money to see a dentist. Otherwise, I'd be gumming my food like an old granny. You'll see. Trust me, you'll see."

The men dozed in the heat. Ernesto moved outside into

the shade of the truck, his head resting back against a tire. Felipe remained in the cab.

"You should come outside," Ernesto called. "You'll find life is less confined and a little cooler, at least."

"I'll stay here," Felipe said. "Someone has to wait for the call."

"Bring the phone with you. It works outside just as well, I think."

"I'll stay in the truck!"

"You don't have to be so touchy."

"I'm not touchy! I'm just not going to sit in the sand like some peasant taking a siesta while a rattlesnake crawls up my pants."

"Is that all!" Ernesto laughed. "Nothing to worry about. The snake will just crawl in far enough to meet the one there between your legs. Then he'll turn around and find his way out."

Ernesto laughed again and then settled back and closed his eyes. Felipe watched the immobile jackrabbit who watched him back. They remained locked in their own private Mexican standoff. Felipe had the gun, but the jack had blinding speed. Neither felt inclined to disturb the balance of power between them.

Three hours passed. The phone's electronic chime sounded harsh and brittle in the dry air, like glass breaking on concrete.

Felipe grabbed it, listened and nodded. "*Bueno*."

He leaned out the window and called to Ernesto. "They're ready."

Ernesto dusted off the seat of his pants as he walked to the truck cab. "It's about time."

He climbed in behind the wheel and turned the ignition key. The engine rumbled to life. The Jackrabbit, at last, decided that caution required him to move away from the ocotillo. Felipe nodded, the victor of their battle of wills.

It required twenty minutes for them to travel the remaining two miles of rough ground to the border. The truck bumped up the final grade and came to a four-strand wire fence. A man, a *gringo*, waited for them. He opened a gap in the wire by lifting out one of the fence posts, swinging it and the wire to the side.

The truck rolled through the opening and across the sixty-feet of dirt road that the U.S. Border Patrol maintained as the boundary with Mexico. The man who had opened the fence approached the truck.

A weathered western hat, boots, dusty jeans, and work shirt made him look like a grizzled cowboy out of a movie. In fact, Sam Bergen's family had settled the area along the Arizona-Mexico border more than a century earlier, laying claim to enough of the arid ground to support a moderately sized herd of cattle. Over the years, the costs of maintaining the herd in that harsh environment had outweighed the financial return. The Bergen Ranch fell on hard times.

"*Buenas tardes*," Ernesto said as the gringo approached.

"*Buenas tardes*," Sam replied in accented but fluent Spanish.

Ernesto looked at Felipe and nodded.

"Hmph." Felipe reached into the glove box and removed a thick envelope, handing it to Ernesto who passed it through the window to Sam.

The rancher hefted it in his hand up and down a couple of times and nodded. "Feels about right." He nodded towards a shed and water tank two hundred yards in from the border.

Another truck waited in the shade, newer and marked with the logo of a local delivery company. The company had no idea that their name was being used for anything but legitimate shipping purposes.

Sam Bergen smiled, tipped his hat and watched as Ernesto put the truck in gear and moved towards the shed. His job completed, he knew it was the easiest part of the operation. There was no way he wanted to be in the hot truck bouncing over the desert on a day like today. All he had to do was open a small gap in the wire fence for Bebé Elizondo's shipments to pass into the United States—that and allow them to transfer the cargo from the old truck to one that would not be so easy to identify as a carrier of contraband.

For that service, he was paid ten thousand U.S. dollars for each truck that crossed his property. Bebé was good on his word and had never shorted him on the payment.

At Sam's request, Elizondo had even ended the illegal immigration problem on his ranch. The *Los Salvajes* cartel had put the word out to the *coyotajes* that the Bergen Ranch was off limits. The flood of illegal immigrants wandering across the ranch dried up almost overnight.

Sam Bergen was a happy man. As costs soared and profits plummeted, he had hit on the way to keep the family ranch in the black, and best of all, in the family and not foreclosed on by the bank.

Ernesto pulled the old truck up to the shed, and they began transferring the cargo to the American truck with the fancy logo painted on the side. Ernesto and Felipe passed the cartons from their vehicle to two men who loaded them on the other. The work went swiftly. They had done this many times.

"I'll bet their truck has air conditioning," Felipe grumbled as he passed a carton over.

"Yes, and dancing girls and *cerveza* too in the back," Ernesto laughed.

They had almost completed the job when a loud crack startled them. Felipe moved to the cab to retrieve the rifle. Sam Bergen stood with a revolver he pulled from his waistband pointed at the sky. A helicopter came skimming over a nearby hill, followed by two more. A line of dust showed a caravan of Border Patrol vehicles bouncing over the desert toward them.

The warning shot Sam fired came too late to be of any help. All it did was get Felipe killed.

One helicopter hovered while the others landed in a swirling, biting cloud of dust. Felipe came from the truck cab with the Remington pointed towards the first chopper. Three sharp reports, like thunderclaps, came from the sky in the direction of the hovering helicopter. Felipe crumpled to the ground, three neat holes in his chest.

DEA, FBI, Border Patrol, U.S. Customs, ICE—there were patches of every type on the various uniforms of the men who surrounded them. Except for Felipe, all the other smugglers had the presence of mind to drop at once to their knees, their hands clasped behind their heads to demonstrate they posed no threat to the officers.

Sam Bergen dropped his father's colt revolver onto the sand and put his hands in the air, old west style. He was arrested, handcuffed, and placed alone in the back of a separate van. The realization that the ranch would not remain in the Bergen family broke his spirit and his heart.

This would be one of the biggest drug busts in Arizona history, and he knew the Feds would seize the ranch and everything on it. They called it private asset forfeiture, and it was routine procedure to take the property of suspected drug dealers, whether they ever got a conviction in a court or not.

Sam was no fool. A conviction was a certainty. They would let the ranch go to waste and ruin, and then when the case was finally closed years from now and everyone, including Sam, was in prison, they would sell the ranch for pennies on the dollar. He wept in the back of the van.

Ernesto accepted his arrest philosophically. He would spend time in a North American prison. This was no big deal. He was older than most of the young roosters working for Bebé, but was fit enough to weather and survive incarceration in an American prison.

At least when he got out and was deported, he would have the pension Bebé promised. Bebé was always good on his word, and Ernesto had no doubts that he and his wife would live out the rest of their lives comfortably in a little village in Michoacán near the coast.

Still, he was not so young anymore and was not looking forward to the years away from his wife. He let out a sigh of resignation. Then they locked the van door and bumped out onto the dirt road.

Through the window, he could see a form covered with a sheet on the ground by the old truck. It was a shame about young Felipe, but the boy was *exaltado*—a hothead. It was only a matter of time for him.

Ernesto knew in this business it paid to remain calm. Emotion got you filled with holes. Just ask Felipe.

THREE

The Munchies

"How the hell do you eat that shit?"

John Sole stopped in mid-bite, a Varsity chili dog hanging precariously out of his mouth, drops of chili and mustard falling to the napkin he had tucked into the front of his shirt.

"Like this," Sole sputtered out around the loaded hot dog and bun.

With that, he shoved the remainder in his mouth. Cheeks bulging, he turned toward Randy Travis, his face spread in a close-mouthed grin, chomping and trying hard not to laugh and spit the whole mess out on the dashboard.

It was his usual order. The Varsity ordering code for it, as every true Atlanta fast-food epicurean knew, was a Heavyweight—hot dog with mustard and extra chili. The rest of the order, a bag of rags—potato chips—and a creamy frosted orange milkshake, sat in the bag between his feet on the floorboard of their unmarked Atlanta Police Department sedan.

"Shit." Travis shook his head. "That's disgusting."

"Best lunch in town." Sole grimaced and with a final enormous gulp, swallowed down the last of the chili dog.

"Did you even taste it?"

"Every last processed pig's tail and chicken foot of it."

"You're shitting me, right? No one uses that shit in people food any more, do they?"

"That's the mystery of it. Keeps things exciting." Sole grinned. "But no, they promise these are made from pure beef … products."

"What the hell is that?"

"Not pig tails or chicken feet, so who cares."

They settled back. Sole opened the bag of chips and sucked on the frosted orange shake. His partner, Randy Travis navigated the busy afternoon traffic. They had worked as partners since Travis arrived in the Major Crimes Unit.

"Heads up!" Clarence Pointer, commander of the unit, called out across the rows of cubicles and investigators huddled over their computers or discussing the cases they were working. "New man joining us!"

Heads swiveled to eyeball the newcomer.

"Fresh meat," someone called out.

"FNG—Fucking New Guy—in town," another said. "A virgin. Just what we need."

Muted laughter rippled through the room as they waited for the introductions. John Sole stood and leaned against the side of his cubicle to better see the FNG.

"Ladies and gentlemen … and I use both terms with reservation," Captain Pointer continued. "This is Investigator Randy Travis. He comes to us from Zone 2 burglary. Ten years in the department."

The laughter was louder now. Tall and lean, Travis waited, the hint of a smile on his face, his brown eyes sparkling, knowing what was coming. He had been through this before.

"You're shittin' me," someone called out.

"What?" Wendell Pearson said, looking around at the other detectives, who laughed louder now. "I don't get it."

"You never heard of Randy Travis?" Pearson's partner Clarence Still leaned his beefy elbows on his desk and shook his head. "Very sad."

"What? Explain Clarence before I toss you out the damned window."

"Randy Travis," Clarence began with a sigh. "Is a famous country singer ... a legend ... you know... *Forever and Ever, Amen ... Deeper than the Holler ... On the Other Hand ...* and my personal favorite, *Hard Rock Bottom of Your Heart*."

"How the hell am I supposed to know that shit?" Wendell held up his large black hand in front of his partner's face. "You see that color, boy. They didn't play that hillbilly shit in my neighborhood."

"That's why it's funny," Clarence replied. "As you can see, Detective Travis is African American, like you." He leaned closer to Pearson, peering at his face. "In fact, I'd say he is a bit more African than you are. You look a little pale. You sure some whitey didn't get in the woodshed somewhere back down the line."

"Fuck you, Clarence." Pearson rose and stepped forward, hand extended to Travis. "Welcome to Major Crimes."

They shook hands, and the rest of the gathering took turns welcoming the new detective to their ranks.

"Alright," Captain Pointer called out. "He needs to partner up with someone. Who's up for it?"

"Wait a minute," Pearson said. "First, I want to know why your mama named you after a white hillbilly."

"Simple. She loved country music," Travis said, smiling. He'd been through this before. "Actually, my first name is Charles, for Charley Pride. She gave me Randall for Randy Travis as a middle name.

"Then why don't you go by Charley or Chuck or Charles," Clarence Still asked. "At least that would make sense ... black face ... black country singer."

"Because I enjoy seeing how it fucks with you white boys when you hear my name and see my face." Detective Charles Randall Travis grinned. "Any other questions?"

"I'll take him." John Sole stepped forward and put out his hand. "Glad to have you on board, partner."

That was three years ago. It was a perfect match, despite Travis' lack of appreciation for fast food.

Traffic had thinned in this part of the city. Dusty storefronts lined the street, some abandoned, plywood replacing the plate-glass windows on many. Others, covered with iron bars, showed the hazards store owners faced here. Some had hasps and padlocks, for additional after-hours security, although their effectiveness was doubtful.

John pointed to a corner three blocks ahead. "That's our boy."

"Got him." Randy wheeled into the curb lane, maintaining speed.

They passed the corner where a tall, thin man stood, hands in his pockets, head down, face partially concealed by the ubiquitous hoodie prevalent in this section of the city. The man ignored them as they passed.

"He saw us," John said.

"Okay."

Travis continued for a half mile then turned from the main street into a side alley. Halfway down the block, they found a spot beside an overflowing dumpster where he backed the car in, concealing it from anyone who might glance down the alley from the main street. Sole opened his door and moved to the back seat. Travis remained behind the wheel.

It took Luis Acero twenty minutes to make his way from the corner that served as his storefront for the sale of marijuana and the occasional eight-ball of cocaine. He slouched down the alley with the same bent posture he had standing on his corner. Hoodie pulled low over his forehead, he pivoted and opened the rear door of the sedan taking a seat beside Sole. To anyone watching from the street, it would have looked like he disappeared into a back door or was standing next to the building taking a leak.

As criminal informants went, Luis was above average. Information he provided had led Sole and Travis to several significant felony arrests. For that reason, they had advised the narcotics division of his status as their CI.

It was a mutual working arrangement between the two investigative divisions. The narc squad had their own informants, some of whom were sought by the major crimes detectives. As long as the CI provided valuable, actionable intelligence about more serious criminal activities, the detectives from both divisions cut them slack.

They couldn't ethically ignore blatant violations of the law, but they could be selective about which violations they focused on. Smart CIs took the hint and kept a low profile.

Dumb ones went to jail. Natural selection tended to weed out the dumb ones. Luis Acero had always been one of the smart ones.

In his case, that meant that he could sell street-use quantities of drugs to his customers on the corner and the narcs looked the other way. If at some point, he failed to provide useful information, or it turned out to be unreliable, the deal would be off, and they would look hard at his operation.

He lived life on shaky ground under terms that would make most people perpetually paranoid. Criminal informants like Luis thrived on it, considering paranoia a cost of doing business.

It was also a risk. Over the years, more than one CI had been found out to be a rat and had gone missing or turned up with a bullet hole through the head or throat slashed and left in a dumpster to rot.

"What do you have for us?" Sole asked as Luis settled in.

"Not much." Luis reached for the pack of cigarettes in the pocket of his hoodie.

Travis sighed and rolled down the window. He hated going home smelling like an ashtray after one of their meets with the CI. Sole pulled out a lighter, spun the wheel with his thumb and lit the cigarette for Luis.

"Not good enough," Travis said from the front seat, watching him in the rearview mirror.

"He's right." Sole nodded. "Been a month since you gave us anything. Time to pay up or lose your good standing."

"What about the pawn shop on Moreland fencing stolen shit? That paid off."

"Small time." Sole shook his head. "We hit it. Couple of flat screen televisions and an old Ruger pistol. We closed the shop, but nothing much came from it. I'd say your account is in arrears."

"Fuck. I ain't got nothin' right now." Luis moved his hands in front of his face holding them palms up to show how empty the criminal information industry was at the moment.

"Got to be something, Luis, my man. Think. We don't want to be forced to revoke your get out of jail free card."

"Shit." Luis lowered his head and took a long drag on the cigarette. After a few seconds, he looked up, letting the smoke swirl from his mouth and nose to encircle Travis' head. "There might be something."

"What?" Sole asked. "Let's have it."

"That's the thing."

"What's the thing?" Travis said from the front. "You're making it sound like we might have to call in your debt."

"There's something ..." Luis shook his head, turning to look Sole in the eye, trying to indicate his sincerity. "Thing is I don't know what. There's talk about some new players coming to town."

"What kind of players?" Sole's mouth twisted into a doubtful smirk.

"Drugs. Not your kind of shit. It'd be for the narcs."

"We'll take it and see how it turns out. If it's good info, it might clear the books for you, for a while."

"But it's like I told you. I don't know what, but the talk is big."

"You playing us, Luis?" Sole's eyes narrowed.

"Naw, man. I ain't playin' you. Uh, uh. No way I'd do that. It's just that the rumors are these big players are comin' in ... gonna change things ... but I'm not close enough to find out who they playin' with."

"Get closer."

"I'll try, man. I'll try."

"Don't try, Luis. Trying isn't worth shit. You get as close to the action as you need to bring us something … something big … something that will get you caught up with us and keep you in good standing. If you don't …"

"Shit, man. You ain't got to say it. I know about the 'if I don't' part."

"What do you think, partner? A week?" Sole spoke to Travis up front.

"Yeah." Travis nodded, looking into Luis' eyes in the mirror. "I think a week is about right."

Sole turned to the CI. "You hear that, Luis? You have a week to get close and bring us something."

"Shit. I can't make no …"

"A week," Sole said and reached across Luis to push the door open. "Get close. Bring us something … something big."

"Fuck, man. I'll do what I can do."

Luis got out as Travis cranked the car and put it in gear. Sole stepped out of the rear passenger door and looked at him over the top of the vehicle.

"Do this right Luis, and if it's big enough, you might be paid up for a while."

"Shit, man," Luis repeated his favorite phrase for every difficult situation. He shook his head and turned away, heading back down the alley to the street.

"What do you think?" Travis asked as Sole sat down in the front seat.

"He was nervous."

"Yeah. More than normal." Travis shrugged. "Maybe because we threatened to take away his status?"

"Yeah, but it felt like more than the usual street jive nerves." Sole nodded. "There could be something big going down, and our boy might be afraid of the fallout if he gets too close. Just have to wait and see."

"Story of our lives."

"Hey," Sole said, energized. "Let's swing by McDonald's. I could use a bag of fries and a Diet Coke."

"You ate that shit from The Varsity an hour ago." Travis shook his head in disgust.

"Yeah, but jerking a CI always gets me high. I got the munchies."

FOUR

Beginnings—1973

He was gone. That was no surprise. Monty was never around when she needed him.

Her back arched, front teeth biting down on her lower lip, Clara Sole's hands clawed and clenched the sofa cushions until her knuckles turned white. The baby was coming.

"Monty!" she shrieked through the contraction. "Where are you?"

She knew where he was. Elvin Lamont Sole was lost. He had been that way since returning from Viet Nam, a twenty-two-year-old veteran of a foreign war that had taken his life as surely as if he had died in a jungle ambush.

Gaunt and hollow-eyed, he returned to Cassit Pass in the mountains of North Georgia. Clara had written to her high school sweetheart while he was away, had continued writing even when his scribbled letters stopped coming.

The homecoming was simple. There were no fanfares, parades, or welcome committees. There was a hesitant knock on her parent's front door. Clara opened it and stared in shock. Monty had come home.

Still dressed in his Marine Green Class A uniform, duffle by his feet, he was suddenly there. No letter. No phone call. One day, he just appeared on the doorstep.

Her parents, her friends, his friends even, told her she should move on. Monty was damaged goods. Viet Nam had taken something from him, sucked it from his soul. Monty never spoke about it.

Clara did not move on. She wrapped her arms around him. Over time, she tried to bring him back from the dark place where his thoughts wandered. A glimmer of the happy boy who had gone off to war would flash across his face. She hoped, prayed, that he was coming back to her, leaving the unspoken pains behind.

The hope was enough. Clara loved Monty, and over the objections of her parents, they scheduled their wedding. For a while, her love was enough. He improved, smiled more often, pushed the darkness from his eyes.

He took long, solitary walks through the mountain passes, following the game trails that switch-backed across the hillsides. When he showed up at the small home they rented five miles out of Cassit Pass, he would sit quietly beside her on the threadbare sofa. Clara would take his hand into her lap and hold on to it, cling to it. When she did, Monty turned his head and smiled. Then his eyes would wander off to the ceiling, and he was away, again, as gone as if he were still out roaming the hillsides. He was out there tonight, somewhere in the hills, lost to her when she needed him most.

She groaned. It wouldn't be long now. No one had coached her on how to give birth, but instinctively she panted and pushed. Legs spread, she leaned back in the sofa, bracing her heals on the cushions. She clenched her eyes shut, unable to pant, the contraction taking her breath away.

Then it was over. In a final torrent of blood and pain, John Sole came into the world.

FIVE

A Man at Peace

Juan Manuel Elizondo was a man at peace. That is not to say he was a peaceful man. He was not. He had learned over the years that there was no profit in peace.

On this bright morning, he stood on the tiled patio of his expansive home in the hills behind Lázaro Cárdenas. The sun rising behind him cast a soft orange glow over the city below and the Pacific Ocean beyond.

The bustling activity in the port pleased him. From above, he could see the trucks service the ships, cranes lifting cargo containers to swing them out over the decks of the giant vessels, men scurrying like ants to secure and ready the cargo for shipment overseas. Some of that cargo was his, and that pleased him more than anything.

The day below brightened all at once as the sun made its final lunge and lifted over the surrounding hills. He smiled at the favorable omen.

Soft footsteps approached from behind and then stopped, waiting for him to turn.

"Yes, Alejandro," he said, his eyes fixed on the activity below.

"It is time, *Jefe*."

"Yes." He stood for a moment before turning with a sigh. "There is business to settle. Unfortunate on a day such as this."

"Unfortunate but necessary," Alejandro Garza said, nodding.

Garza had been with the *jefe* from the beginning, growing up with him on the streets of Morelia. Cara de Bebé—Baby Face as Elizondo was known in those days for his smooth child-like countenance—had been the brains, the innovator behind their schemes.

Serious, grave even, Alejandro had been the enforcer, executing Bebé's will without passion. Feared by their underworld competitors, his unalterable dedication to his assignments was an awesome thing to see. For those who were the subjects of his work, it was terrifying.

"Yes, my friend. You are correct as usual. Let us tend to this business now while the day is young. Then we can put it away from us."

They walked through the mansion, passing through the kitchen where Elizondo's three children sat eating their breakfast. His wife stood at the stove preparing tortillas, eggs, and rice. Even now, she insisted on making the meals for the children although they had wealth enough to hire a hundred cooks if they desired.

"*Papi*! Eat with us," his oldest daughter called out, smiling over a plate and around the school books stacked beside it.

Elizondo kissed his wife, Sofia, on the cheek. She smiled as he nuzzled her for a moment and continued cooking. He turned to the table and kissed each of the children on the forehead, giving each round face a tender pat on the cheek.

"I can't just now, my loves. I must attend to business."

"You always have business," Rosa the youngest pouted. She pointed at Alejandro. "Especially when *he* is here."

"You must not be rude to Alejandro, Rosa." Elizondo spoke softly and leaned over to kiss her again on the forehead. "*Tio*—Uncle—Alejandro is our good friend and protector."

Alejandro watched the exchange without expression or comment.

"Now, say you are sorry," Elizondo said, giving her a stern look.

"I'm sorry, *Tio* Alejandro," the little girl whispered, looking at her plate.

"*Está bien pequeño.*" It's fine little one.

Alejandro relented with one of his rare smiles, if the slight twitching of his cheek could be called a smile. Elizondo noted that only the children had the ability to evoke such a response from his solemn friend and partner.

"Now we must go."

The two men strode through the room to the front door and descended the steps to the expansive yard. Alejandro led the way across the lawn to a small outbuilding perched on the side of the bluff, overlooking the ocean. Stuccoed and painted to match the house, flowers and trees surrounded it. A bird sang in the branches as they passed. Alejandro led the way inside.

The interior was furnished as an office and served as the principal place that Alejandro inhabited when not with Bebé. Descending a circular iron staircase, they came to a room nestled in the side of the hillside. One wall, entirely of glass, offered a dramatic view of the ocean below. In front of the window was a chair. Three men stood around the chair watching the man seated there.

He looked up, wide-eyed, as Elizondo and Alejandro approached. Sweat dripped down the sides of his face, leaving a damp wet ring around the collar of his floral print Hawaiian shirt.

Elizondo stood for a moment before the wall of windows, contemplating the day. He truly was a man at peace with his world. It was a shame they had such work to do this day, he thought.

He shrugged and turned, with a sigh, like a man faced with an unpleasant but necessary chore.

"I understand there is a problem," Bebé said.

SIX

Interrogation

"*¿De donde eres?*" Where are you from?

The Border Patrol officer spoke perfect Mexican Spanish without a hint of the accent most picked up learning Spanish in the *Yaqui* schools.

"I thought you would know that," Ernesto said, shrugging his shoulders. "Mexico, of course."

"You are right. My question was not specific enough." The officer smiled. The DEA agent seated beside her did not. "Where is your village, *abuelo*—grandfather?" the officer asked mildly, showing respect for the old man.

The DEA agent's face remained fixed in a scowl. This particular old man had been caught trying to smuggle a truckload of narcotics across the border.

"Ah, my village." Ernesto nodded. "And how do you know that I am not from a large city?"

Annoyed, the DEA agent leaned across the table, speaking in broken Spanish. "Stop fucking around and start talking." He turned to the Border Patrol officer serving as translator. "Tell him."

"¿*Qué?*" Ernesto smiled at the drug enforcement agent.

"He warns you to cooperate ... to answer our questions," the Border Patrol officer replied.

She peered into his eyes, seeing the relaxed confidence there, not intimidated by his arrest or the bad-tempered DEA agent. There was something else in those eyes. Behind the crinkled folds of his eyelids, the officer detected amusement. The interrogation would be a game for him.

She shook her head, a smile creeping across her face at the mirth in those old eyes. Aware that the DEA agent's eyes were fixed on her, she forced the smile away.

"You should cooperate, *abuleo*. They can make things very difficult for you."

"Difficult." Ernesto shrugged, considering the word. "It is a relative thing, what is difficult and what is not. Still, if he must have an answer ..." He turned his eyes on the DEA agent and shrugged. "I suppose it is not important. Tell him I am from a small village ... Cupuán del Río, in Michoacán."

The questioning continued for four hours. Ernesto spoke at length, providing the same answers to the same questions the DEA agent repeated over and over, hoping to trip him up. By the time it ended, he had spoken many words but said almost nothing.

"How long have you worked for *Los Salvajes*?"

"I don't know any *salvajes*. I drive a truck. That is all."

"Where did you pick up your load?"

"They had already loaded the truck when I got into it."

"Who?"

"I don't know."

"Where did you get into the truck?"

"I can't remember. I am old, you see, and forgetful."

"Why did the man with you carry a rifle?"

"I was not aware he had a weapon until you killed him. Shame on you for that. Felipe was just a boy."

"Are there other ranchers like Sam Bergen, working with the cartel to smuggle drugs?"

"I don't know any ranchers' I drove the truck, and the man opened the gate. I never saw him before."

"How did you come to drive this truck full of illegal narcotics? Who hired you?"

"I have always driven trucks. People call me to drive, they pay me, I put the money in my pocket. My wife is happy. I have no idea who they are or what is in the truck."

"No idea?"

"*Nada.*"

By the end of the interview, he had chatted about life in his village and Michoacán. They knew details about his relationship with his wife and that they were childless. They learned that the lack of children had haunted Ernesto and his wife for many years, but the pain had passed and they had made peace with their bareness as they aged.

They learned much about Ernesto's personal life. They learned nothing about smuggling drugs across the border, at least nothing they didn't already know, or that would aid in the case against the *Los Salvajes* cartel.

"And you, daughter?" He said to the Border Patrol officer. "How long have you lived here, just over the border from your homeland?"

She smiled. "This is my homeland. I was born here."

"Then your parents came from Mexico?"

"My grandparents."

He looked at the name tag on her uniform. "Garcia ... I have known people of that name in Michoacán. Perhaps I knew your grandfather before he came here."

"Perhaps." She nodded and rose. "Now you must go,

grandfather. I think you will not see Michoacán for some time."

They escorted Ernesto to a holding cell in the local county jail, to await transport to a federal processing center. He stretched out on the bunk, hands behind his head, and a smile on his face, certain he had done or said nothing that would help the *gringos*. The young Border Patrol officer had a pretty smile, and he had made sure not to let her trick him with that smile into saying something he should not.

By Mexican investigative standards, the interrogation had been mild. He had not been beaten or threatened. His bones were not broken, and his few remaining teeth were all intact.

Filled with a sense of peace, Ernesto drifted off to sleep warmed by the thought he would return to his village one day to live out the rest of his life with his wife. The pension that Bebé provided them would be more than enough to make them comfortable in the quiet years of their old age, away from border crossings and trucks full of drugs.

SEVEN

Childhood–1978

"I hate him."

John Fitzhugh Sole, named for his grandfathers, sat on the floor of the tiny house outside Cassit Pass with a shoebox full of old photos on his lap. He lifted one for his mother to see and repeated, "I hate him."

"Don't talk like that, John." Clara knelt beside him and took the snapshot of a young man in uniform from his hand. It was Monty, on leave from basic training just before shipping out to Viet Nam. "He is your father. You can't hate your father."

"Why not?" The boy's brow wrinkled like an old man's, his eyes steady and defiant.

"Because he gave you life. You wouldn't be here if he wasn't your father."

The wrinkled brow spread downward into a frown at this idea. The concept that his existence was reliant upon the man in the picture was a conundrum. He considered it for a moment and shook his head, decision made.

"I'd be here," he said with certainty, pointing at the

photo. "I'm here now. He's not." He nodded to put emphasis on his decision, thus closing the discussion of his existence. "I'd be here."

"Maybe you would." Clara smiled. "Still, he is your father. You don't hate him."

"I do." Young John folded his arms to indicate his mind was made up on the matter.

Clara sighed and gathered up the box of photos to put it back on the bookshelf. She looked down at the smiling face of the soldier. Her heart flopped in her chest the way it always did when she thought of him as he was then, before the war took him away from her.

She closed the box and turned back to her son, sprawled out on the floor now, his face in a coloring book, scribbling furiously with a red crayon. They were too much alike, he and his father, she thought, far older than their years.

From his first moments, little John Sole was an old soul. Birthing him alone in this very house, she held him to her breast and looked into his eyes. Those eyes had looked back at her, not as a baby, but like an old man examining this strange creature that had thrust him from the comfort and security of her womb. Even the doctor who came afterward said he had the eyes of an old man.

Whether he wanted to believe it or not, he was like his father in that respect, feeling things, sensing things in a way far beyond his years. As she watched him, the ache built up inside, wishing that Monty was there now to see his son grow.

But he wasn't. Monty had returned from his walk in the mountains hours after his son was born. He looked at the baby and called for Clara's parents to come to the house. Then he took the baby from her arms and sat, gazing into tiny John's old eyes. Something passed between them at that moment. Monty's eyes softened. A single tear formed and trickled down his cheek.

Then he handed the boy back to Clara, stood up and walked out the front door. He never returned.

For months, Clara started at every sound. Wind fluttering against the window pane or the floorboards creaking in the cold had her on her feet peering out the window. She prayed for his return.

His reasons for leaving lay hidden in the depths of his soul, far beyond her discovering, but she knew in her heart they were not malicious. Monty was the love of her life.

EIGHT

Call Me Bebé

Juan Manuel Elizondo turned from the bank of windows to face the man sweating in the chair. He nodded at the three guards who stepped back several paces.

"So we have a problem," he repeated to the trembling man in the floral shirt.

"No ... no problem, Bebé." The man shook his head in great, wide arcs so that the drops of sweat spiraling down his face were flung to the floor with the movement. "I swear to you. This is just a temporary situation."

"Ah, temporary." Elizondo nodded seriously. "And yet, it is two months now since a full shipment has made it across the border."

"It is the North Americans!" The man's hands moved in spasmodic gyrations in front of his face as he explained. "The goddamned *gringos*! They have learned our methods." He leaned forward, glancing from side to side, before continuing in a conspiratorial whisper. "There is a spy. There must be ... someone inside who tells them of our movements ... when the shipments will cross the border.

That is why the *gringos* are there when we cross, waiting for our trucks." He shook his head to show his frustration with the damned *Yanquis* up north. "They know where we will be, sometimes before I know it. I tell you, there must be a spy." He raised his shoulders high in a dramatic shrug to show his frustration. "I am as unhappy about this as you, Bebé. Believe me, I am." He rammed his right fist into his left palm. "When I find the spy, I promise you he will pay, with his life!"

Elizondo listened in silence to the man's sweaty tirade. When he finished speaking, eyes wide and pleading for the *jefe* to understand his dilemma, Elizondo turned back to the bank of windows.

"Join me here, Miguel."

Miguel Diaz had known Bebé almost as long as Alejandro Garza. The trucking company he inherited from his father had opened a path into the North American illegal drug markets. Over time, Diaz had taken on more responsibility, not only providing trucks for shipments but developing new clandestine methods of moving the drugs across the border.

He had been an important part of the *Los Salvajes* drug cartel. As often happens, his importance had made him feel he was indispensable. He was not.

Miguel gave a glance over his shoulder at the three guards who stood nearby. Expressionless and immobile, their eyes betrayed no emotion, only a complete indifference to what was happening. A chill running down his spine, he rose from the chair to join Elizondo at the windows.

"It is a magnificent day, don't you think, Miguel?"

The aqua blue waters of the harbor below and the Pacific Ocean beyond glittered under the morning sun. The surrounding hillsides moved and fluttered with life. A crested caracara, winged past the windows, its black cap over a white throat and orange nose stood out in vivid contrast against the backdrop of the sea.

"Look at him go!" Elizondo exclaimed with obvious pleasure. "He is heading to the water to find a meal." Hands clasped behind his back as he watched the bird drop towards the shoreline below, he continued in a thoughtful tone. "This one is more a scavenger than a hunter, the caracara. He steals from other birds … more industrious birds … he takes for himself what others have worked for."

"I am not familiar with birds," Miguel whispered, a sense of dread swelling in his chest, his heart racing and turning flips that beat against his rib cage.

"Really? That's a pity." Elizondo continued. "And yet, you have much in common … you and the caracara.

"Bebé, I haven't …"

"Don't call me that," Elizondo said mildly. "My friends call me Bebé."

"But … I am your friend … I swear it!"

"My friends do not steal from me."

"Never! I swear I would never …"

"Please, Miguel. Don't speak to me as if I were a fool … your fool." Elizondo turned to face Miguel. "You think we don't know what you do? We have our sources. We can learn anything about you … everything about you." He shook his head, annoyed. "Yes, we are aware of the account in the Banco Mercantil del Norte, the one under your wife's name. The last we checked there were over four million U.S. dollars there."

Sweat soaked through his floral shirt. Miguel's body shook with violent spasms as if some invisible hand gripped his innards.

"I tell you, there is a traitor ... the money in the bank is my wife's she inherited it from ..."

"Who? Her father who worked at the Chevrolet plant in Ramos Arizpe until he died of lung cancer?" Elizondo shook his head and smiled. "I don't think the Americans pay so well as that."

"*Jefe*, yes." Miguel nodded rapidly, tears flowing down his cheeks now. "Yes, yes ... I took the money. There, I said it." He looked at Elizondo, his red, tear-filled eyes pleading. "Please. I beg you to understand. Our business is very uncertain. I only wanted to make sure that there was something for my wife and children if I can no longer provide. There is so much money, and I only took a little."

Elizondo laughed. "I admire your concept of *a little*, Miguel."

"You must believe me!" Miguel's voice rose to a shriek, his brain unable to accept the inevitable. "There is a spy ... a traitor! We will find him!"

"If there is a traitor, you should have found him already, just as we found the traitor in our midst."

"Please," Miguel sobbed.

"By the way, my contacts closed the account. They have transferred the money to an account of mine in the Cayman Islands. It was all very legal, your signature and passcodes verifying the transaction." Elizondo smiled. "You should understand that your wife and children will never see a peso of the money. I fear they may spend the rest of their lives destitute." He shook his head sadly. "You have acted stupidly, Miguel."

Shoulders shaking with his sobs, Miguel struggled to stay on his feet. There was nothing more to say. Elizondo turned to look out at the harbor and ocean through the bank of windows. He gave a small, almost imperceptible nod. Alejandro Garza stepped forward.

It was old fashioned. There was no piano wire or steel cable to cut into the neck, sever arteries and trachea and bring a merciful, speedy death. The garrote was a simple cord affixed to two wooden handles with a thick knot tied in the middle.

Alejandro flipped it over Miguel's head as he sobbed. He gave it a sudden jerk, the cords of muscle in his arms rippling as the traitor struggled, hands at his throat. Alejandro pulled tighter, and the knot crushed Miguel's trachea.

Still, he struggled, feet kicking, on his tiptoes as Alejandro leaned back using all of his strength now. Spit and mucus flowed from Miguel's nose spattering the window before him, and then his struggles became feebler, fading as the life was choked from him.

Alejandro released one end of the garrote. Miguel toppled forward to the floor, face blue, tongue protruding, a grotesque caricature of the man who had stood trembling in front of the windows a few minutes before.

Alejandro turned and nodded to the three guards, watching in silence. Their expressions had not changed. Stepping forward, they took the body of Miguel Diaz by its limp arms and legs and dragged it from the room.

After they left, Elizondo turned and motioned to a dark corner of the room. A tall man stepped forward from the shadows. Neatly pressed Capstone Italian slacks, a starched Stefano Ricci shirt open at the collar, and Gucci loafers marked him as a man of more than average wealth. A full head of distinguished silver hair contrasted with his well-tanned, ruddy complexion that had paled somewhat at the spectacle he had witnessed.

"And so," Elizondo began with a smile at his guest. "We have our own business to conduct."

"Why did you bring me here? To see that?"

They spoke in English although the well-dressed man's accent forced Elizondo to pay attention to his words. It differed from the English of other Americans he had encountered. A rhythmic flow to the words pleased his ears, reminding him of his grandmother's, lowlands Mexican drawl.

"I brought you here for you to understand the nature of our relationship."

"I already understood. I am a businessman."

"Oh, you are much more than that, I think. You will be my partner."

"I know that. I didn't need to see …"

"What? This example." Elizondo shrugged. "It would happen whether you were here or not." He nodded. "You *were* here. That is a good thing I believe. Now there can be no misunderstandings about what is expected."

"It was savage."

"It is interesting that you should use such a term. That is what they call us … our business, our cartel. *Los Salvajes* … the savages."

The tall man refrained from commenting that the name was well-earned.

Elizondo nodded at the spit mingled with blood on the window where Miguel had been standing. "He must have bit his tongue. Please have this window cleaned."

Alejandro nodded, and Elizondo turned back to the tall man. "Come. You will meet my family and stay here in the hacienda during your visit with us."

"I have hotel reservations in the city."

"Nonsense, my friend. There are no good hotels in

Lázaro Cárdenas. You will stay with us." He whirled to lead the way to the staircase. "My wife is an excellent cook and insists on preparing the family meals. A bowl of her *sopa tarasca* followed by a plate of *corundas* will bring the color back to your face." He mounted the stairs that led to the upper room and the door to the yard. "Come! My little ones will be thrilled to meet a real American all the way from Georgia in the *Estados Unidos*."

The tall American had no choice. He followed up the circular wrought iron stairs. "As you wish, Senor Elizondo."

"Oh, call me Bebé!" Elizondo called over his shoulder. "Please, all of my friends do."

NINE

Eruptions

He was in over his head. Luis Acero felt it as soon as he walked through the front door of the Eruptions Lounge in upscale Midtown Atlanta.

In one of the wealthiest sections of the city, Eruptions was an exclusive night spot for local high rollers and affluent out-of-towners staying at the nearby Four Seasons or Ritz hotels. With four bars inside spread out over three levels and several dance floors and private seating areas, there was something for everyone at Eruptions, if they could afford it.

Luis looked around, realized he had underdressed, and tucked in his shirttails. As for the rest of his attire, there was nothing to do about it now. For a second, he considered leaving, but the words of that fucking detective rang in his ears.

Get us something ... get close to the action ... bring us something big ... get paid up with us ... get in good standing ... or else.

The detective had *ojos misteriosos*—mystery eyes. Luis

could never tell what was behind them. All he could do was take the cop at his word. Bring them something big or he would be out of business, or worse, in jail.

He was trapped. He had opened his mouth about something he knew very little about. Now, he had to find out more and hope there was something there.

That meant he had to be where the players were, and those players were far above him in Atlanta's criminal hierarchy. They soared in the stratosphere while he crawled along the sidewalks selling drugs on a dirty street corner. The players were here tonight.

Atlanta's beautiful people swirled by and around him in a blur of color and bling, as he considered his dilemma. He fingered the fake diamond stud in his ear and made his way to a bar on the third level. A ten dollar shot of tequila in his hand, he turned to survey the room as he sipped.

He was in the right place. Private seating areas were spaced around the perimeter of the room. All were occupied.

In one, a group of young executive types, shirt collars unbuttoned to reveal tan lines and well-muscled physiques, sat buying expensive drinks for the sort of women who didn't walk the streets like the women Luis knew, although they performed the same services for their clients. Like the drug hierarchy, these prostitutes were a class above, making more in a night than most street whores did in a month.

Similar groups occupied the other seating areas. Some were older, locals having a night away from their wives.

The faces at one table were familiar, local professional athletes. Luis recognized one, in particular, a member of the Atlanta Falcons football team, known for his expensive taste in jewelry, clothes, and cars.

The table in the farthest, darkest corner was the one he

sought. Bautista Ortega, known on the streets as El Toro—The Bull—sat with his back to the wall so he could see the room. Three others were with him, including a *gringo* in a conservative business suit that might have been expensive but in Eruptions was equivalent to wearing a tuxedo at Mardi Gras. He stood out.

Luis sipped the tequila and focused on the *gringo*. It might be nothing, but a man like that, dressed like that, sitting at a dark corner table with El Toro must mean something.

"Luis, what are you doing here?"

Esteban Moya, a senior dealer and lieutenant in Ortega's organization tapped him on the shoulder. Luis spun, nearly spilling his drink.

Moya stared at him, eyeing Luis up and down as if he were naked. A voluptuous black woman held his arm. She wore a dress cut down the front, exposing most of her breasts, the tips of her nipples just concealed, while her enormous areolas were almost entirely revealed.

Heart racing, Luis paid her no attention.

"Esteban," he said, mind spinning over what to say next.

Moya repeated the question. "What are you doing here?"

"Here? At Eruptions?" Luis gave a shrug he hoped didn't look too nervous. He lifted the tequila. "Just having a drink."

"Bullshit. You come here to have a drink?" Moya shook his head. "I don't think so." He leaned closer. "I saw you watching over there … El Toro. Why?"

"No reason, Esteban. I just …"

"Why?" Moya nodded to one of the goons standing near Ortega's tables.

"Nothing … it's just that …" Luis stammered. "I been

having trouble getting inventory. You know things been slow down on my end. Just thought I'd come by and see if I could find out when things gonna smooth out again." He tapped his back pocket where he kept his wallet and managed a weak smile. "I'm hurtin', man. That's all. Can't bring home the bacon if I don't have inventory. You know how that is."

"Problem?" Ortega's man stood beside Moya.

Eyes fixed on Luis, Moya shook his head. "No, I can handle it."

"Okay." The goon nodded toward the table in the dark corner. "He said, whatever it is, take care of it ... now."

Moya turned and bowed his head politely toward the table and to Ortega who had stopped speaking to the gringo in the suit and was watching from across the room. The gringo turned in his seat for a second to follow Ortega's stare and then turned his back again.

"Tell him it is taken care of," Moya said.

The goon eyed Luis for a moment, turned and went to resume his protective position near Ortega's table. Luis struggled to keep from voiding his bladder in the middle of the floor.

Moya turned to the girl and pulled a hundred-dollar bill from his pocket. "Here, go get yourself something to drink at the bar. I'll be right back."

She smiled, took the bill without speaking and walked away, hips swaying deliciously under the tight fabric of her dress. At any other time, Luis' eyes would have been fixed on her ass as she walked. Tonight he was trying to squeeze his bladder shut, praying they didn't have another goon and a car waiting for him downstairs.

"Come with me," Moya said, taking Luis by the arm,

steering him to the stairs that led to the lower levels. They walked down a flight, Moya still holding his arm. On the landing, he leaned close to Luis. "Don't do this again. Don't come to a place like this again. You don't belong here, and when you come around, it looks like you're trying to start trouble."

"I didn't mean to." Luis shook his head solemnly and emphatically. "I mean it's just …"

"I don't give a shit about your inventory, *cabrón*. We're all hurting right now. There's been problems with supply coming in. What you think El Toro is doing up there?" Moya leaned close enough that Luis felt his bourbon breath on his face. "He's trying to work out the supply problems. You show up like that … watching … you could fuck it all up … Ortega saw you. You're lucky he didn't have that goon take you out and leave you in a ditch with a hole in that fucked up head of yours."

"I'm sorry," Luis whispered, his eyes wide. Personal attention from El Toro was the last thing he wanted. "I mean … I didn't …"

"Shut the fuck up and get out now. Go back to your dirty corner," Moya sneered. "You get your inventory when it comes in, just like everyone. You show up here again, and I'll take you out and slit your throat myself."

Esteban Moya spun and walked up the flight of stairs where a curvy woman with round soft breasts was waiting to make all of his troubles go away. Luis Acero descended the two levels to the street and managed to not fall or pass out. He didn't even stop in the restroom to take a piss.

The fucking cop wanted something big. This might be big. He couldn't be sure, but it was all he had.

Moya said the gringo in a business suit had something to

do with their supply chain to the cartel. It could have been a lie. The gringo might be El Toro's accountant or lawyer.

It didn't matter. The only thing Luis was sure of was that he wasn't going anywhere near Bautista Ortega again.

TEN

On the Edge of Manhood—1990

"John Fitzhugh Sole, you have been found guilty of felony motor vehicle theft." Winscombe County Superior Court Judge Carl Burlson sighed and removed his glasses, rubbing the bridge of his nose. "We've heard the evidence. Do you have anything to say before I pronounce sentence?"

Burlson eyed the seventeen-year-old standing before him. He was a boy really, not able to vote or buy a beer legally, but the State of Georgia considered him an adult, in the matter of taking cars for joyrides.

"Your honor." The young public defender swallowed down the lump in his throat. "My client has nothing to say."

John Sole gazed into the judge's eyes, ramrod straight and defiant. It wasn't in him to beg, never had been. He may have taken the Reverend Mason's car, he may have been driving it when the sheriff caught up with them, but he damned sure would not beg, and he'd damned well spend the next ten years in jail before he'd plead with the damned judge to lighten the damned sentence.

Behind him, Clara Sole sobbed in silence.

"Your honor," the public defender continued. "We would like to ask for leniency in sentencing.

Judge Burlson put the glasses back on his nose and regarded the young man standing before him awaiting his fate. He'd seen too many young men like John Sole, on the edge of manhood, no father to guide them and a future destroyed by a thoughtless act.

Yes, technically, he had been driving the stolen car. The sheriff had asked old Reverend Mason to consider dropping the charges to criminal trespass, a misdemeanor. It was just a joyride, after all. Mason said no. The boys needed to be taught a lesson. Right was right, and wrong was wrong, and he wanted no confusion on the matter. Charge them with theft and let them pay the price for their crimes. They would come out of prison better men for it, Mason had said.

Burlson's experience told him that the opposite was more likely true. John Sole would come out of prison a well-trained young criminal, facing a lifetime of self-destructive brushes with the law until one put him away for good.

Yes, he had confessed to stealing the car, but he hadn't been alone. Billy Siever, a sixteen-year-old friend—one of John Sole's only friends—was there. Siever, still a juvenile under the law, had taken part in the crime. From what Judge Burlson knew about him, Billy had probably planned it, but he would not face the same penalty. In fact, because his father served on the County Commission and played golf with the district attorney, he would face no punishment at all.

"Humph," Burlson rumbled as he shuffled the papers before him.

Billy Siever was a bad apple, spoiled rotten. For all his defiance, John Sole had more character than the whole

Siever clan put together in one squirming lump. Burlson made up his mind.

"Taking into account the defendant's age, I will exercise my prerogative here to delay sentencing for one hour."

For the first time, John's eyes twitched. Clara held her breath.

Burlson nodded toward the courtroom window where the sun shining in made crosshatch patterns on the wood floors. "Across the court square, you will find recruiting offices for every branch of the armed services. If a defendant before me were to present evidence of their impending enlistment in the armed forces of this country, in the branch of their choosing, it would provide some mitigating reason to consider leniency."

There was no mistaking it now. The defiance disappeared from John's eyes. Clara gasped and whispered a prayer of thanks. The public defender stood open-mouthed and amazed.

Burlson picked up the gavel and slammed it down once, sending a resounding bang through the courtroom. "Court recessed for one hour!" He stood and exited through the door into his chambers.

John turned. "Does that mean …"

"It means you best get across the square in a hurry," the public defender said and turned to Clara. "You'll need to go with him to sign and give consent. He may be old enough to go to prison, but he's sure not old enough to serve his country without your say so."

Arms interlocked, they marched across the square and stood before the recruiting office looking through the glass at the trim young uniformed man seated behind a desk. Clara looked at her son. "Are you sure?"

He nodded. "I'm sure."

It didn't take the full hour to complete and sign the paperwork. Clara fought back the sense of foreboding. Would the military change John as it had his father? No, she shook her head at the thought. It was early 1990. There were no wars now. Viet Nam was a distant memory. She pulled his arm closer, wrapping hers around his waist. John would be fine, she told herself.

With proof of his enlistment in the Marine Corps, Judge Burlson suspended John's sentence. Court was adjourned, and three weeks later John shipped out to the Marine Corps Recruiting Depot, Parris Island.

There was no war in 1990. In 1991 there was.

By June, John Sole completed Boot Camp and the Marine Corps School of Infantry. In August, his unit began preparing for participation in Operation Desert Shield. They were deployed to the theater of operations before the end of the year.

Serving with the fabled 3/3, 3rd Marine Battalion, 3rd Marine regiment 3rd Marine Division, John saw action at the Battle of Khafji and was with the battalion at the Kuwait airport when the conflict ended.

Judge Burlson had done John and Clara a great favor. John Sole had found a home in the Marine Corps, and unlike his father, he thrived on the military life and Marine camaraderie.

ELEVEN

Good for Business

"How much?" Eyes narrowed, Bebé Elizondo looked up from the newspaper that Alejandro had placed on his desk

"Altogether, ten and a half million U.S. dollars."

"So little?" Elizondo sat back, chin resting on his hands folded in front of his face.

"It was a mixed load. *Cocaína* ... about ten million. The rest was *hierba* ... grass. Lighter but takes up more space in the truck, not as high market value."

Elizondo nodded. "We were lucky."

That Bebé could be philosophical about the loss of almost eleven million dollars of inventory and count himself fortunate was a testimony to the enormous success of his business. The international sales of his products brought in billions in U.S. dollars each year, with most of that coming from the North Americans.

"Still," he continued. "We have a problem."

"Yes." Alejandro nodded. "Once the *norteamericanos* discover one of our methods of transport, they are relentless. They will cut off other crossings ... find everyone who is willing to work with us."

"So ..." Elizondo smiled. "We must stay ahead of them in this little game of cat and mouse."

"Hmm. I would rather be the cat," Alejandro remarked. "Mice get eaten."

"Alejandro, my friend. Remember the cinema when we were young ... the *Tom and Jerry*, from the States ... the mouse was much smarter than the cat and was never eaten." He nodded, making his point. "We must always be smarter than the cat."

"You are right." Alejandro sat in the chair across from Bebé. "Perhaps I worry too much sometimes."

"That is a good thing, I think. It makes us good partners. You worry for both of us, and I don't have to." Elizondo smiled and changed the subject. "And the men?"

"Three arrested plus the rancher. We lost one killed."

"Killed? By the *gringos*?"

"Yes. He was young ... high strung. He tried to use his weapon during the arrest."

"*Un tonto*." Fool. Elizondo shook his head. "He was there as a protection against other cartels and bandits. How did he expect to win a fight with the Americans?"

"As I say, he was young and hotheaded." Alejandro shrugged. "He learned a hard lesson."

"Yes, he did." Elizondo nodded. "Make sure his family receives ten thousand dollars as compensation for their loss."

"So much?"

"It is a trifle to us. For a peasant and his family, ten thousand dollars is a fortune." Elizondo gazed at his lieutenant the way a patient teacher eyes a willing student, taking the time to explain beyond giving instructions. "In the greater scheme of things a few thousand dollars will reap great rewards when we require loyalty, new recruits ... or silence."

"I'll see to it." Alejandro nodded.

"And the driver?"

"It was old Ernesto. You remember him I think."

"Ernesto. The one who drove trucks across Mexico?"

"The same. They arrested him. No doubt, he will spend a few years in a North American prison before being deported."

"His wife should receive his pension now. I think Ernesto's days driving for us are over. He has been loyal. I think fifteen thousand U.S. dollars a year is reasonable."

"Very generous," Alejandro agreed. "I'll have it arranged for the old woman."

"Good." Elizondo mused, leaning back in his leather chair, tapping the tips of his fingers together. "The *Yanquis* are getting better. They find our tunnels with their listening equipment and ground radar. Their drones patrol in places where we least expect, and now ..." He shook his head. "Now, they have compromised a major point of entry ... one of the few that could handle the tonnage we must send over the border to meet the demand." His eyes moved to the blue sky outside the window and the ocean beyond. "We must move things forward with the American.

"I sent him with a driver to tour our port facilities."

"Good. He will eat with the family tonight. After, we will complete the arrangements. Tomorrow we send him home. In six months, we will be at full operation." Elizondo sat upright, his mind made up on something else. "Suspend further deliveries over the border for now. If they discovered this rancher and the arrangement we had with him, they might be aware of the others."

"That will hurt the dealers who depend on our deliveries."

"It is only a temporary suspension until we have our new arrangements in place. It would hurt them worse if the *gringos* shut us down." Elizondo smiled, hands extended palms up, raising them in front of his face. "Inconvenient as it is, a brief suspension will drive prices up and that, my friend, is very good for business."

TWELVE

Paid Up
___

It was a separate phone, a burner, ownership untraceable. They used it for contact with their informants. The last thing they needed was a snitch with a hot tip having his cover blown because one of his upstanding criminal associates noticed that he had been making calls to the Atlanta PD Major Crimes Unit.

It sat on the edge of Randy Travis' desk when it vibrated and chimed. Travis grabbed it before it vibrated itself off onto the floor.

He answered. "Yeah."

John Sole looked up from his neighboring desk. The afternoon had been too quiet. He was ready to do something besides shuffle papers.

The voice on the other end spoke. "It's all good, bro."

It was the code. Any other words would alert them that someone was listening on the other end or that the informant was in trouble. Leave off the 'bro' and it was a tip-off that things were turning to shit, and the CI needed someone to pull his ass out of the fire. Luis Acero said the words in the correct sequence.

"What d'ya got for us?" Travis got down to business.

Sole motioned him into an adjacent interrogation room. Travis, nodded, followed, closed the door and put the phone on speaker.

"You said big ..." Luis hesitated. "I got something for you."

Sitting on the bed in his one-room, third-floor apartment on the Southside, Luis Acero leaned over, holding the phone tight against his ear, whispering. His eyes darted around the small room as if someone might have crept in a while he slept, waiting to catch him ratting.

Esteban Moya's warning at Eruptions had given him a case of the shakes. Worse, Bautista Ortega—The Bull himself—had noticed his presence. A lump of bowel-loosening fear settled into his gut.

He found a dive bar on the way home and had a drink to settle his nerves. One drink turned into many. He drank until Ortega's stare faded from his memory. Then he cabbed it back to his apartment, stripped to his undershorts, collapsed on the bed, and slept through the day.

He was awake now, shivering on the edge of his bed, goosebumps on his thin, bare chest. He sat hunched over the phone, wearing nothing but his dirty gray tighty-whities.

"Spit it out," Travis said impatiently.

Luis looked at the yellow stains down the front of his shorts where he had not quite managed to open his fly before taking a piss at the bar the night before. He took a deep breath.

This might get him paid up with the cops for a long while, but if Ortega found out he was a rat, he would disappear from sight. There was a street legend that El Toro chummed the waters of Lake Lanier, taking the body parts of those who had betrayed him out on his boat and dumping them overboard to attract fish. Luis believed the legend.

"This could get me killed. You got to be careful." Luis' said, his voice barely audible.

"Why the whispering? Where you at?" Travis looked up at Sole, eyebrows raised. Luis had something, and it had him scared shitless.

"Shit, I'm whispering 'cause I don't wanna fucking die, man! That's why." Luis looked around the apartment. "Home, man. That's where I am. What difference does that make?"

"None. What do you have for us?" Travis spoke quietly now, trying to calm their informant.

"I was at Eruptions last night ... the club over on ..."

"We know where it's at," Travis said. "Speak."

"Well, I ... I sort of saw ..." Luis struggled to force the words from his mouth.

"Let's have it, asshole!" Sole said, losing patience with the jittery informant

"Who this?" Luis said pulling his head away from the phone for a second, startled by the new voice.

"You know who it is."

"Yeah. You that hard-ass white cop. Put the black dude back on."

"I'm here," Travis said, grinning at Sole.

"You said you wanted something big. I went to the place where the people that do the big shit go. Thought I might pick up something to get you the fuck off my back."

"Did you?" Travis asked.

"Yeah ... yeah, I did ... I think so, anyway." Luis paused, standing to part the slats on the window blinds, peeking out at the street below. In his mind, each passing car held a band of El Toro's thugs, coming to bind him with duct tape, throw a blanket over him and cart him off to some secluded spot where they would start slicing off parts of his body.

"Gonna have to do better than that. 'I think so' doesn't cut it, Luis," Travis said. "Let's hear it, and we'll tell you how whether you're paid up."

"You know this man, Ortega … Bautista Ortega?" Luis asked.

"El Toro … The Bull."

Sole and Travis exchanged glances. Actionable information on Ortega might get Luis paid up for a long while.

"What about him?" Travis kept his tone indifferent, masking their interest.

"He was there … at Eruptions."

"That's not news. We don't have any charges on Ortega now. He did eighteen months on an assault charge a couple of years ago, but that's it, and there's no law against partying at a club. You're gonna have to do better." It was time for a little tough cop. "Stop fucking wasting our time, Luis. I think we'll just end this and drop a dime on you with the narcs. They can go check out your little corner drug mart."

"That's not all, man," Luis whined, lowering the blind slat and stepping away from the window. "He was there with someone."

"Who?"

"White dude. In a suit … he didn't belong there … kinda dude that should be having drinks in the lounge at the Ritz, not a club … not at Eruptions."

"Still, not good enough, Luis," Travis said, his voice

tinged with mock regret. "I think our association may be coming to an end."

"Wait!" Luis' voice rose in pitch, pleading. "The thing is ..." He hesitated. "Thing is they was talking about the supply coming in."

"You heard them talking?" Sole asked, leaning toward the phone.

"Naw, not me, but I was told what it was about."

"Who told you?"

"Dude named Esteban."

"Esteban Moya?" Sole and Travis looked at each other. Moya was known to them and every other detective in the city.

"Yeah, that's him. Works for Ortega."

"We know him," Travis said. "So, Moya told you this white guy in a business suit, who didn't look like he belonged at Eruptions talking to a drug lord, was discussing how to bring illegal narcotics into the States. That about sum things up?"

"Yeah ... yeah. That's it." Luis sighed over the phone, relieved that they understood. "I'm paid up now ... right?"

"I'm not feeling it, Luis," Sole said.

"Why not? This is big! A white dude dressed like that talking to Ortega about running drugs ... that got to lead somewhere."

"Or nowhere," Travis said simply.

"I'm telling you ... this is my world ... the street ... I know what feels right and what don't. You got to believe me," Luis pleaded. "You had to see the look in Esteban's eyes. This was big. They didn't like that I saw the white dude there. Fuck, if it wasn't a public place, they woulda stuffed me in the trunk of a car and slit my throat." His voice rose in pitch. "Shit, they still might!"

Travis punched the phone's mute button. Luis peeked out the blinds to scan the street once more.

"What do you think?" Travis looked at Sole.

"Like you told him, might lead somewhere or nowhere." Sole nodded, thinking. "Still, he's right. It is suspicious ... straight-laced looking white male meeting with El Toro. One thing is sure. Luis is shitting himself that they might be after him, and that makes me think there could be something to it."

"Agreed. That's no act. We have to check it out."

Travis unmuted the phone. "All right, Luis, we'll check it out."

"That means I'm paid up now, right?"

"Maybe. We'll be in touch."

Travis disconnected the call. Luis stared at the phone in his hand for several seconds. Fucking cops. Be in touch, my ass.

THIRTEEN

Death and Life—1998

It was the call. He might have stayed in the Marine Corps if it hadn't been for the call.

Staff Sergeant John Sole grabbed the mail from the box outside his Kaneohe Bay Marine Corps Base housing apartment, unlocked the door and dropped it on the coffee table. First things first. He unbuttoned his uniform shirt as he walked, went to the kitchen and pulled a beer from the fridge.

Brew in hand, he plopped on the sofa and picked up the TV remote, flipping the channel to ESPN. A boring discussion about tennis was in progress, but the attractive female anchor held his attention for a few seconds.

After a minute, he dropped the remote on the cushion beside him and reached for the mail, flipping through the envelopes in quick succession. All junk. He had expected nothing else. The only letters he received were from his mother.

He kicked his shoes off and leaned back, one arm behind his head, sipping the beer and admiring the woman on the television talking about tennis, a sport with scoring that totally confused him. He was just drifting into a nap when the phone rang, and his world changed forever.

He reached for the phone and sat up. "Sergeant Sole."

"Sergeant John Sole?" There was a pause before the husky voice with an unmistakable Georgia drawl continued. "From Cassit Pass, Georgia?"

"Yes." John looked at the phone display and saw the Georgia area code. "What's this about?

"This is Detective Gerard with the Winscombe County Sheriff's office, and you are John Sole, son of Clara Sole?"

"Yes!" He was fully alert now, erect and taut. He rose from the sofa, the phone clamped to his ear. "What is it?"

"I'm sorry to have to inform you that your mother has passed away."

The walls seemed to close in around him. He stood staring but seeing nothing.

"Sergeant Sole? Are you there?"

"Yes," John whispered. "How? She was only …" His voice trailed off.

"It was unexpected. A neighbor hadn't heard from her for a few days and stopped by to check on her. The doctor said it was a heart attack, unusual for a forty-six-year-old woman without a medical history, but not unheard of."

"I talked to her two weeks ago. She seemed fine. I was going to call this past weekend, but we were out on training maneuvers. I don't …" He squeezed his eyes, blinking to clear away the tears that clouded his vision.

"I understand," Detective Gerard said, and then waited in silence, giving the young Marine time to process the information.

He had made more than a few death notifications throughout a thirty-year law enforcement career. They were never easy, but he had learned that silence was better than filling the air with unwanted words.

Seconds passed before John spoke. "What ... how do I handle things?"

"We can help put you in contact with a funeral home to make arrangements. If you can come home, it might be easier, but if not, we can take care of things over the phone. Do you ..." Gerard hesitated. "Is there someone else? Another family member ... someone we should call who is closer to home?"

"No." John's answer was abrupt and emphatic. "No one."

His father disappeared from their lives twenty-five years earlier. In all that time, he had done nothing, made no contact, provided no support, had been nothing more than a blank space in their lives.

Clara told John that Monty Sole was the only true love of her life, that war changed him, that he was good and kind, but somehow, he got lost. One day he would return to them. She never allowed John to speak ill of his father. Out of respect for his mother, he never did—to her face. But in his heart, a deep hatred burned for the man who had abandoned them on the day of his son's birth.

A cloud of anger darkened his face. He shook his head and said. "There's no one. My grandparents passed several years ago. I'm coming home."

Two days later, he was in Cassit Pass on a thirty-day family emergency leave. The funeral home had handled all the arrangements by the time he arrived. He picked a simple casket, as his mother would have wished, and then stood near it during the viewing, shaking hands and exchanging hugs with his mother's friends.

There were a lot of them. Cassit Pass was not a large community, but many of those in attendance were unknown to him. He never realized how few people he knew in the place he called home, or how many his mother knew and called friends.

An uneasy idea crept into his mind as he greeted and accepted condolences from the never-ending line of mourners. There might be more of his father in him than he cared to admit. His mother had often said it to him,

Billy Siever stepped forward and took his hand. "John, it's good to see you." He nodded at the casket holding the remains of Clara Sole. "I am sorry for your loss."

"Thank you." He had not seen or spoken to Billy in the eight years since the day Judge Burlson gave him the option of enlisting or going to prison.

"You look good." Billy patted the shoulder of the Marine Green Class A uniform coat. "Filled out some too," he added with a smile.

"You too." John smiled and nodded at the slight bulge of belly pushing Billy's suit jacket open at the waist.

"Too many beers." Billy patted his stomach with a grin. "Bad habit I picked up at UGA." He looked around at the line waiting behind him. "May not be the right time, John, but don't be offended if I say when this is all over, I'd really like to have a beer with you ... sort of catch up."

"I'd like that." John nodded.

"Good." Billy smiled and moved away.

The procession continued. Each mourner had their own personal remembrances of Clara Sole and shared them with John.

"She was there for me when my husband, Marty had his heart attack."

"She didn't leave my side while I was going through chemo for breast cancer."

"Clara never had a bad word to say about anyone."

"Your mother was so proud of you, John. She spoke of you every time we were together."

Everyone who knew her loved Clara Sole, and they made sure her son knew it. When the services ended, the prayers said, and the casket was placed in the hole an old man at the town cemetery had dug with a backhoe, John Sole was more alone than he had ever been in his life.

Clara had always been there, the sun in his universe. Lying in bed that night in the small house where he had been born, his heart ached with guilt over the time he had spent away from her, broken only by short visits home on leave. She never complained about his absence, embracing the time he spent with her, building memories to tide her over until the next visit.

In the dark, he could see her face, smiling, happy that he was home even now. John Sole smiled back at the face and wept.

The next day he met Billy Siever at Gurney's Bar in Sexton, the only place to get a beer in Winscombe County.

"I always felt guilty," Billy said after the first round arrived.

"No need to," John replied. "No one twisted my arm that day." He smiled. "And you sure as hell couldn't have twisted it or forced me to do anything."

They laughed and sipped their beers.

"Still, it didn't seem right. Still doesn't." Billy leaned back and looked at John, his eyes thoughtful. "I get a slap on the hand, go to the university, get a law degree and you …" He stopped and shook his head.

"What? I joined the Marines. That's a good thing, Billy. Best thing that ever happened." He looked at the man who had been a boy eight years earlier, had been his friend, and was still his friend. "You have nothing to be sorry for. Besides, I like being a Marine. I'm good at it."

Billy nodded, regarding his re-found friend. "You would be good at a lot of things, John."

"You trying to talk me out of the Marines?"

"Not at all." Billy gave an emphatic shake of his head. "Just saying you have options. Things you are good at in the Marines may be transferrable to something closer to home. If that's what you want to do." He sighed. "Look, I'm just letting you know that I could help you get resettled if you want to come home. I've joined a law firm over in Dahlonega."

"You saying I should be a lawyer?" John shook his head, laughing. "No way."

"Not that … unless you wanted. I think you'd make a fine lawyer, by the way, but you could do a lot of things. I'm just saying; I got a break eight years ago, mostly because of my father's connections. It seems like you got the shitty end of the stick, and I'd like to help fix that … if you want."

"Like I said, the Marine Corps has been good to me," John said shaking his head and then added philosophically. "We move on. Life happens. It's all good."

"Then here's to life." Billy lifted and tipped his bottle, clinking it against John's. "Anyway, it's good to see you again. How long are you staying?"

"Heading out tomorrow."

"So soon?"

"Yeah." John leaned forward, placing his elbows on the bar top. "Have a thirty-day emergency leave, but there's no reason to stay now. Emergency's over."

"I understand, but I am sorry to see you go so soon." Billy turned on the barstool to face his friend, lifting his beer in salute. "I'm not a Marine, but Semper Fi, John Sole."

John lifted his bottle in return, understanding Billy's intent and the meaning of those words—Always Faithful. "Semper Fi, Billy."

The flight back to Honolulu took fifteen hours and two stops. He could have waited for a Space-A free military flight headed that way, but there would have been more layovers. Besides, he didn't want to wait. A sense of urgency had taken hold of him even though he couldn't determine the reason for it.

The long flight gave him plenty of time to think. Mostly he thought about his mother and what she would have wanted for him. Billy's words kept coming back to him. He had skills that he could do something with in civilian life, but did he?

Three hours after touching down in Honolulu, John was sitting in front of the man who had been his mentor for much of his time in the Marine Corps. Master Gunnery Sergeant Simpson 'Sim' Bradford shuffled through the personnel file on his desk for a few minutes before looking up.

Fifty-two-years-old with short-cropped gray hair, a square face etched from years of service in the field, and a lean, well-muscled physique, Bradford looked like a recruiting poster Marine with a few years added on. In fact, if ever a Marine was an example of everything a Marine should be and what service in the Corps represented, it was Master Guns Bradford.

"So you are considering leaving the Corps?"

"I am, Master Gunnery Sergeant." John sat at attention in the chair Bradford had indicated and fought back the urge to squirm under his stare.

"How does that make you feel?"

"I ..." John hesitated.

"Speak, Sergeant." Bradford's hawk-like eyes never left John's face, reading every thought and emotion.

"Guilty, I suppose. The Corps has been good to me."

"Guilt? Is that what service in the Corps means to you, Sergeant Sole? Is that a good reason to be a Marine?"

"No, Master Gunnery Sergeant. It's just ..." John shook his head. "I think I owe something to the Corps, to the people I've served with. If I hadn't enlisted in the Marine Corps, I ..."

"I know exactly what would have happened." Bradford cut him off. "You would have been in prison in Georgia for taking a joyride in a car you borrowed from the local preacher without his permission. That about the size of it?" He tapped the folder on his desk. "It's all here. Did I leave anything out?"

"No, that's it. I would have gone to prison. Instead I ..."

"You found a life in the Corps, a life of service." Bradford's face softened, and the closest thing to a fatherly smile that John had witnessed replaced his ever-present Master Gunnery Sergeant sternness. "The Marine Corps is not the only place to serve, Sole."

"Yes, but I *am* a Marine."

"You are." Bradford nodded. "An exemplary one, and it

would be an honor to serve with you for the rest of my career, Sole.

"So, you're saying …"

"I am saying that you have served honorably. There is no shame in leaving, and you have nothing to feel guilty about."

"Oh." John was quiet, not sure what else to say.

"Go home, son." Bradford's voice was soft. "You have done your duty, here. You don't have to be a lifer to be a Marine. Whether you remain in the Corps or not, you are always a Marine … always will be."

John nodded without speaking. He hadn't expected this response.

Bradford continued as if the decision was already made. "How long do you have in your enlistment contract?"

"Two months."

"Then take some advice from me. Start now. Make your contacts back home. Find a job you can move into. Don't go home without a plan. Marines plan." Bradford leaned back in his chair in a more relaxed posture taking on the role of counselor. "Have you considered law enforcement?"

"You mean the police department?"

"Seems like a good place to serve … a place where your skills, your initiative, and dedication to duty will be useful."

"I was arrested … for a felony. I'm not sure they will let me …"

"You were seventeen, a boy. You are a man now, a Marine. I'll put a good word in for you. There are others who will." Bradford sat up straight, closed the personnel file and looked John in the eyes. "You are dismissed, Sergeant Sole."

"Yes, Master Gunnery Sergeant."

Two months later John Sole took his honorable discharge from the Marine Corps. A month after that, he took the entrance exam for the City of Atlanta Police Academy, receiving one of the highest scores ever recorded. During the oral board review and interview, it was brought to his attention that Master Gunnery Sergeant Bradford along with several other Marine NCOs and officers had written letters of recommendation. Bradford had even called the chief of police. The final recommendations came from William Siever, Attorney at law, and his well-connected father who had asked Judge Burlson to write a letter of support.

The criminal charges in his record were noted and then forgotten. Once again he took an oath as he had on enlisting in the Marine Corps. Along with forty-five other rookie recruits, he swore to defend the Constitution of the United States, protect and serve the people, and enforce the laws of the State of Georgia and City of Atlanta. John Sole was a police officer.

FOURTEEN

Houseguest

Dinner with the Elizondos was a family affair. The children treated their father's invited guest as a long-lost uncle and not one who had been a complete stranger until this day. When introduced, each stepped forward and politely shook hands. Bebé's wife, Sofia greeted him with a firm handshake and smile, and then bustled off to the kitchen with her two house assistants to organize the evening meal.

True to Bebé's word, Sofia did the cooking, although the opulence of their home showed they could afford many servants and the finest chef if they desired. Instead, Sofia performed the household tasks and cooking with the help of two teenaged servant girls.

While they prepared the meal, Bebé poured tequila into tall, thin glasses, rimmed in silver. The bottoms of the glasses came to a point and rested in small silver cradles when not being held. The children sang for them while Bebé and the tall *norteamericano* sipped the tequila.

Alejandro sat to one side, expressionless as he watched

the children and listened to their singing. Occasionally, the little one, Rosa, would come to his knee and tug on his trousers for attention. Alejandro gave her hand a gentle pat, but his expression never changed.

Still shaken by the day's events and the execution performed just yards away in the little building on the hillside, the American had little to say and kept his mouth safely shut except to answer questions. Mostly, he sipped the tequila and nodded at his host's running commentary on life, politics, and family while smiling at the children's singing. Bebé, on the other hand, was full of genial conversation and anecdotes that flowed from him like water gurgling happily downhill in a mountain stream.

The American avoided eye contact with Alejandro. After witnessing the garroting of the traitor, he was downright terrified of the silent Mexican. His hovering presence was like tornado weather on the horizon back home in Georgia. You couldn't be sure what direction the storm would take or which way to run for safety, but you never forgot it was there.

The evening's tranquil domestic scene was incongruous, surreal even after the day's events. The American wondered if Sofia knew what business her husband conducted so close to their children and the bed where they had conceived them. He sipped more of the tequila and tried to burn away the memories of the day.

Dinner was sumptuous. Sofia called them into a long hall-like dining room. A massive oak table with ornately carved legs was laden with food from one end to the other.

The men went to the chairs Bebé indicated, and Sofia sat beside the American, explaining the traditional Michoacán dishes she had prepared. As the main course, there was *aporreadillo*, corned beef and egg smothered in salsa on the side. This was accompanied by tortillas and heavily seasoned fried pork *carnitas* with *morisqueta*, a mixture of rice and black beans covered in cheese sauce.

When it seemed they could not possibly eat another bite, Sofia introduced the American to *chongos zamoranos*, a dessert made from curd, cinnamon, and sugar. She smiled as he relented and accepted a portion and then did not refuse the second helping she offered.

The meal was like a family party. All of it was washed down by an assortment of Mexican wines, the children tasting the vintages from smaller sampling glasses.

Feeling the warmth from the combined effects of wine, chilies, and spices, the American was ready for bed. Yet, the meal continued and then continued some more.

They had commenced at eight in the evening. It was now past ten. He craved a bed where he could sleep off dinner and perhaps dull the memories of the day's horrors.

At last, the host pushed his chair back from the table. "Come, children. It is time for bed. Kiss your father good night."

One by one, Bebé's three daughters came to him, kissed his cheek and received a kiss from him on the forehead, along with a pat on the cheek.

"Now a kiss for our guest and for *Tio* Alejandro."

The girls performed the duty, smiling as they stood before Alejandro and then the American to plant kisses on their cheeks. Surprised, the American watched and followed Alejandro's example, accepting each kiss without offering one in return.

A little bow and "Good night, *Tio* Alejandro. Good night, *Senor*," and they were herded off to bed by their mother. Elizondo watched them leave the room, a loving paternal smile spreading across his baby smooth face.

"Do you have children?" he asked the American as they disappeared into the hallway to clump up the stairs to their bedrooms.

"No."

"None? Really?" Elizondo turned his curious gaze on the man sitting in the chair beside him.

"None." The American nodded and shrugged. "We wanted children. It just never happened."

"Ah, yes," Elizondo said, a knowing smile on his face. "I hear such matters can be difficult." His smile widened. "I have no problem in that area." He made a fist and pumped his arm to indicate his bedroom stamina.

"Yes, well you have a beautiful family," The American said, ready to change the subject. He yawned. "And now I think it is time for me to head to bed. It's been a long day."

"So soon?" Elizondo's brow furrowed in surprise that the American would end the evening at such an early hour. "We have business to discuss."

The American remained silent for several seconds, unsure about what would happen if he insisted on retiring for the evening.

In fact, it had been a long day. Alejandro and two bodyguards had picked him up at General Francisco Mujica International Airport, in Morelia at seven in the morning, local time. From there they boarded a helicopter to make the leg to Lázaro Cárdenas.

The hour and a half flight over pastoral Michoacán State was restful enough although his companions in the chopper remained silent to the point of surliness. It was apparent that they had been instructed to have no interaction with the *norteamericano*.

On arrival at the Elizondo estate, they hustled the American off to the outbuilding that served as an office. One of the smiling but silent, servant girls came from the house to serve him breakfast that consisted of strong black coffee and pastries, loaded with the Mexican staples of cinnamon and sugar. He ate while taking in the view through the bank of windows. The spectacular views of the harbor and Pacific Ocean beyond were impressive.

After an hour or so of waiting, they brought the man they called Miguel into the building and proceeded down the spiral staircase. The American was instructed to stand in the corner behind the chair where Miguel sat, sweating and wide-eyed with concern.

A few minutes later, Bebé came down the staircase with Alejandro. A few minutes after that, Miguel met his fate, and the guards were cleaning up the mess.

Miguel's execution was followed by a pleasant lunch. Then, Alejandro had dispatched some men to provide him a tour of the harbor and Elizondo's shipping facilities. This had lasted all afternoon, returning him to the hacienda just in time for drinks and then dinner.

"Stay, please," Elizondo said, regarding the American over the top of the glass as he sipped tequila. It was a command, not a request.

"Of course." The American nodded, casting a sidelong glance at Alejandro.

"So, you are still concerned about our demonstration this morning, are you not?" Elizondo smiled.

"Is that what the murder was? A demonstration?"

The American tried to control his voice and meet Elizondo's gaze as an equal partner, but he had come to realize their partnership was anything but equal. Bebe's enormous wealth and power from drug trafficking dwarfed any pretense of riches and influence the American might display. He was terrified by this man who played with his children and then had people murdered just feet away from where they slept.

"Not murder." Elizondo waived a finger, correcting him. "An execution. He betrayed us. I was a friend to him. I trusted him, yet he betrayed me." His eyes narrowed. "For that, there is a price to pay."

"I already understood the price. Your demonstration was …" The American hesitated. "It was unnecessary."

"Very good." The ever-present smile on the babyface widened "We can disagree on this point, but you should know that I think it was necessary. It is important for you to understand the nature of our relationship."

"I understand."

"Good. Now let us discuss business. I have many questions. Your people have spoken to my contacts in the States. Now, I want to hear from you how it will be done."

At two in the morning, Elizondo stretched in his chair, put the glass of tequila on the table and rose. "An excellent discussion! Don't you agree?"

"Yes." The American was fatigued to the point of exhaustion.

"Good. You shall stay here for another day or two as my houseguest."

"But …"

Elizondo raised his hand to cut off any objections. "I insist. My wife has more cooking to feed you and my children have many questions about your home in the United States."

"Fine." The American nodded.

It was a display of power to impress on the American who controlled their relationship. Arguing was pointless. He would remain Bebé's houseguest until Bebé said otherwise.

FIFTEEN

Very Helpful

"We're closed."

"No problem." John Sole shrugged. "Just open up."

Sole and Travis pulled their shirt tails up to display the APD badges hooked to their belts.

"Come back at three. We'll be open then."

Buck Turpin was an imposing figure. A former defensive lineman at the University of Georgia, he had taken up a brief career as a professional wrestler after UGA cut him from the squad. He was one of those large men who cultivate the scowl of a badass and use their bulk to intimidate people into believing they are as badass as their size makes them appear.

At six feet five inches and three hundred fifty pounds, he could block most doors by merely standing in front of them. At nine on this sunny Atlanta morning, that was what he was doing in front of the door at Eruptions.

Sole was not impressed. "Sure you want to play it that way?" he asked mildly.

"Come back when we're open." Turpin crossed his beefy arms and remained planted in front of the door.

"Okay." Sole leaned against the building's brick facade to one side of the door, pulled out a stick of gum and unwrapped it. He bent it in half between his thumb and forefinger and popped it in his mouth, smiling. "Explain it, partner."

"Sure." Travis leaned against the wall on the other side of the door, forcing Turpin to swivel his head back and forth like a bobble-head toy to follow the conversation. "You see, it's like this. We want to review the security video from a couple nights ago. Probably only take us an hour, maybe two, then we'll be out of your hair."

"You got a warrant?" Turpin put on his best tough guy scowl. "You need a warrant for that sort of thing."

"You're not too bright, are you? I suppose that's why they have you out here on the door," Sole said and added. "Don't need a warrant unless you don't cooperate."

Turpin spun his head, eyes glaring at him.

On cue, Travis chimed in, "That's right unless you don't cooperate."

Turpin's large skull swiveled back in the other direction.

"So if you don't want to cooperate," Travis continued. "We'll be forced to get a warrant, as you have correctly pointed out. While we do, one of us will stay here, with our car right there." He nodded at the unmarked Ford parked at the curb a few feet away in the valet drive up area.

"Might take a while to get the warrant … might take all night," Sole said, shrugging and spitting the gum from his mouth in a high arc to land by the curb.

"Hey, you can't …" Turpin began.

"It's true," Travis interrupted. "Of course, after dark, we'll have to turn the blue lights on … as a safety precaution, you know, so people don't run into our parked police vehicle."

"That'll be something." Sole grinned and laughed. "Cop car ... blue lights on ... in front of Eruptions. I'll bet that will make people think twice about coming in tonight."

"Yeah," Travis chuckled. "Safety first though."

They spoke from either side of the door, leaning against the building, like two friends waiting for a bus, chatting about the weather. Turpin's head bobbed back and forth to follow their banter.

"Let them in, Buck. Bring them to me."

The voice coming over the intercom by the front door was sharp, the words clipped and terse.

"Yes, sir." Turpin nodded and looked up at the camera over the door.

Sole and Travis stood up straight and smiled into the camera.

"Gosh, Buck," Sole said. "Your boss sounds pissed. I hope we didn't get you in trouble."

"Shut the fuck up." Turpin jerked the door open and led them to a fourth-floor office just above the upstairs lounge.

Sergei Sokolov sat behind an expansive oak desk in an office with one window. The window looked down through one way glass onto the third floor where the most elite of Eruptions' clientele gathered.

A naturalized former citizen of the Soviet Union, Sokolov had immersed himself in American culture over the last twenty years, putting his years as an assembly line worker in a Russian car factory far behind him. No one knew where a man with his modest origins had acquired the cash to buy and then transform an old building into Atlanta's most fashionable nightclub.

The Atlanta police suspected he had ties to organized

crime and that Russian mobsters had funded him, but the money trail was too well disguised to prove it. Sole and Sokolov had encountered each other on a previous case when the club owner provided information about a human trafficking ring in exchange for a more relaxed relationship with the police. The traffickers were Asian, unconnected to the Russians with whom Sokolov maintained cozy relations and who were happy to see their competition eliminated.

The heavy odor of men's cologne hung in the air as they walked into the office. "Damn, Sergei," Sole said, plopping without invitation into a chair across from the desk as he sniffed the air. "Did you spill a whole bottle of Polo in here?"

"What do you want, Sole?" Sokolov, sat straight in his leather chair, hands folded on his desk, the gold links in his cuffs sparkling in the light from the shaded lamp to the side.

"Understand one of your patrons had a head to head with someone sitting at a booth on the third floor ... a white guy in a business suit ... not exactly the attire one expects here partying after hours."

"So? We don't have a dress code," Sokolov smirked. "Maybe he was just a rich nerd or someone out exploring the famous sights in Atlanta and didn't know what kind of place this is."

"True enough. Could have been any of those." Sole nodded. "What we want to know is who he was ... met with a fellow by the name of Ortega ... Bautista Ortega. You might have heard of him ... street name is El Toro."

"Never heard of him." Sokolov shook his head. "And I don't know anything about a white guy in a suit."

"Figured as much," Sole said, smiling. "In that case, we need to look over your video from a couple nights ago."

"Why?"

"Not your concern."

"The video is mine. That makes it my concern."

"Sergei," Sole said sighing. "Let's not play this game. It's police business. That's all you need to know, and as I pointed out to Bucky while you listened in over the intercom, we can get a warrant if you force us." He smiled and shook his head. "Don't force us, Sergei."

"I doubt you could get a warrant on something that thin … white male in a business suit."

"Maybe not, but I'll still sit here in my car and wait on your doorstep while my partner visits every judge in the city to find out. That could take a while."

"Why are you busting my ass, this morning, Sole?" Sokolov leaned back in his chair straightening his cuffs as he glared at the detectives.

"Relax, Sergei. We aren't snooping into your business. Just trying to identify someone who was here the other night."

"Why? Who is he?"

"Shit. If we knew that we wouldn't be here, would we?"

Sergei turned to Turpin "Take them to the security office and let them see all the video they want. Then escort them out."

"Thanks, Sergei." Sole smiled.

"Let's go." Turpin put a thick hand on Sole's shoulder.

"Don't do that." Sole looked up.

Their eyes locked as Travis and Sokolov watched from opposite sides of the room. Travis tensed in his chair, ready to come to his partner's aid, if necessary. It wasn't.

Turpin released his grip. "Follow me."

The Security office had no windows. Banks of monitors displayed various images of the interior and exterior of the building. A man sat before the monitors watching. The detectives noted that he was younger than Turpin, more of a techie than the bodyguard sort, probably a Georgia Tech engineering undergraduate working part-time to pay off his student loans.

Turpin had him set them up at a table with a monitor and showed them how to pull up the video they wanted. Travis sat down and began reviewing the images, searching for the white man in the business suit who Luis Acero said had met with a drug kingpin.

"What about the third-floor lounge?" Travis asked as he scanned.

"No cameras on the third floor."

"What?" Travis spun around to face the tech nerd. "Why not?"

"I don't know." The techie shrugged. "Privacy, I guess. High-class patrons don't want to be caught on camera at the club." He pointed a shaky finger at the bank of switches. "But there are other cameras ... the doors ... other floors ... should be able to see who you're looking for there."

Travis glanced at Sole and turned back to the monitor, scanning for the man in the business suit as he entered or left or made his way through the building to the third level. He wasn't there.

Sole looked at the young techie, watching from his chair at the main console. "Is there another door? One without a camera?"

"Uh ..." Techie threw a nervous glance at Turpin.

"Don't look at Bucky," Sole snapped. "Answer the question."

"Well, there is one door, on the side ... comes off the alley and goes to a stairway that goes up to all the floors." He shook his head. "There aren't any cameras on that door or the stairs."

"Son of a bitch." Travis turned and went back to searching the video images.

Sole leaned over his shoulder. It took two hours to review the recordings before they knew no camera had recorded the man who had met with Bautista Ortega.

"What now?" Travis looked up at Sole.

"Now you leave." Turpin had been standing by the door to the security office. Taking one step across the small room, he thumped a heavy hand on Sole's shoulder and attempted to spin him around.

He was big and strong, but like many strong, men he was unaccustomed to being challenged, coasting through life by virtue of his bulk. Most people took one look at Buck Turpin and backed away. He had never faced a determined opponent. Now he faced John Sole.

Sole spun and clamped an arm under and around Turpin's forearm as he twisted his wrist into a gooseneck. He jerked hard, and Turpin went up on his toes, howling in pain.

"I told you not to do that," Sole said, maintaining the wristlock.

"He did, he warned you," Travis said, nodding solemnly. "That looks really painful, Bucky. Is it?"

"We'll be leaving now," Sole said, speaking softly into Turpin's ear. "You stay here. We'll show ourselves out."

He released the hold and Turpin sagged against the wall, cradling his sore arm with the other hand. Sole and Travis left the room, closing the security door behind them.

They scanned the hallway. Sergei Sokolov's office was at one end. A door with a lit exit sign over it was at the other.

"What do you think?" Travis asked. "That looks like there might be a stairway down."

"Let's check it." Sole nodded.

As the tech nerd had promised, there were no cameras in the stairwell. They descended to the ground floor and pushed the door open. Bright sunlight flooded inside.

"No cameras inside or outside," Sole said looking around.

"Whoever the suit was, he must have come in this way."

"Yeah, if he came in at all."

"You think Luis was lying to us?" Travis asked.

"Not beyond the realm of possibilities," Sole replied. "Still, I doubt it. He was wide-eyed, scared shitless when he called. It didn't come across as an act."

"What next then?"

"Let's circle back with Luis. Maybe we can jog something loose from his shaky memory."

"Good a plan as any." Travis nodded.

They walked along the alley to the front of the building. As they turned the corner, Buck Turpin came through the front door, accompanied by two other men.

"What do we have here?" Sole grinned and turned to face the trio of goons.

"Mr. Sokolov wants to make sure you leave," Turpin said, trying to sound as tough as he had earlier, without much success.

"We're leaving. We might be back though." Sole smiled as he slid behind the wheel of the Ford. "We'll let Sergei know you've been very helpful."

SIXTEEN

Shaye–2001

"You always drink alone?"

It started with a smile. Life changed from there.

"Only when there's no one with me." Sole looked up and took a breath as her sunlight washed over him.

She radiated warmth. He took it all in. Green eyes that glittered out at the world, lit by some internal source. Brown hair that bounced softly off her shoulders when she moved, like the ripples on a pond moving in slow motion. And there was the smile, soft and warm, firm and beaming, inviting and tempting. The smile became his world as he gazed at her.

"I'm Shaye." She put a hand out.

"John." He turned on the barstool and took her hand. "John Sole."

"I know who you are." The smile grew broader on her face. "Been waiting for you to invite me over for a drink."

The Blue Don was a cop bar. Everyone was welcome, but off-duty police officers made up a good percentage of the clientele. A caricature of The Godfather, shaded in police blue, hung over the bar inside and on the building's exterior. That had garnered some negative press over the years from those with an ax to grind with the police department. The implication that the police embraced the image of the blue godfather provided fodder for the local talk shows.

The cops found it humorous. Despite the department's efforts to make it off limits for officers, there was nothing they could do. The Blue Don's owner—not a former law enforcement officer, although most assumed he was—made sure they always complied with every licensing requirement and ordinance. Having a drink in a legal establishment on your own time did not constitute a violation of law or departmental policy. Besides, the more the administrative staff tried to dissuade officers from going, the more motivated the officers were to be seen there. The department let the issue drop.

"Do I know you?" Sole held onto her hand, immersing himself in her radiance.

"You should." She leaned close and whispered breathlessly in his hear. "2-Bravo15, be en route to a signal forty-two."

"Dispatch!" Sole grinned.

"That's me." Shaye scooted up onto the stool beside him. "Evening watch dispatch, Zone 2 … one of them, anyway."

"So why me, Shaye?"

"I don't know." She shrugged. "Man of mystery maybe. The quiet one … comfortable on his own … doesn't need to be pumped up by all the war stories and testosterone floating around in here." She touched her fingertips to his arm, and he felt a tingle of electricity he had never experienced around another woman. "Mostly it seems like you have nothing to prove. That's different ... refreshing." She moved her hand, and he ached for her to put it back. "Buy me a drink."

He did, and they talked through the evening. They met the next evening and did the same. On the third, she invited him home to her apartment.

For the first time in his life, John Sole felt whole, complete. The sensation of being part of something bigger grew on him. Away from her, something was missing, and all he could think of was when they would be together again.

Six months after that night at The Blue Don, John Fitzhugh Sole and Shaina Ruth Berman were married. The preliminaries were touch and go at first, at least in John's mind. Shaye's conservative Jewish family spent an evening questioning him in their Buckhead home.

What were his intentions?

He loved Shaye and had come to realize his world revolved around her.

What was his income?

He earned what a cop earned. He wasn't rich, but he wasn't poor, and everything he had was hers if she wanted it.

What were his feelings about religion?

He wasn't opposed to religion, but he didn't have any particular religious convictions.

What was his opinion of Judaism?

He had none.

Was he aware of the historical persecution of Jews?

Yes, he knew the history, although he had never experienced persecution in that way.

He answered their questions without any attempt to embellish or explain. That turned out to be the determining factor. John Sole, although a gentile and not of the chosen people, came to them as an honorable man. He would be an acceptable addition to the family.

Saul Berman lowered his glasses, peering at John over the top. He turned to his daughter who had watched the inquisition with barely concealed amusement. "I suppose you will marry him no matter what we say."

"I will." Shaye nodded, her eyes meeting her father's with firm determination. Then she smiled. "And now that you've had your fun, it's time to let my man off the hook."

"I suppose you're right," Berman said, standing and extending a hand. "Welcome to the family, John Sole."

Sole rose to take his hand. Family. The word had always been a distant dream. Shaye had made it a reality for him. "Thank you, sir."

"Call me, Saul."

"Thank you, Saul."

Naomi Berman left her seat beside her daughter on the family's overstuffed sofa and put her arms around him, planting a wet, red lipstick kiss on his cheek. Then she stood back, running her eyes up and down his lean frame. "We need to fatten you up some, though."

It became a family joke, Naomi's efforts to put meat on his bones and overcome Sole's natural tendency toward leanness. To his delight, she worked hard to fulfill her goal, sending a never-ending supply of treats and delicacies his way to put some additional flesh on her son-in-law.

Blintzes and bagels. Gefilte fish and goulash. Lox, whitefish and cream cheese. Honey cake and potato pancakes. They were new and exotic tastes, for a small-town boy from the hills of North Georgia.

While his waistline had thickened a bit over the years, his genes helped him maintain his trim physique. Saul joked and said his gentile blood made him immune to Naomi's cooking. It all made John Sole feel he had become part of something bigger than himself, no longer alone. He was home.

Then one day, Shaye gave him a gift.

"I think you'll do," she said.

"Oh?" Sole smiled as he washed, shaved and readied himself for his evening shift. "That's comforting. I thought you might kick me out once the warranty expired."

"Nope. You're here for the duration. We've got graduation, college, walking down the aisle, you know, the usual things."

"The usual things?" He lowered the razor. "Are you saying …"

"Yes." The smile on her face seemed even more radiant than usual.

They gifts came, completing the work she had started. It was an amazing time. Samantha was born in the spring. Three years later a son, Robert came to them. They were a family. John Sole was whole.

SEVENTEEN

After All

The descent from the Elizondo estate to the city and port of Lázaro Cárdenas took thirty minutes. Views of the harbor and the Pacific Ocean alternated with the mottled green of the hillsides as they made the switchback turns. Sunlight filtered through the tops of tall, spindly trees that the American did not recognize, reminding him again that he was in a strange and foreign place.

The image of the man strangled to death while Bebé Elizondo stood calmly to the side, gazing out over the ocean, lingered in his mind. He shook his head as if that could clear the memory. It did not. It was another reminder. This place was not only alien to him; the rules here were different.

Death came with an unnerving easiness. One minute, a man breathed, sweated, tried to reason with the smiling, soft-faced Bebé. The next, he kicked and gagged, biting through his tongue as the life left his body. After that, they ate and talked as if nothing extraordinary had happened. The murder was merely a storm cloud passing over for a moment. Then the day cleared revealing a bright sun full of happiness and good cheer. He swallowed back the bile that surged into his throat.

The last few days had been a kaleidoscope of emotion, the surreal mixing with the ordinary as each hour passed, like an acid trip taken on a dare while he was in college. One minute, Sofía Elizondo was preparing meals. The children frolicked and climbed on their father's lap or danced laughing in circles around his houseguest. The next they huddled to discuss their business, the need for trust and the punishment for betrayals, leaving no doubt that the consequences of failure would be severe.

Once, as the day and talks progressed, the American had thought about calling the plan off. He could shake hands with Bebé, say no hard feelings, promise to keep all the details in confidence and return to the States on the next flight. The thought flittered away as quickly as it had come. It was bullshit, and he knew it.

He was in too far now to back out. Alejandro's stone-like gaze, watching all, waiting for a word from Bebé, reminded him that leaving was impossible.

Elizondo's congeniality could turn in an instant into something else. He had witnessed it. The smile would fade, and he would stand quiet, imperturbable as Alejandro resolved any problems with the American.

Besides, the American needed the money. The family business he had inherited, and that had made him a wealthy man at a young age was struggling. As costs rose and profits dwindled, he had struggled to find a way to stay afloat.

Then out of nowhere, a call had come from a mysterious man who claimed to represent an investor who could provide much-needed capital for his business. The investor had a product to transport into the United States. As a partner, the American would share a percentage of the profits derived from those imports.

The American was no fool. The sums of money the caller discussed were far beyond what any legal import could provide.

There were several follow-up calls while the American considered the offer. Importing—smuggling—illegal narcotics presented unique risks. The American asked many questions. Sometimes, he received answers.

Who was the investor?

All in good time the caller told him.

He could lose everything, he had said. What about the risk?

There is a risk to every business venture, and that's what this was—a business venture. The money would offset the risk.

Yes. That was something to consider. There was the money. So much money. More money than he would see in a lifetime of running his business, if he didn't go bankrupt first, and bankruptcy was just over the horizon.

The caller suggested he meet with the investor and sent him a first-class ticket to Morelia in the Mexican State of Michoacán, a place the American had never been. He decided it was at least worth a conversation to flesh out the details. Within hours after his arrival, he watched Miguel Diaz struggle, feet kicking as he died. He knew then that the time for conversations had ended.

The car made the final turn from the switchback road into Lázaro Cárdenas. They stayed close on the bumper of the lead car full of armed men to provide security. Bebé was taking no chances that a rival might try to interfere in his business with the American.

They drove by the docks where the big ships were being loaded and through the city center. At last, they came to the *Aeropuerto General Lázaro Cárdenas Del Rio*. The cars went around to a side entrance where a guard lifted a gate and saluted as they passed. Speeding across active taxiways, they came to a remote portion of the airfield away from the main terminal and regular commercial flights.

The helicopter waited, engines already spooling up. The massive main rotor, blades, drooping at the ends from their weight, turned ponderously over their heads.

As they exited the cars, the security men jumped out of the lead vehicle and formed a perimeter around the helicopter. They were serious looking men armed with automatic rifles, eyes focused outward to detect any threats. The American wondered who would dare threaten Elizondo.

The driver rushed around to take his bags from the rear and place them in the helicopter. With a nod of thanks, the American boarded the chopper. He turned in surprise when he saw that Alejandro took the seat beside him.

"You're coming along?"

"Bebé wants me to ensure that you arrive safely at your flight."

With that said, the helicopter eased itself into the sky. The flight to Morelia passed in silence, followed by more silence as the American checked in for his Aero Mexico flight, passed through security and made his way to the gate. He was no longer surprised that the guards and airport staff made way for Alejandro and allowed him to accompany the American all the way to the gate.

They sat side by side in plastic chairs until the plane

boarded. When the flight was called by the gate agent, the American stood.

"Well, that's me. It's been a pleasure." He nodded at Alejandro without extending a hand, repulsed at the thought of touching the hand that strangled other men with such ease. It seemed safer just to smile and say goodbye.

"Goodbye," Alejandro said facing the American. "We will be in touch."

"Looking forward to it." The American nodded, walked through the door and down the jetway.

With his carry-on stowed overhead and his seatbelt fastened, he ordered bourbon from the petite, brown-eyed flight attendant who gave him a glowing white smile and said, "*Sí, señor.*"

Drink in hand a minute later, he sat back and relaxed. For the first time since arriving in Mexico, he felt the tension ease and a sense of normalcy returning. A drink on an airplane. A smiling flight attendant eager to please him. No steely-eyed man with a garrote in his pocket staring at him.

A few minutes later, the plane lifted from the runway, climbed out over the Pacific and then made a long banking turn toward the northeast and the United States. Muscles relaxed and taut nerves loosened with every mile. He wanted to sleep, but first, he had to make a call to his assistant, the only other person who knew of his visit to Elizondo.

Thankful that Mexico had done away with the silly restrictions on cell phone usage in flight, he pulled out his phone and punched the speed dial number. It rang once.

"I've been waiting for your call. Thought I might hear from you yesterday." The voice on the other end was eager.

"Sorry. Calling was not possible. He insisted that there be no calls from his location."

"Understood. So where are we?"

"We proceed." He didn't mention to his assistant that proceeding was the only way to go. "Did you speak to them?" he asked without identifying 'them.'

"Yes, two nights ago, and I have a follow-up meeting today to finalize the logistics."

"Good ... good," the American said, relaxing more. "I need you to arrange something for me."

"Okay. What?"

They spoke for five more minutes as he explained what Elizondo wanted to do to solidify their plans and protect their new business partnership.

"Interesting idea," his assistant said. "I'll have it set up before you get home. Anything else?"

"Not for now. I just need some rest. Been a long couple of days."

"Get some sleep. We'll be ready." There was a pause before his assistant continued. "Do you mind if I ask how ... valuable ... your contacts will be?"

The American smiled. The younger man on the phone was the only other person he had involved. The promise of a small percentage of the profits was enough to gain his unswerving loyalty to the project.

"Very valuable," he answered. "Multiply the estimates we discussed by ten."

There was another pause as the assistant calculated the enormity of their expected windfall.

"That is good news ... very good," he said, his voice suddenly breathless.

"I thought it would be."

The call ended. The American ordered another

bourbon from the smiling flight attendant then stretched back and closed his eyes.

As the miles lengthened from the hacienda on the hillside, he found himself more at ease with their project. Thoughts of strangled men and threatening eyes faded away, replaced in his mind by images of dollars ... enormous piles of dollars.

He drifted off to sleep, telling himself that nothing had really changed. He was the same person he always was. After all, he hadn't killed anyone.

EIGHTEEN

Question of the Day

It was Sole's turn to drive. Instead of passing by the corner without stopping, he pulled to the curb across the intersection from Luis Acero's street-side drug emporium.

Already nervous, the drug dealer tried hard not to look at the car but couldn't resist. He wiped his brow with his sleeve, his head swiveling back and forth casting glances at the unmarked, but plainly identifiable, Atlanta PD car. The asshole detectives inside were watching him, just fucking sitting there staring.

A heavyset woman with two small children in tow came around the corner. She stopped in her tracks as she was about to make the pass to Luis, money for cocaine. Her eyes narrowed.

She shoved the money back in the pocket of her too-tight jeans, grabbed the hand of one of the children and continued past Luis, head lowered.

"Fuckin' five-o across the street watchin'," she snarled and scowled at Luis, her eyes red-rimmed, her face gaunt despite the sagging excess flesh she carried.

"Ow! You hurtin' me!" The little girl she was dragging struggled to release herself from the claw-like grip.

"Shut up!" the woman hissed, jerking the girl's arm. "Takin' you back to your mama now." Then to Luis, she added, "You movin' or what? I need my hit ... need it bad."

"Yeah, I'm movin'. Be an hour then I'll be at the other corner ... you know where."

"I know. I'll be there, you make sure you there too."

"Don't fuckin' tell me what to do, bitch. You want your shit, be there in an hour."

Luis turned and walked inside the corner market that served as his street headquarters as well as the neighborhood liquor store, pawn shop, and source of paycheck loans. He ignored the old man behind the counter who ignored him in return and walked to the backroom. Pulling open the beer cooler door, he deposited his pocketful of drugs in an empty milk crate and stacked several cases of beer on top for safekeeping.

He watched for a minute from the cooler, gazing past the greasy fingerprints, fly specks and window glass to the corner across the street. It was empty, the police car gone.

"Motherfuckers," he muttered, leaving the cooler and walking to the front door.

After scanning both ends of the block through the glass, Luis went out into the street. There was no reason to warn the old man not to touch his stash in the cooler. They had a working relationship. In exchange for the use of his store and cooler, Luis provided the owner a small percentage of his profits. These added up over time, making a nice supplement to the old man's future retirement.

As he made the circuitous walk around several blocks to wind his way back to the alley, Luis' temper flared. Motherfuckers, parked across the street! How the fuck was he supposed to make living, them doing shit like that? By the time he made it to their hidden meeting place and jerked the Ford's rear door open, he was fuming.

"What the fuck …" he began, his voice rising in anger as he thumped into the seat and slammed the door shut behind him.

"Shut up." Sole's voice was quiet, firm and not to be challenged.

They sat without speaking for almost a full minute. Travis stared at him in the mirror. Sole stared at him from the side. Luis stared out the window and felt the urge to squirm and pull his shorts out of his ass. He didn't. Finally, he spoke.

"I gave you …" Luis whispered, changing his tone, trying to bring the tension level down a couple of notches.

The tension level did not come down.

"You gave us shit," Sole said.

"But …"

"Shit!" Sole's voice rose.

Luis reached into his pocket for the pack of cigarettes and placed one in between his lips, trying to hide the tremble in his fingers. He patted his pocket for a light, came up empty and looked at Sole. This time there was no accommodating lighter waiting for him.

Sole broke the silence. "Well?"

"Why?" Luis responded with his own question.

"Why what?" Sole leaned in close. "Don't fuck around with us, Luis!"

"Why you say I gave you shit?" Luis said, trying to maintain eye contact with Sole and reason with him. "It was true. The white dude was there. He didn't belong there, not on the third floor huddled up with Ortega … and then Esteban got in my face." Luis shook his head, the unlit cigarette wobbling between his pursed lips, teeth clamped together as he spoke. "I'm tellin' you; this is something big. They got something planned with that white dude, and it got to do with the supply from down south ... you know Mexico ... Colombia ... wherever."

"Just one little problem," Travis said, drawing his eyes away from Sole's stare.

"What?"

"No way to single out the white dude you saw."

"What you mean no way? You talk to that Russian son of a bitch ... sock-love or whatever the fuck his name is?"

"Yeah, we spoke to Sokolov," Sole said, his voice rising by several decibels so that Luis' head jerked back in his direction. "He doesn't remember any white dude with Ortega. In fact, he doesn't remember Ortega at all ... never heard of him."

"That's bullshit."

"Yep." Sole nodded, his eyes fixed on Luis. "The deepest kind, but doesn't change the fact that we can't name the white dude."

"So why you hasslin' me?"

"Come on, Luis," Travis said. "Do we really have to go back through that again? You owe us something big. You need to pay up before the heat gets turned up on you and your little business."

"Tellin' you," Luis whined, sounding like a child pouting. "This *is* big."

"Maybe, but not unless we can identify the white dude huddled up with Ortega," Travis replied.

"You get us a name," Sole added sharply. "Or you'll be looking over your shoulder for the narcs from now on."

"How I'm supposed to do that?" Luis whined.

"We don't give a shit how. Just do it," Sole snapped

back. "Here's how this works." Sole used his thumb to motion at Travis and himself. "We are the cops. You …" He pointed a thick index finger at Luis. "You are the criminal. That makes you the criminal informant … the one with the connections to other criminals. You use those connections to find out who the white dude is. That might get you paid up. Do that, and we keep looking the other way while you do that other thing you do." Sole smiled. "You know, criminal stuff."

"I go back in there, they figure it was me for sure that ratted. Esteban will make me disappear for good."

"Hell," Sole said with a chuckle. "Probably just a matter of time before he does that, anyway. Moya is one bad-tempered son of a bitch." He nodded at Luis, a somber look on his face, the humor gone from his voice. "Find out who the white dude is, and maybe we can keep Moya and Ortega from dumping what's left of you into the Chattahoochee."

"You gonna get me killed," Luis muttered and pushed the door open.

They watched him retreat down the alley, patting his pockets in search of a lighter for the bent cigarette dangling from his lips.

"What do you think?" Travis asked.

"Longshot," Sole replied. "Identifying the white guy in the suit and why he was huddled with Ortega is the key … to something."

"Yeah, but what?"

"That would be the question of the day."

NINETEEN

Land of Opportunity

Bautista Ortega's cabin cruiser wasn't quite a yacht, but the distinction was lost on most observers. With its name emblazoned in bold gold letters on the stern, the *Águila Real*, or royal eagle, it cruised the main channel and back bays of Lake Lanier cutting a wake that rivaled any seagoing craft.

Wilson Bettis sat in a leather chair on the top deck, enjoying the sun and the breeze blowing in his face. They pulled away from the marina with one of Ortega's men at the wheel and headed north towards the less populated areas of the lake.

Bautista Ortega and his lieutenant, Esteban Moya sat across from Bettis, sipping chilled tequila, watching the palatial houses on the shore pass by. They spoke to each other in muted Spanish and made no attempt to include Bettis in their conversation. It was just as well. He had no desire to know more than was necessary about their business.

When they were clear of the marina and boat slips, the

man at the controls pushed the throttle forward. The bow lifted, pushing them back in their seats. Bettis watched Ortega lift his face into the wind like a dog sniffing the air from the back of a pickup truck.

An hour later, the bow settled, and the engine noise decreased to a gentle, idling hum. The man at the wheel turned to starboard and allowed the boat to drift into a small cove. Another hand went forward and dropped the anchor.

"So what do you hear?" Ortega began the conversation without preliminaries.

"All is well. I spoke to him on the phone a short while ago. He is traveling home today." Bettis nodded and lifted the Modelo Negra beer he had been nursing since leaving the marina. "It was a good meeting. They reached an agreement."

Ortega and Moya exchanged knowing smirks. There had never been any doubt there would be an agreement with Bebé Elizondo.

"So when do we meet your employer?" Moya asked.

"You don't," Bettis said, savoring the opportunity to shove a little of their Latin machismo back in their faces.

"We want to meet with him." Ortega's eyes narrowed, wrinkling his fleshy brow in an intimidating way that made it plain El Toro did not like being denied.

"Sorry." Bettis shook his head. "No can do."

Esteban Moya leaned forward in his chair, staring into Bettis' eyes. "I think you forget where you are." He motioned around the deserted cove. "Who we are."

Bettis looked beyond him to the shoreline two hundred yards away. Pine trees and oaks descended the surrounding hills to the water's edge. No other human was in sight.

"I am familiar with who you are and what you are capable of." He smiled. "You do not meet my employer for your own protection. He is a public man. It would not do for someone to see the two of you together. There would be scrutiny."

"You say this? To me?" Ortega lifted the eyebrows over his hard brown eyes. "You who came to meet me at the club dressed in a suit, looking like a lawyer. Everyone noticed." He smirked. "My friend Sokolov has warned me that there has been some *scrutiny* of your visit to Eruptions."

"Who?" Bettis' smile vanished.

"Police ... two detectives. They were curious, asking questions about the gringo in a suit who was meeting with El Toro."

"I came from work. There wasn't time to change. You told me there were no cameras ... no way for anyone to know, and I used the back entrance as you said."

"Yes," Ortega nodded. "But someone saw you. They reported your presence to the police." He shrugged. "Fortunately, He could not identify you, and you are right, there are no cameras, so there is no concern ... for now."

"Who told them?" Bettis persisted.

"Ah ... that." Ortega's lips pressed into a thin, mean smile. "We aren't certain, but we will find out. When we do ..." He shrugged. "They won't be a problem anymore."

"Still," Ortega continued in a more accommodating tone. "You may be correct that meeting with your employer would be ill-advised." He nodded. "I accept this condition for now as long as we can meet with you and there are no complications in our arrangements."

"There won't be any complications," Bettis replied, his voice calm. "That's what I'm here for."

"Good." Ortega smiled as a breeze came up, rocking the *Águila Real* on a gentle swell. "*Me encanta aquí.*" He looked at Bettis and translated. "I love it out here. It is beautiful, don't you think?"

"It is." Bettis nodded his agreement.

Surrounded by dense woods on the three sides of the cove, the boat faced out toward the opposite shore a mile across the broad lake. Birds flittered in the brush along the shore. A kingfisher dove from high in a pine beside the water to pluck a minnow from the shallows.

The day was warm and sultry. To any other boat that chanced to pass this secluded part of the lake, they would appear to be a group of friends out enjoying the sun and drinks. Gangsters and drug cartels were out of place here. Even so, it was time to get down to business.

"So now we must make our plans," Ortega sighed and continued. "The shipment is due soon, and our inventory is running low."

"Agreed." Bettis nodded.

They spent most of the day planning for the transfer of Elizondo's inventory into the United States. Tensions eased as their plans solidified, and they set a date for the first shipment. Even Esteban Moya managed a smile when Ortega chided him about putting on weight during the lunch served to them on the upper deck.

When the engines roared to life, and the boat turned back towards the marina, Wilson Bettis grinned.

"You told me I shouldn't have attracted attention showing up at Eruptions in a suit!" He shouted over the wind and engine noise. "What about this? Drug lord riding around Lake Lanier in a big-ass boat."

"They only *think* I am a drug lord!" Ortega nodded, laughing. "They have no proof. They can think all they want, but in this country, I am innocent until proven guilty. Isn't that what your Constitution says?"

"It is indeed," Bettis replied, nodding.

Ortega reached over and slapped Moya on the back as they sped across the lake. "You hear? Innocent until proven guilty. America truly is the land of opportunity!"

TWENTY

Fairy Tale

"Now what?" Travis asked.

"Damn good question," Sole replied with a shrug. "I guess now we have to do actual police detective type work."

"Cool," Travis said. "Been wanting to try some of that."

"Yeah, but let's not try too much of it on this one." Sole started the car and pulled from their hiding place into the alley, turning in the opposite direction Luis Acero had taken. "We've spent a lot of time on it with nothing to show." He shook his head. "There is the chance Luis is trying to pull one over on us ... just all talk."

"It's crossed my mind," Travis replied, adding, "But I would have bet anything he was genuinely terrified ... had the shakes ... voice trembling." He shook his head. "I have a hard time believing our boy Luis is that good an actor."

"True," Sole agreed. "If he's lying, he should get an Oscar for his performance." He sighed. "I expect we've rattled Luis' cage all we can for now. Let's give it one more day to turn something up ... a name, a face ... something we can sink our teeth into. If we don't, then we close out his ticket. Call it past due and turn him over to the narcs, no strings attached."

"Fair enough. Where you want to start?"

Sole pondered that for a second as he steered the Ford through the morning traffic. "We already hit the club so let's expand it and check video recordings at every ATM, parking lot, building lobby ... any place in the area our white dude in a suit might have stopped at on his way to Eruptions for a head to head with a drug kingpin.

"That's a hell of a lot of video."

"Got a better idea?"

"Nope." Travis shrugged. "Let's do it. Maybe start with parking lots. He had to get there somehow, and if he drove, he had to park somewhere."

"Right." Sole nodded, glad to have a plan. "If we don't turn anything up, we move out to ATMs and other buildings from there and see what turns up."

Nothing turned up. Two of the four parking lots within walking distance of Eruptions had camera coverage, but only on the attendant's shack, which was of no use for identifying after hours parkers. The other two had good camera systems but no useful images.

They moved on to ATM surveillance cameras at three local banks and in the lobbies of two major high-rise buildings. Bank and building security staff were more helpful than the parking garage attendants, but nothing useful turned up. The ATMs were busy. A few of the customers wore suits, but there was no way to tell where they headed after they left the ATM.

By the end of the day, Sole and Travis realized they could spend years questioning every occupant of the dozens of midtown office buildings and never identify the unknown white male. He was a blank face in a crowd of thousands of possible suspects.

"What do you want to do now?" Travis pulled his sunglasses down from their perch at the top of his eyebrows and settled them on his nose.

The waning afternoon was warm. The car's interior had become uncomfortably hot and stuffy parked in the sun while they sat in the dark rooms scanning video images. Sole opened the driver's door slid behind the wheel, started the car and cranked up the air conditioner to an icy gale.

"I want to stop seeing spots," he said, rubbing the corners of his eyes with his thumb and forefinger. He looked at Travis and shrugged. "Well, it seemed like a good plan this morning."

"Still is." Travis nodded. "Just need more manpower to go through the video, check all the possibles, eliminate the ones who were home having supper, and verify alibis until we come up with a reasonable list of suspects that's not in the thousands." He shrugged. "Simple. Shouldn't take more than five or six years."

"Yeah, simple, but there's not going to be any more manpower." Sole shook his head. "Not on a shaky tip from a CI who might be playing us."

"True." Travis nodded. "Mind a suggestion?"

"Shoot."

"Let's call it a day. Give it a rest and rethink things tomorrow. If we don't come up with anything else, then we turn Mr. Acero over to the narc squad and get back on our cases."

"Sounds good to me." Sole pulled the car into the city's rush hour traffic.

It was after five in the afternoon. The streets and sidewalks were flooded with people pouring from the surrounding high-rises and offices. The odds against identifying one person out of that throng were a Vegas bookie's dream.

Reality settled in. Luis Acero would not be the first informant to concoct a story to lighten the pressure from his handlers. His account of an over-dressed white male meeting with El Toro might be nothing more than a doper's fairy tale.

TWENTY-ONE

Everything was in Order

The American was nervous about making his way through the airport. On any given day, Atlanta's Hartsfield-Jackson International Airport is the busiest air terminal in the world with about two hundred and sixty-thousand people passing through its gates. Thousands more service personnel and airline employees are required to keep the flow of humanity moving.

At first, he thought the mass of bodies congregated in one place would make it easy to disappear into the crowd. His assistant, Wilson Bettis, warned him it also increased the likelihood of an encounter with someone who might recognize him and ask questions. Donning the ball cap and sunglasses Bettis had provided, he walked along the bridge from the Aero Mexico jet to the concourse, head down, avoiding eye contact.

The next hurdle was U.S. Customs. There would be facial recognition technology there, cameras and computers scanning for faces that matched those in the terrorist watch list database. He was a known figure, but he wasn't a terrorist and unless someone recognized him or was looking for him, his passage through the airport should go unnoticed. That was the plan, at least.

"Remove your hat and sunglasses." The customs agent looked up from his passport.

His heart skipped several beats. He reached up and removed the cap with one shaky hand and the sunglasses with the other. You are so fucked, his mind screamed at him. What were you thinking?

The agent leaned forward, peering into his eyes, then looked at the passport and back at his face. After an excruciatingly long period of examination that lasted all of ten seconds, the officer handed him his passport and smiled.

Was it a smile of recognition or just the perfunctory smile he gave a thousand times a day? No, he knows me. This is it. All of the planning, the partnership, the money was about to blow up in his face. Fuck!

The American's eyes darted to the side, to the armed officers lining the back wall. They would take him in some backroom. There would be questions about his unscheduled trip to Mexico.

Why were you in Michoacán?
Why did you meet with a drug cartel boss?
What did you do when they murdered a man in front of you?

"Welcome home. Have a nice evening," the agent said, handing the passport back and looking beyond him to the line of waiting passengers. "Next!"

He managed to mumble, "Thank you," as he pulled the ball cap visor down over his face and settled the sunglasses on his nose.

Exhaling a deep breath, he walked through the door into the main terminal. Thousands of people bustled around him, unmindful of his existence.

Or was it just a show? Were they pretending not to see him, not to know him? Did the customs agent pretend not to recognize him? That's it. It was all a setup, a trap. Somewhere the security cameras were watching, FBI agents following his every move.

Everyone in the crowded terminal stared. He felt their eyes on his back as he passed, imagined he heard their whispers.

Look, there he goes. He's the one who met with the drug cartel murderer.

Who? That tall man there?

Yeah, that one. The one about six foot one, two hundred pounds, graying hair, clean shaven.

See him over there. He's got that stupid ball cap and sunglasses on to fool us, but that's him.

He clenched his eyes for a moment. Stop! The whispers faded.

He had done nothing wrong, he told himself. He had killed no one. It wasn't a crime to see someone else commit a murder, was it? He wasn't sure.

The point was, he told himself, he didn't plan it. He didn't want it to happen. He didn't take part. They planned it. They made it happen in front of him, a *demonstration* of what would happen to him if …

Focus! Calm down!

You are just another anonymous face moving through the airport. Keep moving. Don't stop and let anyone ask you questions. Questions are bad. Bebé won't like questions.

He hurried out of baggage claim to the public transportation curb and tugged the cap brim even lower on his forehead. Outside, the evening air was warm and sultry. A trickle of perspiration formed on his brow. He made his way to the taxi line just as the next available cab pulled up.

Yanking the door open, he tossed his bag across the seat, and climbed in behind it, pulling the door shut with a bang.

"Where to?"

He looked up to see the curious eyes of the driver watching him in the mirror. For a moment, he thought of pulling the door handle and looking for another cab, but that might have drawn attention.

Still, it was disconcerting. The driver—a man of Hispanic origin—bore an uncanny resemblance to round-faced, smiling Bebé Elizondo. He forced himself to relax and examine the man's ID posted by the meter. Emilio Garcia could have been Elizondo's brother, or at least a close family relative.

"Buckhead. Peachtree Road." He gave him the address of a deluxe high-rise condominium.

The driver picked his way through the airport traffic. He settled back in the seat, feeling safe enough to lift the brim of the ball cap and peer out the window. Outside, everything appeared normal. No police pursued. No fingers pointed. No one shouted, stop the drug smuggler! He breathed a sigh of relief.

Emilio braked to avoid another taxi that darted in front toward the passenger departures lane.

"*¡Mierda! ¡Estúpido hijo de puta!*" Shit! Stupid son of a bitch. Emilio lifted his arm, glaring at the other driver as he came even with the car, then gunned the engine and passed.

The American in the back smiled. He was home.

Traffic wasn't bad for that time of day. The drive to Buckhead only took twenty minutes.

He paid the driver and gave him a moderate tip. Not too big or too small to notice and remember.

Usually, he would have had Wilson Bettis, arrange a limo or would have driven himself and valet parked his

BMW at the airport. Those options would leave a paper trail and involve too many people.

A brief nod to the doorman and he was in the elevator on his way to his penthouse condo. He pushed the heavy double oak doors open, dropped his bag on the wood parquet, and went into the living room to stand before the wall of windows that looked out over the Atlanta skyline.

The sun was well below the horizon now. The red-orange glow in the west contrasted pleasingly with the city lights below. On another evening he would have sat on the balcony for a few minutes, sipping bourbon and taking in the view.

Instead, he pulled his phone from his pocket and hit the speed dial for Bettis' number.

"You made it home safe and sound, I trust." Bettis sounded pleased and annoyingly calm.

"Just got in." He changed the subject. "How did your meeting go?"

"Not bad." Bettis smiled. "Good, actually."

He could imagine his assistant's self-satisfied smile over the phone, and it irritated him. "Tell me."

"We made the arrangements for the first delivery. Do you want the details now?"

What he wanted to say was, yes, you little pissant! It's been a long day. I want the fucking details! Don't play coy with me. Without me, your dreams of riches, are just that ... dreams.

What he said was, "Yes. Tell me."

They discussed the arrangements he'd worked out on Ortega's boat that afternoon. It was a simple plan but required careful management of the logistics. He asked a few questions then moved to the other related matter of importance.

"And tomorrow?"

"I have everything set for ten in the morning ... made sure our usual friends will be present up front."

"Good." He nodded and looked out the bank of windows. The western glow had faded now, replaced by the city lights twinkling star-like all the way to the horizon. "If there's nothing else ..."

"There is one more thing," Bettis said.

"What?"

"They wanted a meet with you."

"What did you say?"

"I said, no can do."

He sensed the grin was back on Bettis' face. The smug little bastard. "Good. That can't happen."

"I know. That's what I told them."

"And?"

"And they can live with it. I'll be their point of contact in all matters. You will never be involved, at least not face to face."

"Good. Stop by in the morning. We'll go over together."

He was ready to end the conversation and disconnected the call, asking no more questions. It was time for a drink.

He grabbed his bag and went to the master bedroom, tossing it on a chair as he kicked off his shoes. A minute later, he had changed into jeans and a lightweight pullover shirt. On the way back to the living room, he cranked the thermostat down so the air conditioning blew at full speed.

He stopped at the liquor cabinet, poured three fingers of bourbon into a glass and carried it to the bank of windows, sinking into an overstuffed leather chair. Eyes closed, he put his head back.

The events of the last few days passed by in a kaleidoscope of contrasting images. Bebé's smooth face and

Alejandro Garza's hard eyes. The blue Pacific and green hills surrounding Lázaro Cárdenas. Elizondo standing tranquilly by the window while Garza strangled the life from Miguel Diaz.

The bourbon glow helped push the images away. Everything was in order, he told himself.

TWENTY-TWO

Life Was a Blast

"Dad, are we Jewish?"

"What?" John Sole lifted his eyes from the morning news open on his tablet.

"Jewish ... are we Jewish?" Fourteen-year-old Samantha Sole sat at the breakfast table, books stacked in a neat pile beside her bowl of wheat flakes and plate of buttered toast. Brow furrowed, she had the look of a person contemplating a profound philosophical question.

"Maybe." Her father smiled, amused. "Do you want to be Jewish?"

"I don't know." Samantha shrugged. "Maybe."

"Mind if I ask you why the sudden concern about it?"

"Just some things Grandpa Berman was saying last night. We went over to have dinner while you were at work."

"So, what did he say?" John put the tablet down, leaned his elbows on the kitchen table, listening.

"Well ..." Samantha looked up at the ceiling as she

recalled her grandfather's words. "Jewish tradition ... law ... in the Torah says ..." She hesitated.

He patted her hand. "Go on."

"Well, it says it's not the father that makes you Jewish. It's the mother."

"This is true."

"So Mom is Jewish, but you're not."

"Correct again."

"So that means I am Jewish ... right?"

"What did Grandpa Berman say?"

"He said I should talk to you about it. That he was just explaining things ... letting me know my options."

John smiled. Saul Berman was a wise man. There had never been any pressure to raise the children as Jews or anything else. All he wanted was for his grandchildren to know their heritage.

"Okay. So let's talk," Sole said. "I go back to my original question. Do you want to be Jewish?"

"Sometimes I think I do," Samantha said and then added quickly. "Not that I don't want to be like you too, Dad."

"You don't have to apologize, Sam."

"It's just ..." Samantha folded her hands on the table and looked at them solemnly. "It's just that we don't have your family around. Grandma Sole ..." She hesitated. "Well, I never knew her. She died before I was born."

"You would have loved her, Sam." He set his hand on his daughter's. "And she would have loved you no matter what choice you made."

"Really?"

"Really." He nodded. "It's your choice, so you decide. If you want to be Jewish, then that's what you should do, but be sure. It's not something to decide on a whim."

"I know."

"Jews are a proud people. They have a right to be. They've been persecuted. People have tried to kill them, but they take it all and find a way to overcome. That's a pretty strong heritage, and any father would be proud to have it as part of his family."

"Okay." Samantha contemplated things for a few seconds, quiet, the way she did when thinking through complicated problems.

He watched her, wondering what he had ever done to deserve the children that had come to them. Then he remembered. It was Shaye. She had given it all to him. Children, family, love, a home, everything that made him whole.

"Can I ask you something else?" Samantha said, her brown eyes serious. "I've heard things."

"What things?"

"Things about Jews."

"Oh." John nodded. "I see."

"Not very nice things," she went on. "That Jews are dirty and cheap like Ebenezer Scrooge. That they are cowards, and sneaky."

"Well, let me ask you some questions then," John said. "Is anyone in this house dirty?"

"No." Samantha shook her head. "Mom wouldn't tolerate it."

"How about cheap? Is Grandpa Berman cheap?"

"No." She looked up thinking. "One time I was with him, and he stopped to buy breakfast for a man with a sign at a corner."

"How about cowards? Think your mother is a coward?"

Samantha laughed. The idea of Shaye afraid of anything was too ridiculous to consider.

"Anyone sneaky in this family?" John asked.

Again, Samantha laughed. "No. Everyone around here always knows what everyone else is thinking."

"Right." His face hardened for a moment. "As for the assholes who say those kinds of things about Jews, they can go to hell. They're idiots."

Shaye walked in trailed by Bobby just as he finished. "Watch your language with the kids, John."

"Oh, Mom." Samantha shook her head. "Dad was just telling me about the people who say bad things about Jews."

"Oh," Shaye patted John on the shoulder, leaning over to kiss his cheek. "Those people can go to hell. They're all assholes."

Breakfast ended, and the kids went off to catch the school bus. Samantha kissed his cheek. "Thanks for the talk, Dad."

"Welcome. Have a good day."

"See ya, Dad." Bobby waved.

"Bye, Big Guy."

The kitchen door slammed behind them. Silence settled over the house as Shaye sat down at the table, sipping her coffee.

"What's on your agenda today, Detective Sole?" she asked peering at him over the top of the cup.

"Gonna go in later. We're trying to follow up on a tip from a CI, but it's going nowhere. Might hang out at Eruptions to see what we can see."

"The night club?"

"Yeah. Word is some out of place white dude met with a suspected drug lord there." He shrugged and picked up his cup, gulping down the last of the lukewarm coffee. "Didn't fit the profile so there might be something to it … or the CI might be playing us. Either way, we need to put it to bed and move on."

"Sounds like fun."

"How about you?"

"Same old stuff. Afternoon shift at dispatch."

"Afternoon, huh?" He placed the coffee cup back on the table. "Does that mean we have a little private time to … maybe time to firm up our marital relationship?"

"Detective Sole, are you propositioning me?" Shaye said grinning as she stood. "Follow me." She reached out and took his hand, leading him to the bedroom. "I know just the place to firm things up."

Afterward, she dozed against his shoulder while he stared at the ceiling, contentment washing over him as he thought about his family. The talk with Samantha had surprised him. She was becoming an adult, and he couldn't help feeling it was happening too fast.

Bobby was still young though. He'd never known a happier boy, mostly thanks to his mother. Bobby's perpetual grin broadcast to the world the pure joy of just being. Rain or shine, to Bobby, life was a blast.

He smiled. It was another lesson from his children. Life was indeed a blast.

TWENTY-THREE

Good Drama

Wilson Bettis knew his place. It was clear from the way he walked two paces behind his boss and one to the side.

He didn't mind though. He would soon be wealthier than he could ever be after a lifetime of service as the chief aide to Senator James Sillman.

They rode together in the black limo Bettis had arranged for the event. Seated beside the senator, the short trip from midtown passed in silence. On arrival at the Georgia State Capitol, the driver pulled into a secured private entrance away from the press and visitors.

The senator exchanged pleasantries with the few dignitaries waiting for them, then proceeded along a back hallway to an elevator and up a level to the main floor under the rotunda. Bettis peeled off to one side as his boss strode alone to the center under the dome.

Cameras held on the shoulders of their operators whirred. Flashes lit the room in bursts like miniature novae exploding in their faces.

Those gathered had been promised a major announcement. To underscore its importance to the State of Georgia, the senator would meet with them here and not under another capitol dome six hundred and forty miles to the north.

Members of the media, other politicians, and invited guests leaned forward, curious and expectant. Senator Sillman beamed, pointing here and there to a familiar face, giving a wink to one, mouthing a greeting to another, sending unspoken messages but saying nothing.

He took his place in the precise center of the rotunda, standing alone under the vast expanse of the dome, two hundred thirty-seven feet and four inches above. All eyes focused on the lone figure, erect, distinguished, a god in this small universe. He spoke.

"Thank you all for being here. I wanted to address a topic today that has become a plague on our society. It affects Georgians as much as it does the rest of our great country. That is why I came here, back to my roots, to my home to share with you my thoughts and make an announcement."

Except for the soft hum of the video cameras, the crowd remained silent. Reporters leaned forward speaking into their personal voice recorders or making notes.

"It is no secret. The sale, distribution and use of illegal narcotics affect every corner of our state. They destroy families and kill our children, robbing them of their futures. Efforts in the past have done little to curb the spread and availability of these poisons. Almost every American family ..." He paused and looked into the cameras. "Every Georgia family ... has been exposed to them at some level."

Jaw set, eyes sincere, his voice took on a determined tone. "Any school child can find access to illegal narcotics."

His head bowed, lips turned down in a grave expression of sorrow. "Sadly, many do."

It was classic Sillman, a master at manipulating the emotions of his listeners. The mention of the children had heads nodding around the rotunda. After all, who doesn't love children? A problem that plagues them must be eliminated, and James Sillman, the savior of children, was just the man to do it.

"I, for one, am not going to stand by. I intend to do something about it." His voice took on a good ole boy tone. "With your help, we are fixin' to put a whoopin' on those who think they can break our laws and poison our youth."

Smiles spread through the crowd. Heads nodded. Sillman was one of them.

"I will not stand by any longer." He slammed his right fist into his left palm for emphasis. "That is why next week I am introducing a bill on the floor of the Senate of the United States that will target and eliminate the drug traffickers. We will do more than give it lip service. No more talking about a war on drugs. We are going after the enemy, and we will defeat him … bring him to his knees until he screams for mercy." He pointed a finger at the crowd, jabbing at them with each syllable he spoke. "But there will be no mercy. We will accept nothing less than the total destruction of those who would murder our children with their poison." He lifted a fist to show that the final victory over drugs was in sight. "We will win!"

Sillman turned to stride from the rotunda as the voices of reporters called after him.

"Senator Sillman, can you tell us more about your plan?"

"Senator, give us some specifics about the legislation you are introducing!"

"Senator, what makes your bill different from the war on drugs Nixon declared in 1971?"

"Senator ..."

Hands raised, the media turbulence crashed around him like a storm. As Sillman waded through the crowd, the waters settled in his wake, and some of the more skeptical media representatives tried to decipher what they had just heard. Looking at their notes to decide what they would report back to their respective news publications and networks, they realized he had said nothing new.

Drugs certainly were not new, and the so-called war on drugs was not new or of itself, newsworthy. A few were already thinking maybe that was the story, that this was another political stunt by a seasoned politician to garner votes and fill the media void with drama in order to remain in the spotlight.

Wilson Bettis stepped forward from the side and raised a hand. "Ladies and gentlemen. Senator Sillman has another pressing engagement, but he wanted me to tell you that all of your questions will be answered when you see the bill he brings forward in the Senate next week."

"Do you know what's in it?" A reporter from a local radio station called out.

"Thanks for your time today," Bettis said and turned to follow his boss.

By the time he made it to the elevator and down to the VIP entrance, Sillman was seated in the back of the limo. The engine was running, and as soon as Bettis had climbed in, the car moved down the drive and out onto Capitol Square to merge with traffic.

The Senator from the Great State of Georgia leaned back in the seat, loosened his tie and smiled.

"How'd it go, Wilson?"

"Masterful." He smiled at his boss. "Left them with more questions than answers but put you at the front of the anti-drug fight. A lot of the press will want specifics, but specifics won't matter so much to the public. They want to see the man out front, and that's what you gave them." He nodded. "It was good drama. Everyone loves good drama."

TWENTY-FOUR

I Knew It

The rumble of street noise from busy Ralph David Abernathy Boulevard rose and then ebbed like a tide as the door swung open and shut. Mid-morning sunlight accompanied the sound, flooding into the dark interior of the bar, forcing Luis Acero to squint.

Crouched over a tumbler of cheap whiskey he turned his head to the side to see who had entered. It was no one, at least no one he knew. That was good.

The beer and booze joint was not one of his regular hangouts. He'd been avoiding those for the last few days. In fact, he had been avoiding everyone and anyone who might let Esteban Moya know they had seen him. He had no idea if Moya was looking for him, but Luis was not one to take unnecessary chances.

He held no illusions about himself. He was a rat, and he knew it. He accepted being a rat the way the scurrying rodents in alley trashcans did. It was their life. There was no reason to question why they were rats. They just were, and they lived with it. The dilemma was he didn't know if Esteban Moya knew he was a rat.

Had the fucking detectives figured out who the white dude in the suit was? Had they confronted Ortega and Moya? Would Moya put two and two together and figure out that Luis was the rat?

Too many questions. Best thing for his ass was to lay low like the alley rats when the cat is prowling.

The cops could take away his street corner livelihood. Moya would take his life if there was even the slightest concern that Luis posed a threat to him or to Bautista Ortega.

It wouldn't even take a deliberate thought. A simple passing remark by El Toro, a slight irritation while Esteban was taking his morning shit and the word would be out. Luis would be history and his spot on the corner taken over by another dealer.

Luis would simply cease to exist, and no one would ask questions. No one would dare. Then business would get back to usual while what remained of Luis became dinner for the fish in Lake Lanier.

Huddled out of sight in his apartment, he eventually ran out of booze. Then he ran out of cocaine and pot. After several jittery hours peeking from his apartment window, he decided it was safe enough to go out and get something to calm his nerves.

That's how he ended up in a bar he'd never heard of before, in the west side Mechanicsville district of the city. It was far from his usual turf, and he felt safe enough to sit and have a drink, and then more drinks.

Even so, he cringed every time the door opened. The old woman who had just entered shuffled around the bar in a bathrobe and slippers to sit in the dark at the far corner.

She must have been a regular. Without speaking, the bartender poured a tall glass of bottom shelf gin and sat it on the bar in front of her while she scratched under her arm and then down the front of her robe.

Luis stopped nursing his drink, finishing the last of it in a gulp. He set the glass down with a clunk on the bar top and looked at the bartender who had returned to reading a newspaper beside the wash sink.

"Another ...same," Luis said.

The old man looked up, annoyed. He folded the paper in half, placed it on the bar and walked over to Luis, scratching his belly under the black and gold Georgia Tech tee shirt he wore.

"You gonna keep drinkin' like that, whyn't you buy the bottle?" the bartender suggested, reaching down to the bottom shelf.

"How much?" Luis looked up from his empty glass to the half-empty bottle of no-name whiskey.

The bartender held the bottle up to the light and peered at the level of the liquid inside. "Twenty."

"Here." Luis tossed a bill on the bar. "Leave it."

"Good." The bartender put the bottle in front of Luis, satisfied that this unknown customer would not interrupt him again for a while.

He shuffled back to his post by the wash basin and opened the newspaper. Luis screwed off the bottle's cap and filled his glass. Tilting his head back to take a long swallow, his eyes caught the images on the flickering television over the bar. The glass almost fell from his fingers.

He leaned forward to squint up at the television through the smoky haze. There he was, standing just off to the side and a few steps behind the man speaking. He looked like some politician, but Luis couldn't say who. They were all the same anyway, and he wouldn't have recognized the name if someone had told him.

What he did know was that the man off to the side, standing there smiling in his suit and shiny shoes was the same white dude he had seen huddled with Bautista Ortega at Eruptions. He looked at the bartender.

"Turn the sound up."

"Sound don't work."

It didn't matter. It was him, standing there right in front of the cameras. The politician finished talking, smiled and waved at the cameras, then turned and walked away. The man at the side stepped forward and spoke for a few seconds to the group of people then turned and followed the politician out of camera view.

"Son of a bitch," Luis whispered. Then louder. "I knew it!"

"Knew what?" The bartender looked up, brow furrowed, irritated that the heavy drinker at the end of the bar had interrupted him once again.

"Gimme another bottle ... a full one." Luis stood up from the barstool and reached into his pocket for cash.

"Not supposed to sell takeout ... no liquor store license."

Luis unfolded the last of his cash and threw a hundred on the bar. "This cover it?"

The bartender reached for a bag under the counter and put the bottle Luis was working on inside with another full bottle. "That covers it."

He pocketed the money as Luis grabbed the bag and headed for the door. Outside on the sidewalk, Luis stopped and squinted into the sun to get his bearings. Eyes darting back and forth in case Moya's goons followed, he scurried through back streets and alleys toward his apartment, muttering to himself all the way.

"I knew it. Goddamn, I knew it. That white dude, he somebody ... up there standin' with some politician. Motherfucker got to be somebody, and that somebody been sittin' head to head with El Toro." He stopped at the end of an alley, peering up and down the street before stepping out. "Goddamn if I didn't know it!"

TWENTY-FIVE

A Shock

He thought he was a tough man. His time spent working on his father's fleet of shrimp boats off the Georgia coast in his youth made him think so.

James Jadyn Sillman, JJ as friends and family called him, had indeed rubbed shoulders on the swaying decks of the boats alongside the coarse men with swollen, scarred hands who pulled the nets, manned the winches, oiled the machinery and performed the thousand other tasks required of those who venture out on the ocean to earn their livelihood. JJ had done these things until his own hands were swollen and raw.

He had done these things because his father had insisted. To Sillman senior, it was a *noblesse oblige*, a duty that those of their standing must perform to merit the fruits of the labors of those lower classes who served them.

Anchored at the ports and coastal inlets along the Georgia coastline from Savannah down to St. Mary's, the Sillman shrimping fleet was a significant contributor to the coastal economy. A southern gentleman had obligations by virtue of his birth, and Sillman thought it only proper that JJ should have some acquaintance with the dangerous work and manual toil of those others who had made their family wealthy. So, leaving the soft comforts of his privileged life, JJ went off to work in close quarters with the men who crewed the boats.

In his father's mind, it was a probationary period for JJ, a time to toughen him and teach him about manhood as he learned the family business. For JJ it was a prison sentence.

His parole came when the University of Georgia accepted him for enrollment, fulfilling another family tradition and obligation. Satisfied that his son had paid his dues to southern manhood and the family name during two summers his junior and senior year in high school, Sillman sent JJ to join the same fraternity that had been his when he attended the university thirty years earlier.

In truth, his shrimping experience served him well at the university, at least in a social sense. To his frat brothers from equally privileged families, JJ's toughening experiences on the boats made him unique, a sort of frat boy man of mystery.

They had never clung to the rails of a storm-tossed shrimp boat, the green waters surging over the bow, threatening to wash him overboard. They hadn't known the indignity of being a deckhand under the rule of boat captains and crewmen who had never attended a university or who had any idea what a fraternity was.

His shipmates were told that 'Boss' Sillman, as JJ's father was known among his shrimpers, would not tolerate any accommodations for his son. They must treat him like any other apprentice crewman on the boats. In practice, this meant that some crews, in their zeal to carry out Boss Sillman's instructions, treated JJ far worse than a normal apprentice.

To a few, he was an interloper from a different world. He may have worked among them during the day, but when they returned to port, he went home to a palatial estate on the outskirts of Savannah. They returned to their single-wide trailers and tract homes.

Not long after his arrival at UGA, JJ saw the wisdom in the life lessons his father forced on him. The experience had, in fact, toughened him.

His upper-crust classmates were in awe of him. Wealthy as the Sillman family was, young JJ had been required to perform manual labor in a hard and dangerous industry.

Some would come to his room in the evenings to interrupt his studies and hear the stories he shared, always at their insistence. They leaned forward, passing beers around, fixed on his words.

He recounted the events of his time shrimping. His friends learned with fascination that he had seen death aboard the boats, hands crushed in equipment, shrimpers snared by lines and dragged overboard to drown beneath the green Atlantic.

JJ always welcomed them, trying to make it seem like he did not want the attention. He would shrug and recount his experiences. Each nonchalant shrug enhanced his prestige with the other young men. He learned to pick the right time and the right audience.

The reputation gained in those late night frat sessions followed him as he inherited the family business. JJ Sillman, from a southern aristocratic family, was a man of the people, toughened by hard and dangerous work. He had earned his success and not received it because of the privileged life he inherited. He had his father to thank for that.

Eventually, he ran for public office, always proclaiming to his constituents that he was one of them, a man who understood hard work. He held up the hands that had pulled the nets on his father's shrimp boats and pledged, "These hands will work for you!"

It was soap opera. The voters loved it. After winning three terms in the state legislature, he ran and won a campaign to unseat a longtime incumbent in the U.S. Senate. His campaign posters bore the image of two strong hands with the words, *These Hands Will Work for You!*

These days, he spoke of his days on the shrimp boats over fifty-dollar-a-glass bourbon in the leather chairs of a Buckhead gentleman's club. Like many rich and famous personalities, his ego led him to believe the myth about himself, the one he helped create—a working man, a tough man.

The events of the last few days had shattered that self-image.

The call came soon after his arrival back at his penthouse condo following the press conference. The number showed as unknown, but he knew who it was before he answered.

"Yes." The glass of bourbon in his hand trembled. He lifted it to his lips and gulped it down in one swallow.

"I am instructed to tell you that Bebé is pleased."

Alejandro Garza's voice was emotionless. He could have said the weather tomorrow will be sunny, or you will die, and the inflection would have remained the same, without thought of the consequences of either possibility.

Sillman could not control the cold tingle that ascended his spine. "I … I'm glad Bebé is satisfied. We are setting the stage to …"

"Yes, we are aware of what you are doing," Alejandro interrupted. "It is as we planned. The next phase begins soon."

"Right," was all Sillman could think to say.

There was no further message to relay from Elizondo. The call ended.

The day's events had all been part of the discussion at Elizondo's hacienda. Create the pretense of taking the lead in the so-called war against drugs. Focus the efforts everywhere but on Sillman and his arrangement with Elizondo and *Los Salvajes*.

Bebé had designed the strategy himself, quoting the ancient Chinese military strategist, Sun Tzu.

"All warfare is based on deception. Hence, when we are able to attack, we must seem unable; when using our forces, we must appear inactive; when we are near, we must make the enemy believe we are far away; when far away, we must make him believe we are near."

Bebé had laughed and offered Sillman another glass of tequila as he bragged about the stratagem. Sillman would lead the crusade against drug trafficking, and their dealings would be even more secure. No one would suspect that a U.S. senator was working in partnership with a drug cartel. It was the perfect deception. Sun Tzu would have been proud.

Elizondo bubbled with enthusiasm over it. He said the idea had come to him as he lay beside Sofia one night after making love—adding as an aside that his best ideas always came after sex. It was Bebé who ordered Sillman to stage a press conference.

The senator from Georgia was not as convinced as his new partner that the deception would be useful, or even successful. True, the government was a bureaucracy, slow-moving and usually inefficient. This reality had served him well during his political career.

But those staffing the bureaucracies were not idiots. On the law enforcement side, most were dedicated professionals, zealots even, when it came to ferreting out criminal activity.

The risk that they might see through the scheme seemed unnecessary to Sillman. In the end, he had no choice, and he knew it. With Alejandro Garza eyeing him from a side chair, Sillman smiled and agreed to arrange the press conference and lead the deception.

James Jadyn Sillman stood before his penthouse window, looking out over the bustling city below. The scene was far removed from the hillside hacienda on the Pacific where trembling men were garroted to death on the orders of a smiling, baby-faced monster. An involuntary shiver shook his frame, and he swallowed more bourbon.

He had always thought he was a tough man. Now he knew he was not. The revelation came as a shock.

TWENTY-SIX

Ain't Goin' Nowhere

He was on his fourth mile, sweating hard in the morning humidity. Travis made the turn onto Twelfth Street and took the entrance into Piedmont Park when one of the two cell phones in his pocket chimed.

It was his day to carry the burner they used for communicating with their informants. He pulled it out as he ran then came to a stop, squinting at the display as he caught his breath. The call was from Luis Acero.

"Yeah," Travis said, one hand on his hip, breathing deep as he rested.

"I know this white dude."

"What?" Luis never broke protocol. The correct response was the usual 'It's all good' signal. The question now was whether Luis was in trouble or just so agitated that he forgot to give the all clear signal.

"I know who he is!" Luis persisted, his voice rising in pitch. "The white dude ... from Eruptions."

"You can identify him?" Luis might have a reason to be anxious, Travis decided. "Where are you?"

"Home, man. At home and I ain't goin' nowhere."

"Okay," Travis kept his tone mild. "Say it right, so I know this is legit."

"Oh, yeah ... right," Luis paused then said, "It's all good, bro."

It wasn't textbook protocol, but it would have to do.

"You know him?" Travis continued. "The white dude? How?"

"Well, I ain't met him or nothin' like that, but ..." Luis hesitated, his mind whirling. There was danger here. El Toro was frightening enough, but ratting on a prominent politician would plunge him into dark waters too deep for him to fathom.

He took a breath and said, "I seen him on television."

Travis stared across Lake Clara Meer at the midtown high-rises. Could it be possible that Luis was on to something?

"What do you mean on television? A show?"

"Not a show. One of them news things ... some politician up there smiling and makin' a speech, then they all askin' him questions."

"A press conference?"

"Yeah, that's it. A press conference."

"A politician? You saw a politician from a press conference?" Travis lowered his voice, the phone screwed tight against his ear. "Meeting with El Toro?"

"No not a politician, but I seen him ... the white dude ... standing right beside one on the news, this morning. The press conference, like you say."

"Which politician?" Travis asked, playing it cool to mask the intensity of his interest.

"Shit, I don't know his name, they all the same to me." Luis spoke fast, explaining. "I saw the white dude standing off to the side. That's why I paid attention. Saw it on the screen in a bar. Then the politician left and the other white dude stepped up and said something. Then he left." Luis finished breathless. "I'm tellin' you I seen it all. I *saw* him."

Travis remained silent. There was only one politician in town on the news that day, talking about his crusade against drugs.

To call the information a longshot was an understatement. First, you had to accept that Luis Acero had been sober enough while sitting in a bar to recognize a politician's aide at a television press conference. That was hard enough to swallow.

Second, you had to believe that Luis was also sober enough the other night at Eruptions to recognize the same man meeting head to head with a suspected drug kingpin. Still, if it were true, if Luis's faculties were not dulled by alcohol but instead heightened by fear, he might be telling the truth.

"You still there?" Luis called out to him over the silence.

Travis spoke up. "I'm here."

"So, I'm paid up now, right?" Luis' voice was hopeful.

"Maybe. We have to check things out."

"What you mean maybe? I'm telling you what I saw. I ain't no genius but I know what I saw, and I know a politician's boy hanging with a drug boss means something's up." He nodded to himself, sitting on his bed in the apartment. "It's big. I know it is."

"We'll see," Travis replied. "Stay close to your phone and don't speak to anyone else about this."

"I ain't saying shit to no one. This could get me killed."

Travis nodded. Luis' assessment of the risk was accurate.

"Stay quiet, and don't get killed," Travis said. "If what you're saying is true ..."

"Shit, man. I ain't lyin' ... not about this."

"Okay. Then we will probably want to bring you in ... for protection."

"I ain't goin' nowhere. My ass stayin' right here hunkered down. You do what you got do and get the white dude ... get Ortega ... fuck ... get 'em all. Ain't no safe place for me 'less you do. You put me in a lockup for safe-keeping, and one of Moya's men will get to me and shove a knife up my ass. They got ways. You know that's true."

Luis was right. If word got out that he was in custody for anything, it would reduce his life expectancy to days, if not minutes. Esteban Moya would not hesitate to eliminate Luis if only on the mere possibility he had turned rat on them.

"All right, hunker down there. We'll run it down and call you back, but you be where we can reach you."

"I said, I ain't goin' nowhere."

The call ended. Travis pulled out the other cell phone and punched up John Sole's number. He ran over the information Luis had given him and asked, "What do you think?"

"Question is, what do you think? You talked to him."

"He sounded shaky, but it's a hell of a story. The kind of story that would take real smarts to come up with. Not sure our boy Luis has that kind of brain-power." Travis paused, thinking it through. "I think we have to take him at his word and check it out. I believe him ... or at least I believe he thinks Senator Sillman's aide is the white dude he saw at Eruptions with Ortega."

"Fair enough. I'm on my way. I'll pick you up, and we

can run down Sillman's aide. It's worth that much at least. If it pans out, we make Luis accept protective custody. If he's jerking us around, he's on his own."

TWENTY-SEVEN

Sara Jane

"You know who we are?"

Tolbert 'Tully' Sams eyed the short dark man with the hard eyes and the three men with him. "I know."

"Good. Take us to the boat."

"I'll do that, but first you need to get out of those city clothes." Tully opened the tailgate of his pickup, pulled out two large duffels and held them out. "Here. There's clothes inside ... clothes that won't make you stick out like a sore thumb down here."

Esteban Moya stood in the heat of the early afternoon, regarding the bag for a few seconds, then shifted his gaze to the man. Their eyes locked. The Cessna that had delivered them to Brunswick's Golden Isles Airport lifted from the runway and climbed over their heads, turning back to Atlanta. Neither man moved.

Tully placed the duffel on the ground. "Might as well get something straight up front," he said his voice even and firm. "It's my boat. I'm the captain. Keep that in mind, and things'll go smooth."

"It belongs to the owner. Our arrangement is with him." Esteban replied, wondering if he should just kill the old man now and tell Ortega the deal was off.

He dismissed the thought as soon as it had come. While El Toro might be sympathetic to his desire to dispatch this shabby boat captain, Bebé Elizondo would not be. Moya did not want a visit from Alejandro Garza.

The old captain said nothing, waiting for Moya and his men to comply with his instructions. "Explain," Moya said when it was clear they were at a standoff.

"Fair, enough," Sams said with a matter-of-fact nod. "New crew. You got a right to know the rules." He pointed to the south, standing up straight as if he could see over the horizon to their destination. "We're going down to St. Mary's. It's a lot smaller than Brunswick and a hell of a lot smaller than anything you're used to in Atlanta. I show up there with four Mexicans ..."

"El Salvador," Moya said. "I'm from El Salvador." He nodded at his companions. "They are from Honduras."

Sams smiled and pulled a pack of cigarettes from his shirt pocket, lit one and continued, "Down here you're all Mexicans. No disrespect intended ... that's just the way it is, so get used to it." He inhaled deeply, letting the smoke drift away on the afternoon breeze. "Like I was saying, I show up in St. Mary's with you all ... wherever you're from ... people are gonna ask questions. It's a small town, and everyone is in everyone else's fucking business." He chuckled and nodded. "You can take that to the bank."

Moya's eyes remained firm, fixed on the man's face. This stupid *gringo* had no idea who he was dealing with and what they could do ... would do ... if he gave them a reason. Men had died for lesser insults than this old man's arrogance.

"So you take off those fancy jeans," Sams continued, "and the designer shirts and gold necklaces, high-top sneakers and you dress like y'all are itinerants, looking for work crewing on a shrimper. People there won't care you're Mexican or anything else. They all know how it is to need work. They won't fault me neither for looking for some cheap crew hands … just business, is what they'll say. But you show up dressed like that, and they'll be asking question neither one of us want to answer." He shrugged, flicked the ash from the cigarette between his fingers. "That's the way it is, and like I said, I'm the captain."

They had wasted enough time. Ortega would be waiting for a report. Moya looked at his men and nodded. "Do it."

Tully Sams leaned against the pickup's bed, and continued smoking. One by one, Esteban Moya and his men went into the back of the truck, rummaged through the bags of used clothing, squirmed around on the seat as they made the change.

Suitably dressed as working-class migrants, they piled into the pickup. Moya sat up front with Tully Sams. The others crowded into the crew cab seat behind.

The hour-long drive from Brunswick down to St. Mary's passed in silence. Had they been able to land at the old general aviation airport in St. Mary's the trip would have been much simpler, but that airport closed in 2017 after sixteen years of impact studies over security threats to the Navy's nearby King's Bay Submarine base.

Sams figured it was just as well. There would have been too many questions from locals who saw him pick up a load of fancy-dressed Mexicans, claiming they were deckhands.

Senator JJ Sillman had picked Tully Sams for a reason. Unlike Wilson Bettis, whose primary concern was the promise of riches, Sams was completely uninterested in money, but he was absolutely loyal to Sillman and only wanted the chance to get back out on the ocean.

Their relationship extended back to the days when Sillman was a teenager assigned by his father to work on Captain Sams' boat. The shrimper had been a mentor to the boy, letting him sit in the cabin and drink beer with him when they were in port, talking about life and shrimping. Over the years they remained close, and Sams took particular pride in Sillman's success, bragging to friends at the local St. Mary's taverns how he'd been there when the senator was only a boy just out of short pants.

As for this venture, Sams was thankful for the opportunity to repay a debt that had been weighing on him. After retiring from the Sillman Shrimp Company ten years earlier, he had planned to live out the rest of his life in St. Mary's with his wife, Sara Jane, traveling to visit their grandchildren around the country. They even bought an RV trailer to tow behind the old pickup so they'd have a place to stay on the road and for extended visits to the children.

The retirement hadn't lasted long, and the dreams of a peaceful old age disintegrated when Sara Jane was diagnosed with breast cancer five years after Sams retired. The bills mounted.

Sillman helped cover the expense and had paid for the funeral when Sara Jane's misery finally ended. After, he sat with Sams while the old man wept and begged to go back to work for free to repay Sillman for what he had done for them. Sillman refused, mostly because of their friendship but also because a good politician knows it is always preferable to have someone indebted to them, and Senator Sillman was a good politician.

When the deal with Bebé Elizondo came along, Sillman decided it was time to collect the debt. Sams was grateful. Besides, the money that Sillman was offering was more than he would make in a year of hard shrimping.

Sillman explained what they required and why, leaving nothing out. As far as Tully Sams was concerned, if people wanted to burn up their brains with drugs, who was he to say they couldn't. The world was full of fools.

Besides, his grandfather had told him stories about running rum up from Cuba during the prohibition days. People weren't going to stop drinking then, and they aren't going to stop using drugs now he figured. He was just holding up a family tradition.

As they approached St. Mary's, Moya noticed a sign along the highway.

"King's Bay," he read and looked at Sams. "A Navy base?"

"Yep."

"We are taking a boat out to smuggle drugs right next to a Navy base?"

"It's a sub base, super-secret ... never see the subs. They stay under until they get to Fancy Creek off the St. Mary's River. Then cruise on up to King's Bay."

"Submarines ... and we will have ..." Moya was incredulous. "Are you *loco* ... *estúpido*?"

"First off," Sams began. "We won't have any drugs when we leave St. Mary's, unless you and your boys are carrying any. Once we have your cargo on board, we'll be offloading at a private dock up one of the creeks that come into the sound between here and Brunswick." He turned and grinned at the nervous drug dealer. "Trust me. We'll just be another shrimp boat heading out. Doing it right next to a Navy base ... hell, no one will ever suspect. Couldn't be safer."

"And when the boat comes back without shrimp? What will others say?"

"Already took care of that," Sams replied, with a confident nod. "Spread the word I got a special deal with Sillman, a private customer we sell to and offload somewhere else before we come back to port."

The look on Moya's face was doubtful. Border crossings in the desert, ferrying across the Rio Grande, those were things he knew about. Boats heading out onto the open ocean were something else. He'd seen movies about submarines, peeking through periscopes at boats on the surface. The thought of a big eye watching them from beneath the waves made him uneasy.

"Relax," Sams said, puffing his cigarette. "Everything will be fine."

"It better be." Moya stared at the turn-off to the Navy base as they passed.

They drove through the small St. Mary's town center to the docks along the river. Sams parked in a dirt lot made of crushed shells and sand.

He led the way across the street to the boat Sillman had provided for their enterprise. A couple of deckhands on a nearby trawler looked up and then went back to inspecting nets, ignoring Sams' new crew members. Moya breathed a little easier.

The boat was an old one, and like Sams, had been retired by the Sillman Shrimp Company several years earlier. While Sillman made his arrangements with Bebé

Elizondo, Sams saw to making the boat seaworthy and renamed it the Sara Jane.

"Down Below." Sams pointed to the passage to the galley. "Sit tight. I'll get things ready on deck. Don't need you up here stumbling around like tourists or people will figure out quick you're not real deckhands. I'll get things organized. You can help me cast off the lines, when we get underway. Until then stay out of sight."

Moya could think of nothing to say. He was out of his element and knew it. He led his team out of sight.

Tully Sams puttered around the deck, straightening things up, checking nets as if they were going out for shrimp that night. Satisfied that everything was in order, he pulled a beer from an ice chest he kept in the deckhouse, sat back in the cracked leather chair, and patted the bulkhead beside him, smiling.

"It's good to have you back, Sara Jane."

TWENTY-EIGHT

Heads or Tails

They sat huddled over Travis' desk eating McDonald's Quarter Pounders that Sole had picked up on the way in. Notes they had made on Luis' tip were scattered before them.

"First off," Sole said around a mouthful of burger. "Do we have a name for the assistant that Luis saw?"

"Sillman's got several aides and assistants," Travis said. "A small staff stays here and works out of his Atlanta office full time, handling issues with constituents, granting favors, that kind of stuff. Most of his staff works out of his Washington D.C. office. One of those is his senior aide ... the one at the press conference this morning. His name is Wilson Bettis."

"Bettis? Anything on him?"

"Usual. No criminal history ... not even a traffic ticket since he was eighteen. Appears to be a wonder boy ... gets things done for the Senator ... the kind that never stands in the spotlight but gets close enough to feel the glow and bask in the sidelight. That's why he was at the presser this morning. He's pretty much always there with Sillman when the cameras are rolling."

"So the question," Sole said, crumpling the Quarter Pounder wrapper and sending it in an arc into the trash can beside Travis desk, "is why he was meeting with a reported drug lord at Eruptions."

"Reported but not proven drug lord," Travis reminded him, adding, "And that is, if he actually met with him and Luis is not full of shit."

"Good point," Sole agreed.

"So what do you think? We go over to Sillman's Atlanta offices and meet with Bettis?"

"No. There's a better way. Right now we know nothing, just acting on a tip from a shaky CI." Sole shook his head. "Bettis might have been looking to score cocaine and saw Ortega at the club. Illegal, but no big deal, and if he was after coke, Bettis gets a slap on the hand, and that's the end of it. Sillman gives him a tongue lashing, makes a big deal about it to the media, says that's why he is leading the charge against drugs, etcetera."

Sole leaned forward resting his chin on his hands as he thought it through. "On the other hand, Bettis might have been up to no good, into something that required a head to head with El Toro. It might involve Sillman or maybe not. We don't know that either. Seems we need to find that out too, if there is anything to this at all."

"Agreed." Travis nodded. "So we meet with both alone."

"Correct. Separate and without warning. That way they can't get their stories straight between them."

"I like it." Travis nodded. "You want Sillman or Bettis?"

"Flip you for Sillman, partner." Sole grinned and pulled a quarter from his pocket. "Heads or Tails."

"Heads," Travis called out as the coin flipped in the air.

Sole let it hit the floor and looked up grinning. "Looks like I get to meet a real live senator."

The next step was trickier than flipping a coin. The challenge was to time the interviews without tipping off either Sillman or Bettis and not give them the chance to coordinate their stories.

Bettis was simple. Travis called Senator Sillman's office and scheduled a meeting with his aide under the pretext he represented law enforcement officers interested in possibly supporting the Senator's anti-drug efforts.

Scheduling a concurrent, meeting with Sillman took more creativity. Sole picked up the phone and made a call.

"John Sole, how in the hell are you?" Jimmy Cutshaw answered. He was a friend and retired APD detective sergeant who now ran security for the building that housed Sillman's condo.

"Doing good, Jimmy. Wife and kids okay?"

"They're fine. Jim Jr. graduates UGA next year. Maria's teaching school in Augusta. Your family?"

"All fine. Growing up too fast, and we're getting old."

"I hear that." Cutshaw paused, knowing Sole hadn't called to chat about their children. "So, what can I do for you, John?"

"I need to talk to someone ... a tenant in your building."

"Who?"

"James Jadyn Sillman."

"So why are you calling me? Call his office and schedule an appointment, or get his cell number and call him direct."

"It has to be impromptu ... no advance knowledge."

"Meaning you don't want him talking to anyone about why you might give him a visit."

"Meaning I want to hear what he has to say, not what some aide told him to say."

"Mind if I ask what this is about?"

"Could be nothing," Sole said. "But we have to run it down and put it to rest. You know the drill."

"I know the drill." Cutshaw had policed for twenty-three years before pulling the pin and retiring. He understood the workings of investigations and the reality that most leads went nowhere. "So again, what do you need from me?"

"Just need to know when he's in the building."

"He's here now."

"Alone?"

"For now. Showed up after the press conference show he put on down at the capitol this morning. Hasn't come down for his car or been out since."

"Good. So one more favor then."

"Shoot."

"If I show up unannounced can you get me up to his penthouse? Figure if I show up at the door he's got to talk to me or look like he's got something to hide."

"Might be a brief visit," Cutshaw chuckled. "But yeah, I can get you up to his door. After that, you're on your own."

"Perfect. You won't catch any heat for helping out?"

"None I can't handle. Detective shows up and wants to speak to a resident. I show him where the resident lives. That's within building policy. I mean I'm not breaking and entering for you." Cutshaw paused before adding, "Am I?"

"Nope," Sole assured him. "I'm just going to ring the bell and give him my best smile when he opens the door."

"You've learned how to smile?" Cutshaw chuckled. "Damn, if Shaye hasn't been good for you."

"She has for a fact," Sole agreed. "I'll be there within

the hour. Let me know if he leaves before I get there, will you?"

"No problem. I'll keep an eye on him."

"Thanks Jimmy." The call ended. Sole turned to Travis. "We're set."

"Good." Travis stood. "Let's make like horse shit and hit the road. My meet with Bettis is in thirty minutes. You should be standing in front of Sillman's door about then, ready to flash that smile I heard you brag about." He gave Sole an amused look. "By the way, let's see it … the smile … sort of give it a test drive before you use it on Sillman."

Sole's face twisted into a lopsided smirking grin. "How's that."

"Scary as hell."

"Perfect."

TWENTY-NINE

On the Big Water

Tully Sams stopped and looked into the galley cabin below the deckhouse and called out, "Hands on deck!"

Esteban Moya looked up from a video of Mexican singer Thalia he was playing on his cell phone. "*¡Ándale! Vamonos,*" he called out to the others, sprawled on the bench and chairs around the galley table.

Sams didn't speak Spanish, but he didn't have to. It was clear that their leader had told them to get their asses in gear. He moved out on deck as the men jumped to their feet, looked around for direction and then followed Esteban up to the deck.

"Okay, we're gonna cast off," Sams said when they, had gathered in front of him. He eyed his crew and wondered just how they would react once they were out on the ocean swells. "Follow me."

He stepped along the narrow planks between the deckhouse and gunwale. Behind him, Moya spoke in staccato Spanish.

"I'll show you how it's done." Sams reached for the line on the stern cleat.

"*No. Permítame por favor señor.*" One of Moya's men rushed past him to leap to the dock and loosen the line, leaving a turn on the cleat to hold the boat in place.

Surprised, Sams turned to Moya, a question on his face.

"He says he will handle it," Moya said, leaning against the side of the deckhouse, smiling.

Forward, a second man hopped to the dock and worked the bow line. They stood waiting for Sams to give the order to cast off.

"You didn't mention your men are seamen," Sams nodded with respect for their apparent skills.

"It was not important for you to know."

"Lots of things can be important out on the water," Sams replied. "Would have been good to know up front."

"Would knowing have changed what we are doing tonight?" Moya's eyes narrowed.

"I suppose not," Sams nodded and reached for the pack of cigarettes in his pocket. He lit up and stood for a minute in the center of the deck, feeling the gentle tidal swell come up the river to rock the boat. "Wouldn't have thought there were many sailors where y'all come from."

"There are many types of people where I come from," Moya said matter-of-factly, amusement on his face. This dumb *gringo* must think everyone below the border rides donkeys and wears sombreros. "Some are sailors, like these two. All need money, and we have money. So now, they work for us."

"And him?" Sams persisted, nodding at the fourth member of their party.

Moya turned his head toward the man standing in the

middle of the deck. "Julio?" He nodded and folded his arms across his chest. "Julio has special skills … for later."

Moya offered no further information. Sams took a deep puff on the cigarette, flipped the butt overboard and stepped into the deckhouse to start the engines. He let them idle for a few minutes to get the oil circulating, then leaned out and waved at the man on the stern line.

His Mexican—no Honduran, he reminded himself— deckhand released the last turn on the line, and with a nimble flip sailed the line to the boat's deck and hopped aboard after it. He turned and nodded, lifting a hand at the forward deckhand who released his line with equal agility and took up his watch in the bow.

Sams saw the forward deckhand say something to Julio who nodded and moved to stand amidships beside Esteban. Probably told him to get the hell out of the way before he got hurt, Sams thought, smiling. He reversed the engines and turned the wheel, sidling the trawler away from the dock with gentle touches on the throttles.

The engines thrummed and rumbled through the deck boards as he idled along, working his way out of the port and into the St. Mary's River channel. He watched with appreciation as his two new deckhands coiled the lines by the starboard cleats. By the time they passed Cumberland Island, he figured he'd had worse crews in the past.

He wondered where they had gotten their experience. Probably deep-water fishers, maybe on the big tuna or salmon trawlers out on the Pacific, he thought.

Now, they worked for a drug cartel. How did that happen? What had they done to earn their way into that life? He'd heard stories. The two men standing watch on the deck didn't seem the type to be cold-blooded killers. But then, who did? For now, they were his crew, and they were beginning to earn his respect. That was enough.

Warm salt air blew through the deckhouse. Tully Sams smiled and nudged the throttle up as they pushed into the Atlantic swells.

An hour before sunset, he motioned to the two deckhands, calling them to him. They left their posts in the stern and bow and came amidships, obedient and deferential.

"We gonna be working together. I reckon we should put names to the faces." He patted his chest "Tully ... Tully Sams."

The two sailors nodded. One, older shorter and darker than the other nodded, and pointed at Sams saying, "*Capitán*."

"True enough," Sams nodded. "But out here you can call me Tully ... long as you mind what I say."

Esteban Moya poked his head out from the galley dayroom, and said something in rapid Spanish to the men, then looked at Sams. "I told them to call you *Capitán*. They don't need to know your name. They don't need to know anything about you. They do what I tell them. For that, they will be well paid."

"If that's the way you want it," Sams said with a shrug. "Gonna be kinda tough giving them instructions when we're underway if I can't call them by name to get them doing what I need done."

Moya frowned, said something to the men, and disappeared back inside.

The short man patted his chest and said "Hermilio." He pronounced it Hair-mee-lyo.

Sams gave it a try, twisting the name around on his

tongue. The man laughed and tapped his chest again, saying. "Hermie." Hair-mee.

"Hermie," Sams repeated the Americanized version of the nickname with a grin. "Reckon I can handle that."

The other man, as tall as Sams and thin, tapped his chest and nodded, saying his name, "Paco."

"Good." Sams nodded. "It's a good start. Hermie and Paco ... names I can remember." He gave each a friendly slap on the shoulder, indicating they were now part of the team. "Good sailors too."

They understood that word at least. The two fishermen grinned their acknowledgment and nodded emphatically.

Hermie patted his chest and said, "*Sí, Capitan. Buenos marineros* ... good sailors."

The Sara Jane was an eighty-two-foot trawler and had been in the Sillman fleet for thirty years. Sams put in two months hard work, refurbishing her Cummins diesel, going over every inch of wiring, couplings, and fixtures. Happy to be doing something after losing his wife, he threw his heart into the project.

It mattered little to him what their cargo would be. It mattered a lot that when the Sara Jane sailed from St. Mary's she was a credit to JJ Sillman who had given him a second chance at life.

The empty days after his wife's death were gone. No longer was he some forgotten piece of sea trash washed up on the shore, waiting to die. He had a purpose, thanks to Sillman, and Tully Sams would repay the favor. His boat would be as ship-shape as one man could make it.

He turned to the east, heading offshore, to deep water, feasting his eyes on the expanse of ocean stretching to the blue-green horizon. In the bow, Hermie grinned at him and Sams realized it was because he was grinning too.

Tully Sams threw his head back and laughed. You old fool, you're grinning like a damned idiot, he thought. Why not, his mind shouted back? You're alive! Out on the big water!

The high bow of the trawler sliced through the waves, rising and falling on the swells, keeping tempo with the thrum of the engines. He felt his sea legs returning, knees flexed to absorb the movement while his eyes remained focused on the horizon.

There was freedom here. Freedom in the movement, in the rise and fall of the bow, in the rumble of the engines, in the wind blowing fresh and salty through the deckhouse. He relished it all and thanked God for JJ Sillman.

Not everyone on board was as thrilled as Tully Sams. Cruising the river and the sound past Cumberland Island was one thing, but once the first swells lifted the bow, the trawler began to rock like a cradle. Esteban Moya and Julio with-the-special-skills made their way to the deck, pale and sick. They clung to the supports around the deckhouse to keep their balance while they worked at keeping the contents of their stomachs from spewing out in front of the others.

Moya leaned against the deckhouse door, face pale, eyes clenched shut. He wasn't giving orders now. The *Capitan* of the Sara Jane grinned wider. Out here on the big water, Tully Sams was in command.

THIRTY

Dirty

"Your press conference is getting attention. It's all coming together just the way we planned!"

We planned? Wilson Bettis was gloating over his good fortune. Sillman could visualize him on the other end of the call, rubbing his hands together, counting his share of the money that would soon flow their way. At some point, he would have to remind the little peacock of his place. Nothing had changed. He was an aide, not a partner, and any share of the profits was thanks to Sillman's benevolence, nothing more.

That would come later. For the now, Sillman asked "What kind of attention?"

"Just had a call from an Atlanta cop. He's putting together a law enforcement group to get behind your anti-drug efforts." Bettis chuckled at the irony. "He'll be here in a few minutes to go over plans and see how they can support us … I mean you."

"So soon?" Sillman was suddenly uneasy. Despite

Elizondo's fascination with Sun Tzu's *Art of* War, deceiving the cops shouldn't be so simple.

"I guess they watch TV too," Bettis replied.

"Just seems a little convenient." Sillman rubbed his jaw, thinking it over and reached for the ever-present glass of bourbon beside his chair.

"Relax," Bettis reassured him. "Our friends wanted misdirection and deception. They sure as hell got it." Unlike his boss, Bettis was thrilled. He had to give Bebé Elizondo credit. "They bought it, boss … hook, line, and sinker. With you leading the anti-drug charge and the cops backing your legislation, they will be looking everywhere except at us. It's perfect."

"I suppose so," Sillman said, uncertain but trying hard to feel the same exuberance. It was easier for Bettis to be excited and sure about things. He hadn't stood in a corner and watched while Bebé had a man strangled.

"Gotta go, boss," Bettis said, excited anticipation in his voice. "He's here. I'll call you after and let you know how it goes."

Bettis was gone. Sillman could picture him bouncing out to greet the Atlanta police officer. Things were moving fast. It might be best to go to the office and check in with Bettis after his meeting with the police officer.

Sillman stood and went to the bedroom to retrieve the tie and suit jacket he had discarded after returning from the press conference. He was sliding the jacket over his shoulders when the knock came at the door.

In a downtown high-rise not far away, Bettis marched across

the reception office, hand extended to the tall, plain-clothes detective. "Wilson Bettis," he said, introducing himself.

"Randy Travis," the detective replied as they shook hands. "Thanks for meeting with me, Mr. Bettis."

"Glad to do it, and call me Wilson." Bettis smiled and leaned toward Travis, lowering his voice. "Interesting name you have."

Travis nodded. "Been told that a lot."

"Any singers in your family?"

"Nope," Travis shook his head grinning. "Not a one."

"Me neither," Bettis said. "That's something we have in common."

"Yep. We have that."

It was the routine opening for Travis. His name coupled with his black face had broken the ice more than once before he dropped the investigative hammer on an unsuspecting head.

"I guess I was expecting someone in uniform," Bettis said as he led the way to his office.

"Sorry." Travis nodded and smiled. "Forgot to mention that I'm a detective."

"Narcotics?" Bettis asked, a look of hopeful excitement in his eyes as he stood aside for Travis to enter the office in front of him.

"No." Travis shook his head. "Nothing that glamorous. Major Crimes Unit. Not a problem, is it?"

"No, no. No problem. Always glad to have support from the law enforcement community." Travis nodded and motioned to two upholstered side chairs facing each other across a small coffee table. "You have a uniform though, right?"

"Yep, with a badge and everything," Travis said, amused

at Bettis' obvious disappointment that he was not decked out in APD blue.

"Good. If we get to where we want to do publicity events ... promos, public service announcements with the Senator, that sort of thing ... it might be good to have you and some of your colleagues standing with him in uniform. You know, for the visual effect."

"Sure, I get it," Travis said and sat in one of the chairs. "If we get to that point. First, we need to understand a little more about what the senator is promoting and what his initiatives will be ... so we can determine how we might help."

"Absolutely." Bettis plopped down in the chair across from Travis, crossed his legs and leaned forward.

He was expansive, bubbling with excitement and information about the legislation Sillman planned to introduce. The plan was three-pronged.

First, there would be immediate, mandatory increases in the lengths of prison terms for those convicted of trafficking in narcotics. Next, Sillman planned to decrease demand by helping users break their addiction, funneling unheard of amounts of federal money into local programs for counseling and addiction rehabilitation.

"And most important," Bettis said, leaning forward, his eyes intense, staring earnestly into Travis'. "We will end the import of narcotics across our southern border."

"How?" Travis asked, flipping a page in the notebook he had filled as Bettis expounded on Sillman's plans.

"By sending troops to the border. We are going to lock the fucker down once and for all." Bettis leaned back, having spit out this last bit of information with orgasmic delight.

"Not sure that's legal," Travis said mildly. "Lock the

border down, sure, but using federal troops. That will get a lot of opposition."

"Doesn't matter." Bettis shook his head. "We have a president who will do it. We need the legislation to give him the authority. That's what Senator Sillman is trying to do … give him what he needs to get the job done."

It all became clear. It was all bullshit.

Sillman would introduce legislation, make speeches, appear in television spots and get his name out in front of everyone, supporting a popular president. Most important, voters would take note. Even those who might disagree with him on other issues would be drawn to his holy crusade against drugs.

That Congress could never pass into law what he was proposing, or that challenges in federal courts would tie it up for years was irrelevant. Like most politicians, the only result that concerned Sillman was the vote count, and he would no doubt garner votes for his initiative and support of the president.

Travis found the pretense distasteful. He put his feelings aside. Sillman was a politician, no different from any other.

It was time to get to the real reason for the visit. He flipped to another page in his notepad and tossed the question out without any preliminaries.

"Wilson, I was wondering if you could tell me why you were meeting with Bautista Ortega a few nights ago."

The uncontrolled twitch in his jaw and the color draining away from his forehead told Travis that it was true. Bettis had met with a suspected drug trafficker. Sober or not, Luis Acero had hit this nail dead center on the head.

"I don't …. I mean … I didn't …"

Bettis shook his head, his mouth agape like a child caught with his hand in a cookie jar saying, *'Who me?'*

"Video cameras, Wilson," Travis said with a sigh. "The club has video cameras."

He did not mention they were useless. Bettis' face twisted, the pallor replaced by red cheeks that grew darker as the seconds ticked. He struggled—almost strangled—trying to come up with what he would say next. Travis waited, content to let Bettis stew until he filled the uncomfortable silence with whatever bullshit spewed from his mouth next.

"I mean," Bettis stammered. "You see, it's like this ..."

Travis repressed a laugh, and looked solemnly into the man's eyes where the truth was revealed. Bettis was blinking fast, eyes darting from side to side, a caged animal seeking an escape. There was none, and his mind whirled, trying to come up with a plausible explanation.

"Okay, right ..." Bettis put his hand up as if to ward off a blow. "So, yeah ..." His head bounced up and down. "I met with Bautista Ortega the other night at Eruptions. It was a brief meeting, just sat down with him for a few minutes. I mean I wasn't asking for a donation or anything like a bribe or something to get Sillman ... I mean the Senator ... you know, to back off from his legislation. That would be illegal, right?"

"Right." Travis nodded. "That would be illegal."

The attempt at misdirection was almost laughable. Randy Travis wasn't just any questioner, and he had never asked about bribery or even implied it. In his clumsy way, Bettis was trying to throw him off the scent ... of something. But what?

"Okay, so you need to know that this is all completely innocent." Bettis paused and licked his lips as he gathered his thoughts. "So I was doing research ... all part of the anti-drug initiative." A light came on in his eyes. He'd found the angle he would use. "You know ... looking for support for the Senator's initiative in the Hispanic community. That's not illegal is it?"

"No. That's perfectly legal."

Travis had to hand it to Bettis. He was overcoming his shock and trying his best to recover.

"So, Ortega's not wanted for anything, is he? I mean if he is, I didn't know about it, and I certainly wouldn't have ..."

"He's not wanted," Travis cut in.

Bautista Ortega—El Toro—had managed to keep his hands legally clean through the years because his hands never touched the drugs his organization peddled. He let others do that for him and serve the time when necessary.

"Not wanted," Bettis continued, "So, it was perfectly legal for me to meet with him and try to get his support for the Senator's program. I mean he's a prominent member of the Hispanic community. You understand I was just ..."

"Never said it wasn't legal." Travis smiled.

"Good. I want that to be clear." Bettis had the relieved, gut-sick look of a man who had driven off onto the shoulder and almost over the cliff before pulling the car back onto the pavement.

"What did he say?" Travis smiled again.

"What?"

"Bautista Ortega," Travis looked down at his notebook, pen poised as if to record Bettis' response for posterity. "What did he say to your proposal ... your request for support?"

"Oh ... he ..." Bettis was suddenly at the cliff edge again, straining to keep things together, frantic, tugging at the wheel. "He ... uh, he said he would take it under advisement ... talk to others in his organization and get back to me."

"Did he get back to you?"

"No, not yet," Bettis said, his breathing more regular now, feeling he had handled the detective's questions well, all things considered.

"Who?" Travis asked, not letting up.

"Who?" Bettis shook his head. "I don't know what ..."

"Who was Ortega going to speak to ... the others in his organization?"

"I don't know, Detective. He said he would take it under advisement. I did my job."

"For the senator." Travis nodded and looked up from the notebook.

"That's right," Bettis said, recovering some of his earlier bluster. "For Senator James Sillman."

"You met with Bautista Ortega as part of your job for Senator Sillman, as his senior aide." Travis made a note on his pad. "He knew of the meeting then?"

"Well, I didn't say ..."

"You met without his knowledge?"

"I didn't say that either. I just ..."

"You and Sillman are close?" Travis was unrelenting. "You speak often?"

"Of course. We speak daily."

"Okay." Travis closed the notebook and stood. "I'll check with the Senator. I'm sure everything will be fine."

"What do you mean ... fine?" Bettis jumped to his feet. "Who the hell do you think you are coming in here under false pretenses, asking me questions like that ... no, not asking ... making insinuations. Who the hell ..."

"Goodbye, Mr. Bettis. I'll be in touch."

Travis walked from the office and smiled at the receptionist and office staff as he passed. Bettis sagged back down into his chair like a boxer leaning against the ropes after having his ass whipped.

In the hall waiting for the elevator, Travis checked his phone and sent a text to John Sole, then descended in the elevator to the building's below ground parking garage. Fourteen stories above him, Wilson Bettis frantically punched the Senator's speed dial number on his phone. No one answered.

It was unusual for anyone to knock at his door unannounced. In fact, it had never happened before.

Senator Sillman pulled the penthouse door open just as Wilson Bettis escorted Detective Travis into his office. A smiling John Sole greeted him, holding up his badge.

For a moment, Sillman recoiled, unsure about the twisted grimace on the detective's face. From his reaction, Sole figured he should have taken Travis' advice and given the smile a few practice runs first.

"Senator Sillman," Sole said mildly. "I'm Investigator Sole with the Atlanta Police Department ... Major Crimes Unit."

"Is there a problem?"

Sillman fought to control the quiver in his voice and sudden fluttering in his left eyelid. Neither was lost on Investigator Sole.

"No. No problem." Sole shook his. "Saw your press conference today and thought I would drop by to talk to you about your efforts, since we're both fighting the same battle."

"Yes, but they're supposed to let me know when someone is here ... coming up to my door."

"Oh, don't be upset about that." Sole held the badge a little higher. "I sort of pulled rank on building security and told them I was here on official police business."

"Yes, but ..."

"May I come in for a few minutes, Senator," Sole interrupted. "Just to talk about your new anti-drug initiative."

Sillman hesitated. If he didn't invite the detective in, it could signal that something was wrong. Bettis was meeting with another detective at that very moment. They were committed.

Fuck Sun Tzu, Sillman thought, and his bullshit ideas about deception, but he opened the door wider and stepped back. "I suppose so. I was just going out, but always happy to meet with our law enforcement friends."

He escorted Sole into the penthouse living room and pointed to a chair in front of the bank of windows. "Have a seat Investigator ... what did you say your name was?"

"Sole ... John Sole."

"Investigator Sole, please sit." Sillman sat in a chair by the window.

"Nice spot," Sole said, sitting in a chair that faced Sillman at an angle and gave him a view of the city.

"Thanks." Annoyance replaced Sillman's initial surprise at the intrusion. "Perhaps you could get to the point of your visit, Investigator Sole."

"Sorry," Sole nodded, the grimace-smile back on his face. "Like I said, saw your press conference and we are very interested in your anti-drug initiative. We are on the same team, fighting the same battle so to speak."

"Yes, we are. In fact, one of your fellow officers is meeting with my assistant as we speak. No disrespect, but I would prefer to coordinate all interaction between the police department and our initiative through him."

Sole nodded. "I completely understand. Your assistant ... that would be Wilson Bettis, right?"

"Yes, Mr. Bettis coordinates all public relations matters for me, while I work to push the legislation through," Sillman said, impatient and imperious.

"You work closely with him."

"Very closely. He is my chief aide."

"All right then. Sorry to bother you." Sole put his hands on his knees, leaning forward ready to stand. "Oh, just one more thing before I go."

"Please," Sillman nodded, polite but curt, annoyed and sending the message for the investigator to ask his question and get the fuck out of his penthouse.

"Why did Wilson Bettis meet with Bautista Ortega at Eruptions?" Sole leaned back, not ready to leave, the grimace-smile gone now.

The eyelid began fluttering again, and Sillman's eyes widened like a deer staring into the bright beams of an oncoming truck.

"I ... I'm not sure who that is." Sillman shook his head. "No, I'm certain I've never heard the name before."

"Really?" Sole's brow furrowed as he pulled his notepad from his pocket and scanned a page.

There was nothing on the page about Bettis or Ortega, but James Sillman didn't know that. Too flustered to question the contents of the notepad and hold his ground, his face paled. The empty pit in his gut grew into a chasm. His breaths came in shallow pants that he tried to control. He was panicked.

The furrows on Sole's brow grew deeper as he scanned over the page containing the grocery list Shaye had given him that morning. He shook his head and looked up from the note pad.

"Are you sure about that, Senator? That you've never heard of Bautista Ortega?" He said the drug lord's name deliberately, pronouncing each syllable as if Sillman may not have understood it the first time.

"Well ... let's see." Sillman looked up as if trying to recall the name, resisting the urge to loosen the tie that seemed to tighten around his neck like a noose. "I ... uh ... I might have misspoken. I think I do recall that name ..." He nodded, his head moving up and down fast to acknowledge his innocent error. "Yes, that's it. Wilson ... Mr. Bettis ... told me he had arranged a meeting with this Ortega person."

"About what?"

"Pardon?"

"The meeting with Ortega, what was it about?"

"Oh ... that. I couldn't say."

Sillman realized his rigid posture and body tension must make him look guilty about something to the investigator. He tried to recover, waving a dismissive hand. "I have no idea why Mr. Bettis met with this ... what was his name?"

"Ortega."

"Yes. This Mr. Ortega." Sillman shook his head.

He leaned back in the chair, crossing his legs with an air of indifference. It was not a convincing performance.

"You have no idea why Wilson Bettis met with Bautista Ortega?"

"No, I don't."

"And Bettis works for you ... very closely, I believe you said."

"Well, yes, but that doesn't mean that ..."

"That you would know why he met with a suspected

drug dealer?" The first bead of sweat appeared above Sillman's left eye. Sole smiled. "After he told you he was meeting with him, you never thought to ask why?"

"As I said ..." Sillman's hand lifted and started to tug at his collar to loosen it. He forced it back down to his lap. "There are many things happening in my office ... much to coordinate. Perhaps you should ask Mr. Bettis why he met with this Ortega fellow because I don't remember the details."

"I will. Thanks for your time, Senator."

Sole stood, turned away and walked down the hall to the front door. Sillman remained seated, staring through the windows, his face blank, oblivious to the bustling activity below. His gut and balls tightened suddenly, like a man stepping from a tall building onto a ladder only to find the ladder gone, and he was in free fall.

Sole pushed the button for the elevator. A text message from Travis beeped in on his phone. It contained a single word.

Dirty

Sole typed a message back before entering the elevator

Ditto

THIRTY-ONE

Fixing Things

The red in his cheeks had faded to a dull, mottled pink by the time Wilson Bettis arrived at the penthouse. He punched the doorbell. It swung open almost before the ringing chime faded away.

There was no red in Sillman's cheeks. They were gray tinged with yellow around the eyelids and corners of his mouth. He looked like a man taking a walk to the gallows while the mob shouted, *'Hang the bastard!'*

Sillman stepped aside to let Bettis in, then glanced down the hall to assure himself that it was empty before closing the door. Bettis was speaking fast, even before they reached the living room. Sillman did not invite him to sit.

"Okay, let's not overreact. Everything is under control," Bettis chattered, sounding more than anything else like a man trying to convince himself that all was well. "There isn't anything to worry about. All things considered, I think we handled it well. They don't have any…"

"Stop!" Incredulity spread across Sillman's face. Could his senior aide really be this stupid?

Bettis took a deep breath and nodded. "Right. I only wanted to …"

"You met Ortega in a public place … at a club … at Eruptions? What the fuck were you thinking?"

"He said it would be okay, no cameras anywhere. It only took a few minutes. I came in through the alley." Bettis threw the words out like a machine gunner spraying bullets, trying to keep the enemy away, hoping one would hit a target. "It was just a preliminary meeting. He invited me out on his boat where we could finalize the details in private. Then I left." He shook his head. "No … I don't see how anyone could have …"

"No cameras?"

"Right." Bettis forced himself to slow down and breathe.

"Then why did you admit to the cop you were there when he said they had you on video?"

"I … I was …"

"You were had," Sillman said, eyes blazing. "They set you up to get a reaction, pretended they had something … you fucking walked right into it."

The senator tried to calm himself. The truth was his performance had been just as inept. He should have known better, done a better job of answering the trick questions from that asshole detective.

Cops see through lies. That's what they do. They planned their visits to find any holes in the stories Sillman and Bettis concocted, and there were plenty. He knew their bucket of lies leaked like a sieve. Worse, the cops knew it.

"But I …"

"Shut up!"

Sillman slumped into a chair by the windows. Bettis

remained standing, trying to retain a grasp on his vision of riches before they were blown away by the wind.

A minute passed, and he tried once more. "When you think about it, I don't think we have a problem."

"Are you insane?" Sillman's eyes widened. "Two cops question us … separately … making sure we don't speak to each other first, using a pretext to get a sit-down and you think it was just random chance?"

"No, no. Not that." Bettis shook his head rapidly. "All I'm saying is we can get through this. We stick to our stories." He raised his hands, palms up to show how simple the answer was. "I was just looking for support for your initiative from a community leader. You didn't know what I was doing. You're busy … lots of things on your plate … what your aide does, who he meets with is not something you keep close tabs on."

Bettis' head moved up and down in rapid nods, trying to convince himself as much as Sillman.

"You think this will pass?" Sillman sighed and shook his head. "No, they caught us in a lie … set us up so we would have to lie or admit a connection to Ortega. They won't give up."

"Still," Bettis' voice was almost a whisper, working to reign in his emotions. "We can hold to our stories. They can't prove anything because we recall events differently. No crime in having a bad memory."

"And when they question Ortega?"

"They won't do that, will they? Why would …"

"Of course they would!" Sillman interrupted, irritated. "They probably already are!"

"Then we have to let Ortega know, right? I mean …"

"Stop talking. I have to think."

Sillman stared out at the darkening sky. Bettis stood to the side, meek and silent staring at the floor.

A minute passed, then two. A man's face floated before him, reflected in the glass. It was his face. It turned red, then purple, gagging, teeth biting through his tongue, blood flowing from his mouth over his starched shirt.

Sillman shook his head until only his reflection remained in the glass, gray and frightened. Unlike Bettis, he knew there was a reason to be frightened. There was only one thing to do.

He turned away from the glass. "I'll take care of it."

"How?" Bettis' brow rose, concerned and relieved at the same time.

"Don't worry." Sillman rose from the chair to pat his assistant's shoulder and led him down the hall to the front door. "I'll take care of things. Like you said we'll get through it."

Sillman gave a reassuring smile. The door closed behind Bettis, and the smile faded. It was time to fix things.

THIRTY-TWO

They Had a Plan

It was thin. Seen from one way, it seemed clear there was something there. From another, it was just behavioral nuance, not much at all.

That Sillman and Bettis were nervous was an understatement. They had responded to questioning like long-tailed cats in a room full of rocking chairs.

But a case of nerves proved nothing. Any defense attorney would point out to a jury that their client's nervous behavior was understandable. Lots of people were nervous talking to the cops. That wasn't a crime.

What they had was a glaring lack of evidence of any crime. There was not one shred of probable cause that would allow them to go to a judge and obtain a search warrant to find more corroborating evidence. Even if they convinced a judge to sign a warrant affidavit, they had no idea where to search or what to search for.

This wasn't television. Warrants aren't magic wands. They don't mysteriously produce evidence, and they do not give the police carte blanche to go on fishing expeditions in pursuit of criminals.

They focus on evidence relevant to a particular crime. There must be sufficient probable cause—evidence—that reasonably points to a particular person or location being associated with criminal activity.

Reasonable was a moving target with some judges, but Sole and Travis had no illusions. They were a long way from meeting the minimum probable cause standards for any judge, reasonable or not, to issue a warrant, especially one to be served on a sitting senator.

"What do you think," Travis asked, turning the Ford at a random corner. They were in the city car, alone, the place they retreated to away from distraction when they needed to hash things out in private.

Sole looked up and noticed they were on West Paces Ferry Road, passing the governor's mansion. He flipped through the notes he made during his interview with Sillman. Beyond the undeniable nervousness, he had said nothing that could incriminate him in any crime.

"Honestly," He sighed. "Part of me says this is just a big nothing burger."

"Yeah, Travis agreed. "Hard to believe a senator ... wealthy one at that ... is doing business, legitimate or otherwise with an organized crime boss ... even a suspected one. So where do we start?"

Sole looked out the window. The stately homes of Atlanta's rich and famous lined the road. There was old wealth here, family fortunes passed on through generations. Sole wondered how far back the Sillman family could trace its roots and wealth.

"Let's start with what you said." Sole looked at Travis. "Is he really wealthy?"

"Sillman Shrimp Company has been around a long time," Travis mused, thinking things through. "Still, it's worth a shot. I'll do some research on his financials. Could be the good senator is not as well off as his penthouse lifestyle makes us think. Might give us a motive for ... something." He shrugged. "Still not evidence of any crime though."

"No," Sole agreed. "Not evidence. Just another piece of the puzzle."

"Right. Any other ideas?"

"One." Sole nodded. "There's a third party here that we haven't talked to."

"Ortega."

"Yeah. I think it's time to have a conversation with El Toro ... see how his memory lines up with Bettis and Sillman." Sole nodded. "You see what you can do to find flaws in their stories. I'll go chat with Ortega. If nothing turns up, we cut it loose and move on."

"Sounds like a plan," Travis said, spinning the wheel to turn back towards downtown and their office.

It wasn't much of one, Sole thought. Look for flaws in the line of shit Bettis and Sillman had fed them, come up with a motive. The face-to-face with Ortega might open a few cracks in their stories. If they could widen the cracks, drive a wedge in with some cold, hard facts, the whole bucket of lies might crack open and spill out into the light of day.

THIRTY-THREE

Progress

The sign over the storefront read *Taqueria Ortega*. The tiny restaurant in a fifty-year-old shopping center in northeast Atlanta was the first of a chain of such shops that Bautista Ortega had opened. Since then, a dozen more had sprung up around the city, but this one remained his headquarters.

Authorities suspected but had not proven that he used the proceeds from smuggling narcotics into the United States as his seed money. There was also the strong assumption that the chain of popular cafes served as a tool to launder his illegal profits from the drug trade.

So far, it was only an assumption. Like everything else Ortega touched, he kept any scent of drug trafficking away from his legitimate affairs. Like a mafia don, he was always careful to cultivate an image as a simple owner of a business, *Taqueria Ortega*, with no ties to organized crime.

John Sole opened the door and stepped inside. Succulent aromas of chilies, onions, and meats simmering on the griddle behind the counter engulfed him. The place was small, fifteen feet across to a counter with a half dozen tables lining the walls and in front of the window. The kitchen and rooms behind the counter took up most of the shop's space.

A pleasant-faced woman in her fifties greeted him. Dark hair hanging to her shoulders and a brilliant white smile spreading across her face made her look younger. Her confidence and poise made Sole wonder if she was a family relation of El Toro.

"What can I get for you today?" she asked.

"Two tacos ... soft flour tortilla ... one beef and one chicken."

She punched the order into the register as he spoke. "Anything to drink?"

"Diet Coke."

He put a ten-dollar bill on the counter. The cashier gave him back two dollars and a quarter. Ortega's weren't the cheapest street tacos in town, but they were worth the money. Whatever else El Toro might do in his other life, Sole had to agree he made a hell of a taco.

The smiling woman placed the two tacos wrapped in paper, the drink and a stack of napkins on the counter. Sole scooped them up and found a vacant table by the front window, sitting so he could watch the door and people passing on the sidewalk at the same time.

His choice of seats was an occupational precaution, but in reality, unnecessary. He knew that by now everyone within a half mile had been made aware that a police detective was eating tacos at Ortega's. He also knew Ortega would tolerate no one interfering with him or causing him to remain one second longer than necessary in the shop. Sole was as safe as if he were sitting at his in-laws for Sunday brunch.

The other tables remained empty. Several customers came in and ordered, taking their food to-go in paper bags, casting sidelong glances at the detective watching them as he munched his tacos.

When he had finished his meal, Sole tossed the wrappers and drink cup in the trash and stepped up to the counter again. The woman's smile broadened. A knowing look in her eye told him she knew he was there for more than tacos.

"Mr. Ortega in?" Sole asked. He nodded to the black Cadillac Escalade with the fancy wire rims and oversized hood medallion in the parking lot outside. "His car is here," he added to encourage her not to make excuses for her boss.

She didn't try. She smiled and said, "Of course. He waits for you to finish your meal. This way please." She nodded at a door in the wall to the side of the counter.

Sole followed her past the kitchen, walk-in cooler and storeroom to the back of the store. There, in an eight by ten office seated behind a desk too large for the room, he found Bautista Ortega. El Toro lifted his head as Sole came to the doorway.

"Come in. Have a seat." Ortega did not rise to shake hands. He folded his thick arms on the desk in front of him and nodded. "I've been expecting you."

"Expecting me?" Sole said, taking a seat in a wooden chair so close to the desk that his knees banged against it as he sat.

"Of course." Ortega nodded to the side table where a monitor showed four images—front door, rear door, kitchen, and dining area where Sole had eaten his lunch. "So, I suppose we should get the formalities out of the way ... Detective."

"I suppose we should." Sole pulled his badge holder and ID card out.

"Investigator John Sole," Ortega read aloud, then looked up. "What can I do for you today, Investigator Sole?"

"Just a few questions for you."

"Questions?" Ortega smiled. "Do I need a lawyer?"

"That's up to you."

Sole's eyes bored in, watching for any reaction, a nervous tic, an involuntary reflex. There were none.

He had to give him credit. El Toro held himself together without flinching, unlike trembling Sillman or his wonder-boy assistant, Wilson Bettis.

No doubt, he had vastly more experience dealing with law enforcement investigations—had been the target of more than a few. The prospect of being asked a few questions by investigators constrained by the protections of the U.S. Constitution did not intimidate him.

Or, maybe, Sole had to admit, there wasn't anything for Ortega to be nervous about. It was time to find out.

"Well, Detective Sole," Ortega lifted his beefy hands, palms up in a shrug as he smiled. "I have nothing to hide. Ask your questions." He looked at his watch, "But please get to the point. I have appointments later today, and your visit was … unexpected."

The smile spread wider across Ortega's face, enjoying the little game of cat and mouse. Sole recognized the arrogance as for what it was—a dare—testing him to find out what the cops knew and what they didn't. The truth was they didn't know much.

Ortega may have even realized that the dare, his smug arrogance, was as much a signal as Sillman's nervous tic or Bettis' stammering. The difference was, Ortega knew his arrogance would not prove a damned thing in court.

Fine. Sole decided he'd play the game.

"Why did you meet with Wilson Bettis at Eruptions?" Sole launched in with no preliminaries, going for shock value. Platitudes and prolonged small talk would not lull Ortega into making a mistake.

"Who?" Ortega replied without blinking.

"Wilson Bettis ... aide to Senator James Sillman. You were there together a few nights ago."

"Senator Sillman? You think I met with his aide? What was his name ... Bet ... something or other?"

"Wilson Bettis," Sole replied evenly, his eyes never wavering from Ortega's face. "You were seen together."

There was no need to pretend there was a recording of the meeting. It would not work with Ortega. His men would have verified there were no cameras on the third floor at Eruptions, and his friend Sergei Sokolov would have guaranteed it for a customer like El Toro.

Pretending otherwise would just make the questioning appear weak, grasping at straws. Ortega would be in control then. It was best to just say it, blurt it out and see the effect.

The effect was minimal, but it was there. A slight furrowing of the wrinkles in his forehead, an almost imperceptible downward turn of the eyebrows, a hardening in his stare. Was it annoyance? Anger? Sole decided it was both. Either way, it sent the message that there was something there.

Ortega was not happy. He would never admit that he met with Bettis, but his eyes told the story. When their conversation ended, El Toro would have questions of his own. Sole felt a momentary pang of pity for the person who would be asked those questions. Someone would pay for putting Ortega in the hot seat.

The smile reappeared on Ortega's face, the brow rose

again, and the defiant but playful look returned to his eyes. "Do you mind if I ask who told you such a thing?"

"I don't mind at all," Sole replied. Now the smile was on his face. "You can ask. We both know I won't be releasing the name of our source."

"You're right. We both know the rules here." Ortega leaned back in his seat. All pretenses had evaporated. They had played the game. Both came away with something. Time would tell who had won.

Ortega rose, nodding at the door to his office, inviting Sole to get the hell out. "Well, as I said. I have other appointments and must call this to an end. I wish you well in whatever investigation you are conducting, and I hope our discussion was helpful."

Sole rose from the wooden chair, tucked his notepad in his pocket and nodded. "Thanks. I think I got what I came for."

Ortega allowed Sole to make his way through the back of the store unescorted, sending another message. He had nothing to hide. You leave with what you came with—nothing.

Sole smiled at the woman behind the counter as he came from the back and left the store. Outside, he stood on the cracked sidewalk, gazing up and down the line of shops.

He had the feeling that eyes watched him from the storefronts, the cars in the parking lot, the small groups of men gathered at either end of the strip center. Let them watch, he thought, walking to his car in the first row across from Ortega's shop.

He started the engine and hit the Bluetooth button on the wheel to call Travis.

"Where we at partner?" he asked when Travis answered.

"Made some progress. Turns out, Sillman Shrimp Company is not doing so well."

"How so?"

"Checked UCC filings in Chatham and Fulton Counties ... Savannah and Atlanta ... for Sillman's known company's. That's Sillman Shrimp Inc., Sillman Enterprises and James J. Sillman, LTD. All three are heavily leveraged, borrowing money to continue operations."

Travis paused, shuffling through his notes. "Looks like he's been using a sort of pyramid scheme to keep things afloat ... no pun intended. Sillman Shrimp borrows from Sillman Enterprises which then receives funds from Sillman LTD, which includes the family fortune plus funding from credit obtained on the good senator's family name ... a lot of credit."

"Another piece to the puzzle," Sole said as he pulled onto I-85 headed downtown. "Sillman is on shaky financial ground."

"The shakiest," Travis agreed. "Liens filed on equipment, a good portion of his shrimp boat fleet, even a couple of houses. Bottom line ... Sillman is a few bad shrimp hauls away from bankruptcy."

Travis put his notes away and leaned back in his chair, hands behind his head. "How about you? Did Ortega crack?"

"Yes and no."

"Elaborate please. I'm too tired to play guessing games."

"Well, he didn't break down and admit to being a narcotics dealer, but it's not so much what he didn't tell me. It's the *way* he didn't tell me."

"The way?"

"Yeah. He denied any meeting with Bettis, but was clearly annoyed that someone had spotted them together."

"That's something." Travis agreed.

"Yep. I'd say it's enough. Luis Acero gets to keep his get out of jail card one more day."

THIRTY-FOUR

A Damned Fine Feeling

The last of the sun flashed brilliant orange in the east, its glow undulating across the water. It had been a perfect day. It would be an ideal night for the Sara Jane's maiden voyage.

After leaving the St. Mary's river channel, they moved into the main shrimping grounds that began just offshore, extending out about eight miles. Tully Sams pushed on to the limit, then had Hermie and Paco lower the net cranes to give the appearance they were trawling for shrimp. Even without deploying the nets they would look like any other trawler cruising along the coast.

The last of the sun dipped below the horizon. Stars appeared in the darkening sky. They had lost sight of land five miles out. At eight miles even the tallest buildings along the coastline were below the horizon. Within a few minutes, the glow from the coastal lights was nothing more than a hazy ribbon on the horizon. Overhead, a billion stars burned in the inky black night.

Tully checked the radar scope for any nearby traffic,

then stepped out from the deckhouse and lit a cigarette. He stood smoking in the night breeze, turning three hundred and sixty degrees as he flicked ashes into the air. No other navigation lights were in sight. Nothing on radar and no visual signs of other boats or ships. Best to be safe though.

He motioned to Hermie and Paco, to join him amidships. After offering each a cigarette—Hermie accepted with a grin, Paco declined with *no gracias*—he used his finger, pointing at his eyes, then their eyes, then the surrounding horizon to communicate that he wanted them to check for lights from other trawlers and ships.

They nodded and turned to scan with their younger eyes. After a minute, each looked at him and said, "*Nada, Capitán.*"

"Good," Sams smiled. "That's what I figured. Just making sure."

He leaned in the deckhouse and cut the switch for the Sara Jane's running lights. They were black now. He stood with his small crew for a few more minutes finishing his smoke, enjoying their silent company, seamen, like him who felt alive out on the ocean.

He tossed the butt overboard, stepped back into the deckhouse and called down into the galley. "It's your show. Best bring Julio and his special skills up on deck."

Esteban Moya poked his head into the deckhouse, gave a quick look around, turned and said something in Spanish and stepped up beside Sams. Behind him, Julio grabbed the sides of the door and pulled himself out, in better shape than earlier, but still a touch of green around his gills.

"Where to?" Sams asked.

"East," Moya replied. "Julio will show you.

"Right." Sams spun the wheel, and the Sara Jane rocked

on the swells, turning from her northerly course along the coast to head out into the Atlantic.

Julio took a book-sized device from the cargo pocket of his trousers and pressed a power button on the side.

"GPS?" Sams said with a shake of his head and motioned to the dashboard at the front of the cockpit. "Got GPS onboard. That's his special skill?"

"He is in contact with our target, through his device. You are not. You never will be. Your job is to steer the coordinates that Julio provides. That is all you must know." Moya's fingers tapped the pistol tucked into his waistband. "Questions?"

Sams shrugged. "Whatever you say."

Radar scanning in all directions, running dark, the Sara Jane proceeded out into the vast Atlantic. At twelve miles off the coast, they reached the limits of United States territorial waters. Still, they continued east. At twenty-four miles, they arrived at the boundary of the U.S. contiguous, legal enforcement zone.

Thirty-five miles out, they were still within the two hundred mile economic zone claimed by the United States. Julio made a circular motion with his hand, showing Sams that he was to orbit the trawler in this area until given further navigational instructions.

Throttling back, Sams let the Sara Jane cruise in a two-mile-wide circle. Standard trawling speed was between four and five knots. He had bumped the throttle up to seven knots, covering the twenty-seven miles out from his usual trawling distance in just under four hours. Now they turtled along at about 3 knots, just enough to make headway.

Julio sat in a chair beside Sams, huddled over his two-way GPS communicator. He typed a message into the device and pressed send. A minute later, it beeped with a reply. With meticulous care, checking to verify what he wrote, Julio printed a set of coordinates on a piece of paper and handed it to Sams.

"Go here," he said in broken English.

Sams nodded and spun the wheel to line the bow up with the coordinates, bumping the throttle up again. He wondered how much Julio-with-the-special-skills was being paid for his part in their venture.

As he made the turn, a blip showed up on the radar screen, sailing in their direction. The fifty-thousand-ton Panamax class container ship closed until they could see the glow of its lights just below the horizon.

After sailing from Lázaro Cárdenas, the freighter passed through the Panama Canal. From there, it navigated through the Caribbean shipping routes, an innocuous cargo ship sailing amid the swarm of drug enforcement ships and aircraft from the United States.

Turning to the north, sailing past Cuba and the Florida Keys, it ran another gauntlet of anti-drug smuggling craft operated by several agencies. Coast Guard and U.S. Customs authorities were alert to ships offloading containers with drugs in ports, but this one did not sail into port. Its passage was noted, filed and forgotten.

It sailed north along the Florida coast, staying fifty miles offshore, bound for a common transatlantic crossing route. By the time it reached the waters off the Georgia coast, the ship was just a blip among hundreds.

Sole Survivor

As Sams guided the Sara Jane toward the mid-ocean rendezvous point, the captain of the cargo ship slowed engines allowing the huge freighter to coast under its own momentum. Then he sent the watch crew below. They asked no questions. It was no secret that Bebé Elizondo was a part owner in the shipping company.

Only the first mate and a cargo crane operator remained above deck with the captain. While the captain stabilized the ship, the first mate went to one cargo container and broke open the seal. Inside, he attached the lifting chains to the steel framework supporting a tarp-covered bundle resting on three pontoons. These sat atop conveyer rollers installed in the container's floor.

It took skill, and this operator was one of the best on two continents. Moving the crane laterally, he slid the secured cargo from the container over the rollers, until it hung from the end of the crane. It was an immense pontoon raft loaded and covered with a tarp.

The operator waited a full two minutes for the swaying load to stabilize. Then with subtle movements of the controls, he swung the raft overboard and lowered it to the water.

A twitch of control here, an almost imperceptible nudge there, and the precious cargo settled into the water. The raft floated, perfectly balanced, not too high in the water or it could capsize, or so low it might swamp.

After releasing the cables, the operator repositioned the crane over the deck. The mate closed the container and resealed it with an identification tag registered and purchased from the cargo master in Lázaro Cárdenas.

The Captain called the crew back to the deck, and the freighter increased speed again. The whole operation had taken thirty minutes. It was nowhere in sight as the Sara Jane approached the cargo floating on the swells.

If the engineering and planning going into the operation were intricate, its purpose was simple—avoid any of the common points of interdiction by the many law enforcement agencies, patrolling the coasts. The solution was to make the transfer at sea to a registered U.S. craft outside the usual points of interdiction. That's where the Sara Jane came in, a known shrimp trawler, operated no less by a U.S. senator.

Bebé Elizondo demanded the best and paid for it. To execute the plan, cargo handlers concealed a military-grade, heavy-duty pontoon cargo raft capable of carrying forty thousand pounds inside a cargo container. Nestled amongst hundreds of others on a cargo ship, the container was unidentifiable from those carrying other Mexican exports like tropical fruits and vegetables, vehicle parts, electronics, medical instruments, alcoholic beverages, even gold, and silver. The only difference was that the contents of Elizondo's special cargo container far exceeded the value of the others.

After making the passage through the Panama Canal and working its way to the north, the captain prepared for the transfer at sea. He monitored weather conditions and the movements of drug interdiction ships and aircraft that might wander near their route.

When the weather conditions were favorable and the skies and waters clear of encroaching shipping and law enforcement activity, the captain identified a precise set of

GPS coordinates as the drop point and sent them to Julio on the Sara Jane.

Fees paid to the captain, first mate, crane operator, cargo handlers and engineers to design and execute the operation soaked up three hundred thousand dollars of Elizondo's profits. Another hundred thousand went for the custom-built pontoon raft that could handle the load. It was pocket change.

The base value of the five thousand kilos, a little over ten thousand pounds, of cocaine at the current market rates figured to be about one hundred and twenty-five million US dollars. Once the pure cocaine was cut and repackaged in one gram hits, the street value would soar to almost a billion dollars, give or take a million or two.

Elizondo was a lot of things, but he was no fool. With transport and delivery costs well below one percent of the street value, he was more than happy to cover shipping and delivery.

The process was more complex than running a truck across the border, but if this shipment was successfully delivered, future loads would be larger and bring even greater returns. Bebé was going to be a very happy man.

Sams steered for the coordinates Julio indicated, making slight adjustments as the pings on the raft's GPS transponder sent signals of its drift in the current. By the time he pulled alongside the raft, the freighter was miles away. They were alone on the black ocean.

Moya was now in command. At his nod, Paco secured the raft to the trawler and climbed over the side while Hermie got the starboard net crane operating.

Ten separate five hundred kilo bundles were packed with Colombian cocaine. One by one, Paco fastened the hoist chains to a bundle, and Hermie lifted it and deposited it on the deck, taking care to distribute the cargo evenly and maintain the Sara Jane's trim in the water.

It took less than an hour to complete the transfer. When the last bundle rested on the Sara Jane's deck, Hermie hooked a chain saw to a safety line and lowered it to Paco. With the saw in hand and safety line securing him to the crane's hoist chain, Paco went to each pontoon, cutting into the industrial grade laminated fabric along its length. A loud hissing filled the night air as the pontoons deflated.

When he finished, the raft was almost below the water. By the time Hermie hoisted Paco up to the deck and deposited him gently beside one of the bundles of cocaine, the steel frame of the raft had dragged the deflated pontoons down to the ocean floor three hundred feet below.

Tully Sams turned the Sara Jane to the west, making for a tidal estuary along the coast between Brunswick and St. Mary's. They would wait for high tide and then cruise inland to offload into vans at a small private dock on a piece of land Bautista Ortega had purchased through a third party. From there, Bebé Elizondo's cargo of cocaine destined to the United States markets was only a few hours away from hitting the street.

Tully Sams wondered if his grandfather had felt the same rush of adrenaline surging through him, during his runs from Cuba loaded down with rum. He couldn't help grinning and sticking his head out of the deckhouse into the breeze, sucking in the salt air and relishing the tingle in his spine. It was a damned fine feeling.

THIRTY-FIVE

Acting Stupidly

"I have to speak with Bebé."

Sillman imagined Alejandro Garza's cold eyes peering at him through the phone. He felt like a squirming lab specimen awaiting dissection.

"A moment," Garza said without question or comment

The line went dead. For a moment, Sillman thought he had disconnected, wondering what he would do if that were the case. He had mustered all his fortitude to make this call. The thought of phoning a second time tightened his sphincter and sent a shiver up his spine.

Elizondo came on the line. No doubt he had discussed the possible reasons for the call with his lieutenant while Sillman waited.

"Yes, James," Bebé said in a voice as smooth as warm butter. "What would you like to speak about, at such a late hour? I have reports that all is well with the first shipment."

Sillman had almost forgotten. Tully Sams had sailed today with Ortega's men to make the transfer from the freighter to his trawler.

"Yes, I am sorry for calling so late," He continued, trying to sound confident, knowing that he sounded just the opposite. "There is … uh, something we should discuss."

"Something that cannot wait for tomorrow? It must be important."

"It might be."

"Please tell me."

He could see Bebé, his smooth, round face relaxed, sitting back in his leather chair smoking a cigar, a glass of wine on the table beside him. Alejandro Garza would be watching, intent, fixed on what his *Patrón* might say, waiting for orders.

"There have been some … inquiries," he began, trying to find a way to say it without choking on the words.

"What sort of inquiries? Please be direct, James. The hour is late."

"Yes, I know. Sorry." He took a deep breath. "I was … we were visited by detectives today."

"Detectives? You mean the police."

"Yes, that's right, the police."

"And what did these detectives inquire about?"

"They wanted to know why Wilson Bettis was meeting with Bautista Ortega. In their words, Ortega is a suspected drug lord."

"Oh, I would say that is an overstatement," Bebé said, sounding amused. "He is far from being the lord. Still, he plays a valuable role in our organization." He returned to the point, his voice sounding more serious now. "How did these detectives know your assistant met with Ortega?"

"He was seen there … at the club … at Eruptions."

"Yes, I know this club. I have been there myself with Ortega on a visit to Atlanta. There are no cameras to record and a secure back entrance, so you say he never had a meeting with anyone there ... that whoever saw him is mistaken. They have no proof, and all is well." Elizondo paused. "This is what you said, correct?"

"I ...uh ... I'm afraid not." Sillman wiped at the beads of sweat breaking out along his hairline. "You see ... they set us up."

"You mean they tricked you."

"Yes," Sillman said, his head bobbing up and down to emphasize the unfair tactics the detectives employed. He realized that Bebé could not see him over the phone and continued, "They tricked us. They met with us alone using the pretext they wanted to know more about the drug trafficking legislation ... said they wanted to support the idea."

"That sounds harmless enough."

Sillman took a deep breath. "Then out of the blue, they said they had information Bettis had been at Eruptions with Ortega. It happened so fast, the way they came at us. We couldn't coordinate ... had no idea what they were asking or how the other answered the questions."

"Yes, the police can be deceptive," Elizondo said dryly. "What did you say ... you and your assistant?"

"Bettis said the meeting with Ortega was to get support for the anti-drug program. They confused him."

"Your chief aide, the man you trusted, was confused?" There was acid in Elizondo's voice.

"Well ... I mean they surprised him. They implied they had a video of the meeting."

"Obviously, that was a lie," Elizondo said.

"Yes, they lied about that, but they were so adamant about it ... said someone noticed him because he wore a business suit and didn't fit in ... drew attention and got recognized."

"Who is the someone who recognized him?"

"I don't know." Shit. Sillman felt the earth crumbling away beneath his feet.

"He wore a business suit to this nightclub?" Elizondo persisted. "To meet with Ortega? That seems foolish. Still, he could have simply denied being there and all would have been well."

"Yes, but like I said, they tricked him ... confused him with their questions. They came at us out of left field. We didn't expect it ... weren't prepared for it."

"You must always be prepared," Elizondo interrupted, his voice taking on a harder edge now. "And you, James. What did you say to the detective who visited you?"

"Why, I was as surprised as Bettis. Maybe more so. No one questions a senator like that without some advance notice. There are protocols ..."

"You could have said so to the detective and told him to follow the protocols ... ended the conversation until we had spoken."

"I suppose I could have," Sillman whispered. "I see now that I should have."

"But you didn't." The hard edge in Bebé's voice had ice on it now. "So what did you say?"

"Not much ... I, uh ... I told him that Bettis does many things for me." He took a breath to calm himself before continuing. "I was boxed in, you know. Without knowing what Bettis said, so I ... I mean I might have said I knew Bettis had arranged to meet with Ortega." He added quickly, "But I told him I had no idea of the purpose."

"In other words, you confirmed the meeting between Ortega and Bettis," Elizondo said his voice rising in volume.

"Well, when you put it like ..."

"Do not interrupt! You confirmed that whoever had given them the information was correct ... that Bettis was at

Eruptions in a business suit meeting with Bautista Ortega! *Estúpido!*"

There was a pause of several seconds. Sillman had the sense that there was a slow fuse burning at the other end of the call. He didn't want to be there for the detonation.

"I expected better from our partnership and from you," Elizondo said, his voice controlled and flat.

"Yes," Sillman nodded to himself. "I see that now. They won't surprise me like that again. So … uh …" He hesitated to ask, afraid to hear the answer. "What should we do? Just tell me, and I'll take care of it."

"I think you have taken care of enough for the moment." His words clipped, his tone harsh, the melted butter was gone from Bebé's voice. "Do nothing. Make no more calls. If the detectives call on you again, you know nothing more than you have already told them. You have acted stupidly … you and your assistant. We must correct things now."

"All right, I'll do as you …"

The call ended. Bebé was gone.

Slumped in the same chair where he had answered questions from Detective Sole, Sillman looked out over the city lights. They were a whirling blur.

Elizondo's words rang in his ears. They had acted stupidly. Sillman had seen too much to have any illusions about what that meant.

THIRTY-SIX

Resolving Problems

"What has happened is unacceptable!"

"Yes, I understand, but ..."

"Do not interrupt me!"

The ice in Bebé Elizondo's voice froze Bautista Ortega.

"There, in the north," he continued. "They may call you El Toro. To me, you are the little boy I took from the gutter. I fed you, clothed you, sent you to school ... taught you the ways of our life ... what it means to be part of our world. I taught you the price for failure."

"You have my apologies," Ortega said El Toro, the bull, meek before an even bigger bull.

"Your apologies mean nothing!" Elizondo took in a deep breath and waited a moment before continuing. When he did, his voice was calmer, but the tone remained icy. "Someone saw you with Sillman's man. The police are now questioning why a senator would have contact with you. We based our entire operation on the relationship with Sillman, and you have the police looking into that relationship!"

"But they learned nothing, Bebé. I spoke to an investigator."

"You? You spoke with an investigator!" The fire was back, and Elizondo pounded his fist on the side of his chair as he shouted into the phone.

In the hallway outside, Sofia hustled the children away from their father's office. Inside, Alejandro Garza sat across from Bebé, dispassionate and implacable, waiting for his orders.

"Yes, but please hear me out," Ortega said. He was walking through a minefield, and the next step might be his last.

"Speak!" Elizondo shouted. "Explain why I am finding out only now you have spoken to the police!"

"Because it only just happened yesterday afternoon. I did not want to disturb you in the evening. I know how important your family is to you." Ortega took a breath to slow his pounding heart. "I was going to call you this morning, but you have already spoken to Sillman. I swear to you, Bebé. They have learned nothing."

"And why are you so certain they learned nothing?"

"Because of the questions he asked ... or didn't ask."

"Explain."

"It is a simple thing. The detective did not use subterfuge in his questions. He only said they had a witness who saw me with Sillman's man."

"And to you, this means what?"

"It means they are trying to confirm the witness' story, but they have nothing as long as we deny it." Ortega nodded at the phone on his desk and said. "I denied it."

"Yes, well Sillman's man was not so insightful when they spoke to him," Elizondo said, disgust in his voice. "He admitted to having met with you.

"That is his word against mine, and I will continue to deny any such meeting. There is no proof."

"You keep saying that." Elizondo shook his head. "I am not so certain."

"There is no proof. I understand that there are some weak links." Ortega knew it was time to play the card that might yet save his life. "The weak links are the only ones that can harm us," he said, his tone fervent, making it clear he was not one of those weak links.

Elizondo glanced at Alejandro who nodded to confirm the truth of Ortega's words. Failure had a price. It was the rule that Bebé had employed with ruthless abandon while putting together *Los Salvajes*.

"All right," he said, quieter now. "The mistake has been made. We will overlook how it was made for the moment. We must eliminate the problem it created."

"Would you like me to handle the problem?" Ortega asked, already knowing the answer.

"No. I am sending Alejandro. He will guide you."

"Very well."

"Look for him tomorrow evening. When he arrives, he has total control. Provide whatever he requires. You understand?"

"Understood."

Bebé punched the button ending the call and turned to Alejandro. "Difficulty?"

"Nothing I can't handle." Garza's brown eyes narrowed. "Ortega?"

"No." Bebé shook his head. "Not now. We need him." He added with a shrug. "And he may be right. There may be no cause for concern."

"Sometimes it is better to eliminate concerns before they arise."

"This is true. But we must be careful not to overreact." Elizondo nodded. "The operation has just begun, and we have had our first success with the shipment last night. We must take care not to jeopardize the future in dealing with the present situation."

"As you instruct, Bebé," Alejandro nodded out of respect.

"Do you expect any problems?" Elizondo asked, bringing them back to focus on the issue at hand.

"There are always intricacies to work out ... contingencies to plan for." Alejandro said calmly. "Nothing I can't handle. There will be no connection to *Los Salvajes* ... or to you."

"I am confident you will see to things with your usual efficiency."

"One question," Alejandro said, focused on the task at hand.

"Yes. Alejandro. Ask it."

"You wish me to resolve ... all issues?"

Resolving all issues, as Alejandro put it, was one thing in Mexico where they owned the police and much of the government. North of the border, it was something else entirely.

Bebé thought about it for a moment then shook his head. "Not just yet."

THIRTY-SEVEN

Too Damn Late

Tully Sams let the Sara Jane idle its way around the back of Cumberland Island to Fancy Bluff Creek, the sound that separated the island from the mainland. Mainland was more of a technical term than a physical reality. The land here was salt marsh and saw grass stretching in places for miles to the western horizon.

Sams navigated around the islands at the mouth of the main creek and headed inland. At high tide, the water was deep enough to handle the trawler's draft, but they had to work fast. Once the tide ebbed, they had only an hour or two before they risked being grounded in the mud until the next high tide.

Hundreds of small channels and waterways cut through the marshes. Some deep, some nothing more than paths where deer, feral pigs, and sea turtles made their way through to firmer ground and better foraging.

Sams spun the wheel to head into a no-name channel that cut off to the south out of the main creek. After a hundred yards, he cut the engine and let the Sara Jane drift to a small dock extending out ten feet from the shore.

The tiny finger of dry ground extending into the marsh had been selected with care, paid for through a third party who was paid for his services by another anonymous party, leaving no trail back to Ortega or Elizondo. Surrounded by the swaying saw grass, it was invisible, unless you knew where to look.

Sams wondered what would happen if some early morning fisherman out in his johnboat happened to come along. He put the thought out of his head and said a silent prayer that no unlucky soul would spot them.

As they neared the dock, Hermie and Paco bustled about the deck, readying the lines without waiting for orders. The Sara Jane drifted in closer, and they tossed the lines to a group of men waiting on the dock.

Within seconds and without instruction, they organized the work party. Hermie and Paco loosened the bindings around the bundles of cocaine. Three others joined them, leaping from the dock to the deck, and formed a conveyor line.

The shrink-wrapped, kilo packages moved from hand to hand to the men waiting on the dock. Another line relayed them to the panel vans. The drivers supervised, checking their manifests to ensure the count was correct.

As they loaded each van, the door slammed shut, and the driver behind the wheel pulled away from the dock, disappearing into the marsh. From there, they followed the narrow finger of dry ground inland to an unmarked gravel road. The gravel road led to a paved county road. Five miles farther on the county road intersected with Interstate 95.

The vans dispersed, some heading north, some south, to

cities up and down the east coast. Others only went as far as Savannah and turned west on I-16 toward Atlanta and the markets farther inland.

The entire operation took less than forty minutes. Sams kept an eye on the time, anxious about missing the tide.

As the last van door closed with its load, Hermie and Paco retrieved the mooring lines and coiled them neatly on the deck. Moya nodded, indicating that it was time to go. Sams relaxed. They had more than enough time to get to deep water and avoid being left mud-bound as the sun rose.

By the time they made the ten-mile trip back out Fancy Bluff Creek to the sound and then along the coast to St. Mary's, the eastern sky was showing a faint tinge of pink along the horizon. Stars still burned bright in the overhead blackness, but the sun would soon spring above the horizon and wash the world in a burst of morning light. He sidled the Sara Jane up to her berth at the St. Mary's dock and cut the engines, letting his two new deckhands do the work of tying off without comment from him.

There was no celebration or slaps on the back over a job well done. Hermie and Paco nodded, respectful of their captain. Esteban Moya snapped something at them in Spanish, and they hastened to the pickup. Julio followed close on their heels.

An hour later, Tully Sams had dropped the four at the Brunswick airport. He stood alone in the parking lot and watched the small plane leave with them, soaring two hundred feet over his head as it climbed into the morning sky.

He lit a cigarette and watched until the plane was just a speck, dwindling in the distance. Mixed emotions nagged at him. The earlier thrill of accomplishment and elation he had experienced out on the water was replaced by something else.

What would the real Sara Jane think about the night's activities? He knew.

Stubbing the cigarette butt out on the ground, he climbed in the pickup, muttering, "Too damn late for an attack of conscience now, Tully boy."

THIRTY-EIGHT

The Odds

"Do we have enough?" Travis looked up from the pile of notes and financial records he was sorting.

They had decided to wait a day, let everything percolate in their heads overnight, and give everything a once over with fresh eyes in the morning. Now, it was time to cut bait or fish with Luis Acero's tip.

"I think so." Sole nodded, sipping black coffee. "At least it's time to let them decide if they want to follow up. We're getting beyond a simple major crimes investigation. This is specialized … drug trafficking … international smuggling. If this pans out, a lot of agencies will want a piece of it."

Huddled together in Travis' cubicle, they made a list of agencies they should include in their briefing. The APD narcotics squad was a given. They were on the same team, and now that they had more confidence in Luis' information, they could let him off the hook, at least a little.

Next on the list was the Georgia Bureau of Investigation. The GBI had an interest in any significant statewide criminal activity. They also had additional resources to allocate to the investigation if needed.

The DEA and FBI were included as a matter of routine. Crimes that crossed state lines or originated from international sources would involve them. There was no absolute proof that the investigation involved smuggling or transport of drugs to any location outside of Georgia, but with Sillman's shrimp fleet in the mix, there was a strong possibility.

The final addition to the list was U.S. Customs and Immigration Enforcement. ICE had jurisdiction over people or material coming across the U.S. borders. They were experts at interdicting drug smugglers.

"That about covers it." Travis looked at the list he had printed in neat block letters. "When do you want to do it?"

"Soon as possible," Sole replied. "Set it up for tomorrow."

"Okay, why not? I figure we're either going to look like heroes or fools." Travis' face twisted into a wry smile. "I'd say right now, it's a toss-up."

"I think it's better than that. I figure the odds are sixty-forty we won't come out of this looking like a couple of chumps." Sole shrugged and grinned at Travis. "What's the problem? You worried about your future here in Major Crimes?"

"Worried about both our futures. I've become attached to your surly ways." Travis smirked. "But mostly, I don't want to end up checking parking meters and chalking tires for the next twenty years."

"Nothing to worry about." Sole said. "It's all automated now ... meter checkers drive these cute little cars with cameras and tag recognition technology built into an onboard computer. Just drive up and down the block and the computer reads the tags of the parkers who have overstayed their welcome. Really high tech stuff. You'll love it."

"Thanks, asshole."

THIRTY-NINE

Pray

"You see what problems your incompetence has caused me!" Bautista Ortega glared across the desk in his small office in the *taqueria*.

The Americans have an expression. *La mierda rueda cuesta abajo*—Shit rolls downhill. Now, a heavy load of it was rolling right down from Elizondo, to Ortega to land squarely on Esteban Moya's ass.

He lowered his head to avoid eye contact with El Toro. The man was in an evil mood, and no good could come from challenging him, even by attempting to defend himself from his wrath—*especially* by trying to defend himself.

Just back from overseeing the transfer of Elizondo's first shipment, he was exhausted. There had been no time to rest since the plane from Brunswick had landed.

The first order of business was to contact his network of dealers and reassure them that their supply problems would soon end. He managed to reach all by cell phone on the drive to the *taqueria*—except one. Luis Acero was nowhere to be found.

"Any idea who I have been on the phone with today?" Ortega roared, his rage building as he recalled the conversation with Bebé Elizondo. "He is sending someone to correct your mistakes?"

Moya lifted his eyes and ventured a one-word query, "Who?"

"Garza is coming." Ortega let the name hang in the air between them, watching with satisfaction as fear crept into Moya's eyes.

"Is it so bad that he must come?" Moya whispered, more to himself than to Ortega.

"You tell me." Ortega placed his beefy arms on the desk and leaned toward Moya. "Detectives visited Sillman and that peacock of an assistant ... Bettis."

"All they had to do was say they knew nothing. There is no evidence. They remained silent, right?"

"What do you think?" Ortega spat back at him. "A peacock and an aging rooster with his tail feathers falling out. The detectives came with their questions, and they stood there with wide eyes and their dicks in their hands." He shook his massive head. "They might as well have said they had made a deal with Elizondo."

"Still," Moya ventured mildly. "There is no ..."

"Are you fucking listening?" Ortega roared. "They didn't have to give them proof. Everything they said ... everything they didn't say ... the way they swallowed, stuttered, the sweat on their faces ... it was all proof ... enough at least for these detectives to keep digging."

"Yes, but what the detectives are thinking is not ..."

"He came and visited me!"

"Who?"

"A detective." Ortega leaned back in his chair like a balloon with the air escaping. "He knew."

"That is what he said?"

"He didn't have to. I could tell. We looked each other in the eye ... *mano a mano* ... this is not one to trifle with." Ortega nodded. "He knows. He will keep searching until he finds something."

"What was his name?"

"John Sole."

"I've heard the name." Moya nodded. "But he doesn't work in narcotics."

"So you feel he will just walk away because he is not a narc?" Ortega smirked.

"No, not that, but because he is not a narc, it may take him time to put things together."

"We don't have time. Garza arrives tomorrow."

"Then we must plan," Moya said, leaning forward with more confidence now that he had survived El Toro's initial tirade.

"There is no time to plan. It is out of our hands now. That is why Elizondo is sending Garza to clean up. We can only hope he doesn't tell him to clean us up."

There was no talk of running. Escape from Alejandro Garza was impossible. Even if they evaded him for a few days or weeks, he would find them. When he did, the punishment for running would be even more severe than standing and accepting their fate.

"You will pick him up at the airport tomorrow."

"Yes." Moya nodded. "And then?"

"And then we do whatever he fucking tells us to do and pray it will be enough to satisfy Bebé."

FORTY

It Had All Been Said

Sole walked in, and his world righted itself again. He was always amazed at how just walking through the front door brought everything into perspective.

"Dad's home!" Bobby looked up grinning from the floor beside the hall closet. He sat with his back against the wall lacing up his sneakers.

"What's up, sport? Jog time?"

"Yep, and you're just in time." Shaye came to the bottom of the stairs, turned around, and bent over propping a foot on the third step as she tied on her Nikes. "You're home early. You can join us."

"I shoulda stayed late," John sighed, smiling.

Shaye was a fitness addict, and her addiction had spread to the kids. With an afternoon off from the department, they were heading out on a jog around the neighborhood streets. They never followed any precise course. They just ran until Shaye thought they'd sufficiently exerted themselves for the day. Sufficient was a moving target and could range from a couple of miles to six or seven, depending on time and schoolwork waiting for them.

Sole walked up behind her firm, round bottom as she tied her shoes. A hand sliding along the tight fabric of her bike shorts, he bent over and whispered in her ear.

"I can think of another way to get our workout in."

She swatted his hand away, finished tying her shoes and turned to face him. Leaning close, she whispered in his ear, teasing him by letting her breasts under her sports bra rest against his chest. Electricity surged through the fabric, and he took a deep breath to quell the stirring that arose in him.

"Later." Shaye smiled and backed away.

"You are a tease," he said, face twisted in disappointment.

"Geez. You guys get a room." Samantha came down the stairs in her running clothes, her face twisted in a grimace at her parents' public display of intimacy. She pushed past them and went to the front door. "You coming today, Dad?"

Sole looked at his family. There was evil in the world. Sometimes it was hard to see past it, but Shaye banished it from their home.

"I'm coming." He jogged up the stairs. "Give me a minute."

By the time he trotted down in shorts, tee shirt, and his running shoes, Shaye had the kids out in the front yard doing warm-up stretches. "I'm ready," he said, trotting up to them. "Let's go."

"Don't you think you should warm up first, big boy," Shaye said, bending over in a side stretch.

"Naw. Let's get this over with."

"Suit yourself."

Shaye led the way down the street. As they reached the

corner, five houses down the block, John was puffing, wondering what he had gotten himself into. When they hit the three-mile mark, she took pity on him.

Lifting a hand, she jogged in place as the others pulled up beside her. Samantha followed her mother's example, keeping her legs pumping up and down. Bobby stood with his hands on his hips breathing heavy. Sole jogged up last and bent over, hands on knees, panting.

"What's up Marine," Shaye taunted. "What happened to Semper Fi, Do or Die?"

"Yeah." John nodded, sucked in some air and looked up. "I'm working on the dying part right now."

Shaye laughed. These were the days she loved, together as a family. The kids were growing faster than she and John liked, especially John. Soon, they would move on with their lives, but the memory of days like this would hold the family together.

"You two go on home," she said. "Dad and I will walk the rest of the way."

"Okay, Mom." Samantha turned and started off at a sprint, calling over her shoulder. "I'll race you, Bobby."

"Not fair!" He took off down the block after her. "Cheater!"

Samantha laughed and turned on more speed.

"They're showing me up," John said, standing up straight but still puffing hard.

"It's all about conditioning." Shaye patted the bulge over his waistline. "Something you could use a little more of, Mister."

"This?" John patted his belly. "Emergency rations."

She laughed and took his hand. "Come on. I'll walk you home, old man."

He nodded, grateful for her mercy. "I feel old."

They talked about the kids, about, the weather, about nothing. It was good just to be together. John put his arm around Shaye and pulled her close, savoring the feel of her thigh against his as they kept pace together.

They made dinner together. The kids did their homework. Shaye got the salad and vegetables ready. John grilled burgers on the back patio.

The talk during dinner was small, about the little things that, in reality, are big things, the things that added up over time to make a life. His mother had given him that understanding although it had remained buried somewhere inside until he met Shaye. Now he understood.

Samantha chatted with them about her friends' problems and a boy she met in English class. She spoke like an adult, with ideas and thoughts of her own. He couldn't repress a smile at how grown up she sounded.

"What are you grinning at?" Samantha stopped mid-sentence, her fork halfway to her mouth.

"Nothing," he replied, the smile widening. "Everything. The day ... being here with you all." He shrugged. "It just makes me smile."

Later, when the house was quiet, and they lay in the dark with the night folded around them, Shaye turned and slid a bare leg over him.

"I promised you something before our jog. Remember?"

"I do." He turned and held her bare body against his under the sheets.

"You ready to collect, big guy?"

"I believe I am," he said.

His hand slid down to touch her. She moaned and spread her legs, pulling his hand deeper between them.

They made love like two people accustomed to the touch of the other. There was no hurry. Rushing would have cheapened the moment. The seconds and minutes flowed around them, sensuous and delicious, their passion building, moving in unison until they shuddered in each other's arms.

After, they lay touching, awake but not speaking. There was no need. It had all been said.

FORTY-ONE

Stay Out of My Way

Tall and lean, dressed in a business suit, with the shirt collar open and no tie, he could have been an affluent South American, arriving in the U.S. to oversee his business ventures and investments. In fact, Alejandro Garza arrived at Atlanta's Hartsfield-Jackson Airport to see to the business affairs and investments of his employer, Juan Manuel Elizondo.

He passed unchallenged through immigration. The Customs and Immigration officer who scanned his passport asked, "The reason for your visit to the United States, Senor …" The officer flipped back to the identification page of the forged Argentine passport. "Senor Hernández?"

"Business." Garza nodded and gave one of his rare smiles, the perfect Latin *hidalgo*—gentleman.

The officer flipped through the passport one more time, stamped and recorded the arrival of Tomás Hernández within the sovereign borders of the United States, and waved for the next person in line to step forward. Garza picked up his carry-on bag and walked to the customs inspection area where he placed the bag on a conveyor that ran through an x-ray machine scanning for contraband. There was none. Alejandro Garza traveled light, relying on local contacts for anything he might need to fulfill Bebé's assignments.

As he stepped through the doorway into the main terminal, the noise level increased. People scurried to the security lines to catch trams to the concourses, hurried to baggage claim or searched for their traveling companions.

Garza paused for a moment and stood holding his bag in his left hand. He eyed the crowd of people waiting to greet arriving international passengers. A man he had never seen before, but whom he knew by reputation and from a photo that Bautista Ortega had sent to him, lifted a placard that read 'T. Hernández' printed in large block letters.

Esteban Moya recognized Garza at once. There was no handshake, no greeting, formal or otherwise. Moya turned to lead Garza through the terminal and to his car parked in the short-term lot.

They did not speak during the drive to Ortega's office. Garza went through messages on his phone, all from Bebé Elizondo, while Moya made his way through the early evening traffic.

Moya might as well have been alone in the car. He kept his eyes on the road, not daring a glance at his passenger. At least, Garza had not ordered him to some secluded place where no one would hear the bullet he put into Moya's brain, a possibility he had considered as he waited for Bebé's fixer to arrive.

After what seemed an interminable amount of time but was only forty minutes or so, they arrived at the shopping center. Moya pulled around to the rear and used a key to open the back door of Ortega's *taqueria*.

El Toro waited behind his desk and stood as they entered. Beads of sweat glistened on his broad forehead. His nerves made him look less like a *toro*—bull—and more like a steer headed to the slaughterhouse.

This visitor was far different from the police investigator. Even a hard-nosed detective would not harm him. The law would not permit it. Alejandro Garza was under no such constraint. Bautista Ortega, the bull, swallowed and extended his hand.

"It is good to see you, Alejandro." Ortega hoped a familiar greeting would lighten the tension. It did not.

Ignoring the outstretched hand, Garza looked around the small office selected a chair, and sat, taking his phone from his pocket. Esteban Moya standing just behind exchanged a concerned glance with Ortega then took a seat in the only other chair in the room.

"I am instructed," Garza began without preliminaries, "to resolve the business issues that have arisen here in the last few days."

"Everything I have here is at your disposal. Just tell me what you require, and I'll have it done."

"You will do nothing," Garza said, his eyes boring into Ortega. "You have done enough."

The lump in Ortega's throat grew until he thought he might choke. "I only meant to say …"

"There is nothing to say. I will correct the problems here, and then I will return to Mexico." Garza's eyes were small black daggers piercing into Ortega. "You will never see me again. If you do …"

He left the threat hanging in the air. Ortega's eyes widened with understanding. Moya remained deathly silent, hoping not to receive any attention from their visitor. It was an empty wish.

"I will require one person to assist me." Garza turned his head to look at Esteban Moya. "This one."

"Yes, yes … of course," Ortega stammered. All pretense of being El Toro, the bull of Atlanta, had faded. His only wish now was to survive the night.

Moya's eyes widened, but his mouth remained shut. He fought down the desire to plead with Garza to allow the honor of assisting him to fall to another.

"Is there something else that … may I, uh … ask …"

"You may ask nothing. I require nothing else. I will advise you when my work here is completed. Until then, stay out of my way."

Ortega remained mute, giving only a nod, acknowledging the instructions that were, in reality, a warning. Garza rose, looked at Moya then turned to the door. "Come with me. We have plans to make."

Moya followed Garza from the office without chancing a backward glance at the man who had been his boss until this moment. Bautista Ortega placed his sweating hands on his desk and tried to will them to stop trembling.

FORTY-TWO

You're In

Coffee and the ubiquitous box of doughnuts sat on the side table where the investigators stood chatting. Yeah, cops like doughnuts. Doesn't everyone?

Sole had picked these up on the way in from a Krispy Kreme store where the 'HOT NOW' light burned bright. The attendees ransacked the box, and poured coffee into Styrofoam cups, consuming it in various shades from black to light tan.

Sole watched from one end of the conference table while everyone got through their hellos and morning chatter. He nudged Travis, seated beside him.

"See. I told you," he whispered.

"What?" Travis looked up from the notes in the briefing file open on the table before him.

Sole nodded at the side table, and Travis understood, widening his eyes in semi-exasperation. "You never give up."

"Nope."

It was nothing really, just part of an ongoing—and

inane in Travis' opinion—discussion about the curiosities of human behavior. Sole maintained that the blacker the coffee, the plainer the doughnut selection. He contended that those preferring their coffee watered down with milk and sweetened were predisposed to take the glazed and cream filled ones.

"See," Sole nodded, grinning.

"You're obsessed." Travis shook his head.

"On the contrary, I am an observer of human behavior."

"Whatever," Travis smirked. "Who's winning out today?"

"Black coffee ... plain doughnuts." He nodded at the group, like a professor lecturing a class of freshmen. "These are seasoned cops, experienced in the ways of the world and the benefits of early morning caffeine to focus the mind. Too much sugar is a distraction and detracts from the experience."

"Good God. You've actually given this some thought."

"I told you ... I am an observer, recording the facts as I see them." Sole lifted his head and looked down into Travis' coffee cup. "So, what shade of tan would you call that in your cup? Is that ecru?" The grin widened on his face. "Looks like ecru. I know because ecru is the color Samantha wanted her bedroom painted." He nodded. "Yep. That's ecru."

Travis lowered his head in exasperation. "Jesus, give me strength."

Sole chuckled and stood to get everyone's attention. The clock showed eight AM. "Okay, everyone. Let's get started."

Chairs scraped across the floor. Papers shuffled. Everyone gathered closer, coffee cups and doughnuts positioned on the table, notepads, and pens extracted from pockets and held at the ready. Heads turned toward Sole and Travis.

"This won't take too long, but could be important."

"Better be," a burly man with long blond hair and arms covered in tattoos grumbled.

"What's the matter, Chuck? Get you up too early?" Sole grinned.

Chuck Rayburn represented the Atlanta narc squad. "Damn right it's too early. Worked all night."

"Getting old is a bitch, isn't it, Chuck?"

"Fuck you, Sole," Rayburn growled.

"Not if I get a running start."

Laughter broke out around the table. Rayburn leaned back in the chair, arms behind his head, his broad face breaking into a satisfied grin. Sole nodded. It was a good start, with everyone loose, primed and ready to hear what they had to say.

"Let's get to it." Sole picked up his notepad. "We have a reliable tip that a senior state politician may be involved with a suspected drug dealer."

He paused and looked around at the faces. There were nine, including Travis and Sole.

Besides the Atlanta narc squad, DEA had sent along a representative. ICE had two people there and the GBI one. In typical FBI fashion, the Special Agent in Charge was not impressed by their invitation and had responded that the DEA agent present would brief him later.

"How senior?" Bill Lance, the GBI agent, asked.

"Before I get into that," Sole answered, "I need everyone here to understand this is confidential ... need-to-know basis only. If word leaks out, the investigation goes to hell. Worse, people could die."

Heads nodded around the table. No one here would be talking.

"I'll have to brief the FBI SAC," Gene Cusins, the DEA representative, chimed in.

Fuck the arrogant FBI pukes, Sole wanted to respond, but instead said, "Make sure they understand the need for confidentiality." He added one small dig. "No headline-grabbing here. They want credit later, fine … who gives a shit at that point, but the Bureau best not queer our investigation."

Everyone present had experienced it. They did all the leg work, took all the risks, and put the case together only to have the FBI take it over at the point they were ready to make an arrest. Most were philosophical about the FBI's tendency to steal the show at the end of a big case. With a senior politician involved in this one, it was a sure bet they would grab headlines if charges were filed.

"I'll do my best." Cusins nodded and smiled.

"All right," Sole continued. "The investigation involves Senator James Sillman."

He had their attention. The chatter ceased, and all eyes focused on him.

"Our CI reported his senior aide, Wilson Bettis, had a meet with Bautista Ortega."

Pens moved across notepads.

"Sillman knew?" Chuck Rayburn looked up from his notes.

"We're convinced of it. We interviewed both alone. Bettis almost swallowed his tongue trying to explain. Sillman looked like he might have a stroke." Sole nodded. "They're dirty."

"Corroboration?" Bill Lance asked.

"I met with Ortega. He wanted to play cat and mouse.

Standard stuff, but despite his denial, he wanted to know who reported the meeting. That and the fact that he was more intent on finding out what we knew than he was worried about giving it away confirms there is something to it."

Sole gave them the case history. He reviewed the reliability of the intelligence Luis Acero had provided in the past, the lack of video evidence and how Acero identified Wilson Bettis at the press conference with Sillman.

Travis picked up the briefing, reviewing Sillman's financial situation and the possible motive for the contact with Ortega.

"Holy shit," Chuck Rayburn muttered.

"We're in," Bill Lance said.

"Us too," Cusins added. "We need to set up surveillance on Sillman's fleet of trawlers. If they are being used, we should be able to figure out how it's being done ... interdict a shipment and take them all down at once."

They spent the next hour planning the surveillance and joint operation. Ice would have officers working with DEA and the GBI on the interdiction ships. DEA already had a close working relationship with the Coast Guard and would bring them into the loop when they were ready to move out on the water.

The meeting was wrapping up when Sole spoke.

"We want to stay in." He looked at Bill Lance and Gene Cusins.

"Me too," Rayburn chimed in.

There was no evidence that Sillman had committed any crime within their jurisdiction. The investigation had expanded across the state and into the territorial waters of the United States. Sole and Travis had done their job, but they weren't about to just walk away, and as the resident narc on the team, Rayburn naturally wanted a piece of it.

"I don't have a problem with that." Lance nodded and looked at Cusins.

"Me neither."

"What about the FBI," Sole asked.

Cusins looked around the table, gave a shrug and grinned. "Seems they missed the party. I'll brief the SAC today, but don't worry. You're in."

FORTY-THREE

These Will Do

Alejandro Garza lifted the Glock 19 from the table, held it in a one-handed grip, old-style military stance, arm straight, level with the shoulder, feet at a forty-five degree angle to the target and sighted along the barrel. Esteban Moya wondered where Garza had learned to shoot. The stance looked awkward and clumsy.

Garza stood for several seconds, sighting along the barrel towards the plate-glass window in Moya's condo. He was a statue. Moya could not even detect the rise and fall of his breathing. After thirty seconds, his motionless stance no longer looked antiquated. It was menacing.

Garza remained like that, almost trance-like as the seconds passed. Moya was about to ask if all was well when Garza turned the pistol over in his hand and checked for the serial number. It had been removed with a power grinder to make it unreadable.

It was a routine precaution, but given enough time, the American FBI would take the pistol to their forensic lab, apply chemical reagents and recover the serial number. That was why the pistol would vanish once they completed their work, rusting away in the silt at the bottom of the Chattahoochee River. Nature would accomplish what they could never do.

Garza thumbed the magazine release button, dropped it into his hand, and laid it on Moya's dining room table. A brisk pull on the Glock's slide ejected the round in the chamber. It landed in his open palm, and he placed it beside the magazine.

Pivoting with the grace of a dancer, he held the pistol straight out in front in a two-handed point and shoot combat stance. Moya marveled at the fluidity of his motions contrasted with the statue-like posture of a few seconds earlier.

Garza squeezed the trigger, allowing the firing pin to fall on the empty chamber. Moya blinked. The metallic click echoed louder than expected in the silence.

Relaxing, Garza placed the pistol on the table. "We will use these."

He motioned to the Glock and a Beretta Model 92-F nine-millimeter pistol.

"These others are of no use." Garza's arm swept over the assortment of assault rifles and machine pistols spread out on the table.

Esteban Moya's personal armory was impressive and included two Tec-9 machine pistols, an Uzi, an AK-47 and two AR-15s. None were legal. No firearms registrations existed, and no background check records named the owner. Two had come to him thanks to the ATF's Fast and Furious gunrunning operation, intended to aid in identifying illegal arms dealers but which had only added to the arsenals of the cartels.

"Are you certain?" Moya asked, eying the assortment of weapons. Compared to the other weapons, the two pistols looked like toys.

"I'm certain," Garza said, eyes like flint.

"But," Moya hesitated. "Why not make sure that …"

"We are not here to fight a war," Garza explained quietly. "We are eliminating a problem. Excessive force could draw attention." He nodded at the pistols, putting the issue to rest. "Leave these out and put the others away."

"As you say." Moya nodded, taking the hint that the discussion of weapon choice was concluded. "May I ask how we will do this? I suppose we must make an example."

"We must only end the problem. There should be nothing else left behind, not even an example."

"But I thought … I mean in Mexico …"

"This is not Mexico," Garza said. His voice was quiet, but his eyes remained intense, signaling Moya to pay attention. "It is true; in Mexico we might torture then hang a body from a bridge or lamp post with a warning not to cut the body down. This would be a threat to others, an example not to interfere with *Los Salvajes*."

"That is what we intend, no?" Moya ventured. "To set an example … send a warning?"

"As I have said," Garza continued as if he were lecturing a dim-witted student. "We are correcting a problem, not making an example or sending a warning. Who would we be sending a warning to?" He shook his head. "Besides, such tactics do not work here. People here rely on the government authorities and the law for their safety. In Mexico, authority does not always come from the government. The one who has the power is the one with authority, the one who makes the law for the people. That is who they follow. To do otherwise is foolish and dangerous for them."

Moya nodded without speaking, asking no further questions that might annoy Alejandro Garza.

A pistol in each hand, Garza dismissed the array of weapons on the table. "These will do."

FORTY-FOUR

Satisfying

"You don't really buy into this bullshit, do you?"

FBI Atlanta Bureau Special Agent in Charge, Chester Fields, looked from Gene Cusins to Bill Lance and back to Cusins. The scowl on his face turned to incredulity when how realized they did, in fact, buy into the bullshit.

"We work closely with Atlanta PD," Cusins replied. "Their work is solid. They buy into it … so do we."

"And you?" Fields threw a sideways glance at Lance. "You are going to step off into this … swamp … for lack of a better word? This is quicksand, the kind of shit that sucks you under and sends you to law enforcement purgatory."

"Only if we're wrong," Lance said. "I know the Atlanta Major Crimes Unit. They are pros. John Sole is a solid cop. If he thinks Sillman is dirty, I'd bet on it."

"Would you bet your career on it?" Fields smirked. "That's what you're doing."

"What I'm doing is my job. We have a solid tip on criminal activity. We will investigate." Lance shook his head in disgust. "The GBI ... the Georgia Bureau of *Investigations* ... it's what we do ... investigate."

"Don't get smug with me," Fields bristled. "I was investigating crime while you were still trying to get laid in the back of your daddy's sedan."

"Maybe so," Lance said. "But what have you done lately?"

"Go fuck yourself." Fields tossed the briefing paper they'd given him on the desk. "This is too risky ... too much potential for fallout with no real evidence of wrongdoing." He leaned forward, his voice rising. "Sillman is a sitting senator for God's sake."

"That doesn't place him above the law," Lance said evenly.

"No, you're right, it doesn't." Fields' voice became quieter, trying to reason with them. "That doesn't make him a target either. What if he is being set up?"

"That's what the investigation will discover." Lance waited for his next objection.

"You're overreaching." Fields shook his head. "It might seem like a feather in your cap to bring down a senator, but there would be ... there are ... repercussions to consider."

"Jesus, only the FBI would frame an investigation that way," Lance sneered. "This isn't about feathers in caps. This is about a credible tip from a reliable source with corroborating evidence that a crime may be in progress or about to be committed."

Fields slapped his hand down on the briefing paper. "You call this corroboration? So Sillman's business is in financial trouble. So are a lot of others. Why aren't they all being investigated?"

"Because they didn't have a head-to-head meet a suspected organized crime boss."

"*Suspected* crime boss," Fields snapped back. "Not convicted."

"That's right," Cusins said. "Suspected. You know, like Vito Genovese, or Carlo Gambino, Paul Castellano, John Gotti, all suspected crime bosses, until ... guess what?" Cusins smirked. "They became *convicted* organized crime bosses." He shook his head before Fields could reply. "We may not have a case on Ortega yet, but the evidence is mounting, and now we have information he has been in contact with a man who owns a fleet of boats that could bring drugs into the country."

"Sillman denied meeting with Ortega."

"No. He said he didn't know what his aide met with Ortega about. That's different."

"Still not proof of anything." Fields leaned back arms crossed, his body language as closed as his mind about taking part in an investigation of a popular U.S. Senator.

"There's no sense wasting time here." Bill Lance rose. "For the record, the GBI will be working with the other agencies involved. If at some point you want a further briefing on the investigation's progress ..." He nodded at Cusins. "Get it from the DEA."

He walked from Fields' office, leaving the door open. Gene Cusins stood to follow.

"You're not going to fall into this trap are you, Gene?" Fields' puzzled expression matched the disbelief in his voice.

"I was wondering," Cusins said as he gathered up his briefing papers.

"What?" The corner of Field's mouth turned down in a smirk.

"I was wondering when you forgot what it is we do ... what *you are supposed to do* ... investigate."

"I understand investigations and when to open one!" Fields' eyes blazed. "This isn't it. There are too many downsides. The fact that you can't see that, Gene, is ... disappointing."

Cusins shook his head. "You say there is no proof, and I'll grant you that, there is no evidence to take a case to court, but there are a hell of a lot of red flags and arrows pointing in that direction. Isn't that why we investigate ... to gather the evidence ... get the proof, or does the Bureau just wait for everything to be wrapped up nice and neat. If that's the case, then what's the point?" He shook his head as he stepped to the door. "For the record, there won't be any more briefings on this. Next time you want a report on what the hell is going on, you can get it from the news."

In contrast to the FBI's reluctance, the other involved law enforcement agencies were eager to get started. They dug in with gusto, nicknaming the case the Surf and Turf Investigation, Sillman Shrimp being the surf and Ortega—El Toro the beefy turf.

ICE and DEA brought the Coast Guard in to begin surveillance of the Sillman fleet of trawlers. Lance and the GBI compiled a list of known Sillman assets and boats so they could track their movements. Sole and Travis along with Chuck Rayburn and the Atlanta narc squad assisted where they could, staying close to things to make sure they were there when the time came to move forward with an arrest or interdiction. Both came faster than anyone expected.

Three days later ...

Gene Cusins huddled over a conference table in the DEA offices in southwest Atlanta pointing at a map of the

Georgia coastline. He drew a circle in red marker around a small town in the southeast corner of the state, just above the Florida line.

"Here. We think this might be our target ... one of them at least."

"So soon?" Sole said, leaning over the map.

"Wasn't that hard to come up with it ... assuming our logic is correct." Cusins shrugged and smiled good-naturedly "And that is debatable."

"St. Mary's." Travis peered at the small dot on the map. "Down next to King's Bay sub base." He looked at Cusins. "You think they would run a smuggling operation so close to a Navy base?"

"I think it would be the perfect cover." Cusins nodded. "Who would suspect a shrimp boat using the same channel that nuclear subs use to enter and exit a secure naval facility?"

"Okay," Sole said. "But how do you know one of Sillman's boats in St. Mary's is involved?"

"We don't," GBI's Bill Lance interjected. "But here's what we do know. All of Sillman's boats have been in the water operating for fifteen to twenty years each ... except for one." He put a piece of paper on the table and tapped it. "Registration shows that Sillman's company mothballed one boat a few years back ... used it for spare parts ... that is until a couple of months ago when it was re-registered under the name of the Sara Jane."

The group around the table leaned forward looking from the sheet of paper to the map.

Lance continued, "That trawler, the Sara Jane, is based out of St. Mary's."

"Still thin," Travis said. "Sillman just might have needed

another boat in the water to make up his losses … increase his haul."

"Maybe." Lance nodded. "Although it would have been more likely that he would take one out of service to reduce costs. Either way, we did some checking on this one boat, since its re-registration coincides with the time frame we're dealing with."

He looked up from the map. "We took a couple of investigators from our Savannah office and sent them down to St. Mary's a few days ago, to scope things out … posing as fishermen looking for a charter. They've been hanging out in local taverns, getting the lay of the land and asked around to see whether the Sara Jane might be available for a fishing charter, since it was idle, tied up at the docks. Locals told them to ask a guy named Tully Sams. He's the guy runs the boat. Locals called him Captain Tully.

"They went to Sams with their fishing gear to see if they could charter him for a day. He was friendly, and in a friendly but firm way said hell no. In his words, he is a shrimper, and the Sara Jane is a working boat, not some damned tourist fishing charter."

"But you don't believe that," Sole said.

"No. We don't," Lance and Cusins said in unison.

"Tully Sams is a local legend, an old-timer with lots of ties to the community. His work fixing up the Sara Jane for Sillman has raised eyebrows in town. Word is, Sams spent a good bit of time and Sillman's money getting her seaworthy, but she's only been out once since."

All the heads were nodding around the table now.

"So the question is why fix her up if she's not going out on regular trips to bring in a haul of shrimp? We figure, if she goes out again, we should track her and see what she's up to."

"I want to go," Sole said before Travis could.

"You're in," Cusins said with a nod.

"Hey, not fair," Travis griped.

"I'll flip you for it." Sole grinned.

"Hell no, not with your coin. Use mine." Travis pulled a quarter from his pocket. "Call it."

"Heads," Sole said as the coin flew airborne and then clinked onto the table.

"Son of a bitch." Travis shook his head and retrieved the coin. "Hope you get seasick."

"Not me, but the good thing is if this turns into anything, guess who gets the first shot at Sillman?"

"Didn't think of that." Travis smiled. "Hooking the cuffs on a senator might be satisfying at that."

FORTY-FIVE

There is Always a Way

"Anything?" Senator James Sillman held the phone tight against his face, his voice low, almost a whisper.

Since the visit from John Sole, he had remained alone in his penthouse condo, canceling appointments and delaying his trip back to Washington D.C. Wilson Bettis protested that it made them look guilty, as if they had something to hide from the police. His sudden reclusiveness would only increase their scrutiny.

"Nothing," Bettis sighed, giving the same response he had five other times that day. "The detectives have not tried to contact me. There is no sign they are looking at us for anything. I told you; they have no proof of any illegal activity. It's likely they are moving on to a case with some real evidence."

"What about ..."

"Nothing there either." Bettis was losing patience with his timid boss. "Our friends from south of the border have made no efforts to contact me. I'm sure we would have heard something by now if it was a concern to them."

"Good," Sillman said, not sounding relieved.

"We have to talk," Bettis said. It was time to get things back on track.

"What about?"

"About getting you back to work. That's the whole point, isn't it ... your position ... influence ... the anti-drug initiative and legislation? No one will be looking at you, but if we let it all drop now, if you stay locked up in your condo, it will raise suspicions." He didn't add his worries that the Senator's behavior over the last couple of days may have already signaled to the cops that something was up.

"I can't ..."

"You have to!" Bettis raised his voice with Sillman and didn't care.

The man was weak, he thought. That weakness was a threat to all of them. He wondered what Ortega and Moya, or Elizondo back in Mexico, would think if he made them aware of the Senator's weakness ... how shaky and untrustworthy he was becoming. They might look around for someone new to work with, someone younger and unafraid. Someone like Wilson Bettis.

He smirked and pushed the thought away. They weren't working with Sillman because he was strong. They needed his fleet of trawlers and the business he had inherited from his father.

That's the way it always was. Those with money prospered. Those without had to find success and make their own way in the world. Wilson Bettis was determined to make his way in the world.

He should be the one dealing with Elizondo. He wondered what the hillside hacienda was like. He pulled himself away from his reverie.

"Let me schedule a flight back to D.C. for you," Bettis said, his tone milder. "We need to get you back to work."

Sillman remained silent for several seconds. It was true. Hiding out here only made him look guilty.

You are guilty! One side of his brain screamed at him. The other side, the rational side, had to admit that Bettis was right. They were committed now.

Sillman held no illusions. There could be no turning back. Maintaining the façade, leading the charge against the drug traffickers while steering the authorities away from the smuggling operation was his only value to Bebé. Without it, Elizondo would find another partner, devise another snuggling scheme. Sillman would be expendable. Worse, he would be disposable. Every trace of their partnership would be eliminated along with Sillman.

"All right," Sillman said. "Get me on a flight tomorrow evening."

"Why not in the morning? Just jump right back in and let them see you fighting the good fight against illegal narcotics."

"No. Make it tomorrow evening. I have some things to … ah, take care of tomorrow."

What he didn't say was he was planning to finish off the bottle of I.W. Harper fifteen-year-old bourbon the building concierge had sent out for and delivered to his penthouse. Tomorrow morning he would be sleeping off the hangover. Tomorrow evening would be soon enough, and at that, he would still be feeling the effects.

"Fine," Bettis said, his tone curt and annoyed. "I'll text you the flight arrangements."

The call ended. Wilson Bettis set about making the senator's travel arrangements. The senator worked on the I.W. Harper.

The office had emptied by the time Bettis called it a day. As a final task, he texted the flight information to Sillman. He smirked, knowing the message would not be read until the next day. By now the old man was probably three sheets to the wind and unconscious.

He loosened his tie and headed for the elevator, descending to the below-ground parking garage. Senate office staff parked on a private level, monitored by security cameras and patrolled hourly by a building guard. At this hour, it was deserted.

Bettis always made a habit of leaving the office last. He thought it made a good example for the others to follow. The other staffers just assumed he was a kiss-ass trying to curry favor with the senator.

Heels clomping on the concrete, he made his way to the four-year-old Japanese car with a dent on the rear bumper he had not had the time to have repaired. He clicked the remote to unlock the door, giving the dent and car a disdainful look.

That would be the first thing to change, he thought. There would be a new car to go with his newfound wealth. Nothing too ostentatious that might draw attention. Just something more upscale, with leather upholstery and a sunroof.

A sunroof. He smiled, thinking of tooling around Atlanta on a summer day, breeze in his hair and maybe a girl by his side. Like the car, the girl would not be anyone who would draw attention. No models or beauty queens. Just a reasonably attractive woman to be seen with—and to sleep with when he felt the need. Red hair would be nice, he thought.

He reached for the door handle, pulled it open and tossed his briefcase in. Behind him, the sound of soft-soled shoes shuffling over the concrete caught his attention. He started to turn.

A pair of muscular hands shoved his head from behind, slamming his face into the edge of the car's door frame. The hands spun him around. Blood gushed from lacerations in his forehead and on the bridge of his nose. Stunned and wobbling, he stared wide-eyed at the two men.

They wore hoodies over baseball caps with the bills pulled low over their faces to prevent the surveillance cameras from getting a look at them, but Wilson Bettis recognized one. His jaw gaped at the grin on Esteban Moya's face.

The other man, the one who had struck him from behind, was unknown to him. Tall and angular, his cold, passionless eyes sent a shiver through Bettis.

He tried to focus through the blood streaming from the gash over his eyes. He squinted through the pain at Moya and the terrible dark thing in his hand.

"No … don't," Bettis shook his head. "You don't have to …"

But he did. Esteban Moya squeezed the trigger of the Beretta three times. The first two slugs punched into his chest, breaking through the sternum and piercing his heart's right ventricle before exiting his back to lodge in the Japanese car. The third crashed into his skull.

Wilson Bettis, a young man of so much promise, thudded to the concrete as if they had cut his legs out from under him. As the blood pooled around him, Moya jerked his wallet from his pocket and took his watch and cell phone. Then he reached into the car, grabbed the briefcase, opened it, shuffled through the papers then turned it upside down dumping the contents over Bettis' body.

The papers floated to the pavement to become saturated

in blood. They adhered to Bettis' body like wet gauze. Moya and Garza turned and jogged to the stairwell. Climbing to street level, they exited the parking garage through an emergency fire door into an alley. A block away, traffic and people bustled by on Peachtree Street, unaware of the two men. Five minutes later, they were in Moya's car blending with the evening traffic. He was careful to obey the speed limit.

"*Eso fue perfecto!*" Moya exclaimed. That was perfect! He pounded the steering wheel in triumph and looked sideways at Garza who remained silent. "*¿No?*"

"*Si perfecto.*" Garza agreed. "*Por lo que va.*" As far as it goes. Then he added, "The next will be harder."

"Yes. I suppose it will." Moya felt the exhilaration subside. His brow furrowed in concern as the adrenalin high dissipated. "Is there really a way to do it ... the next?"

Garza nodded, turning his head to the window where the upscale shops and bistros of Buckhead flowed by in a ribbon of light and motion. He was neither excited by the murder they had just committed nor concerned about the one they were planning.

"There is always a way."

FORTY-SIX

Soon
─────────

"*Papi*, see what I've drawn!"

"Why it's beautiful, *chiquita*!" Bebé Elizondo lowered the phone from his ear to pat little Rosa on the head. "But may I ask, what is it?"

"*Papi*! You know! Can't you see it? It's *Tio* Alejandro!"

"Oh yes," Elizondo held the paper out at arm's length, nodding seriously as he studied the almost random collection of lines drawn with different colored crayons. "Yes, I see it now."

The lines depicted a long thin body, long arms that hung almost to the figure's feet and eyes. Over the eyes were two black lines drawn in a downward angle.

"See," Rosa said, excitement in her chirping voice, as she pointed. "These are the eyes."

Elizondo lifted the phone to his ear again. "Little Rosa has drawn a picture for you."

"Is that *Tio* Alejandro on the phone?" Rosa jumped up and down, excited, her hand out for the phone. "Let me speak to him. Please, *Papi*!"

Elizondo handed his daughter the cell phone and watched, smiling as she began chattering at once to Alejandro Garza. He could picture Garza's face, staring straight ahead, listening without comment. Elizondo found it humorous that the deadly, quiet man who never knew what to say or do around the children was so beloved by them. They doted on him when he visited and looked forward with anticipation to his return when he departed.

He was a man of mystery to them. Perhaps that was what they liked about him. A mysterious presence, yet solid and always there, watching without judgment. Elizondo had given up trying to understand the reasons for their affection. It was enough that Alejandro Garza was accepted by his children as one of the family and that he was their protector.

After several minutes, Rosa finished her description of the picture she had drawn for Garza, listened for a moment and then handed the phone back to Elizondo.

"And what did *Tío* Alejandro say about your picture?"

"He said, thank you very much, young lady." Rosa's face spread into a gap-toothed grin. "He called me young lady!" she called out as she scampered off to find her sister and brother.

Elizondo lifted the phone to his ear. "You have a fan."

"The picture was a nice."

"You haven't even seen it!" Elizondo laughed. "If you had, you might not think it was so nice."

"The gesture was nice."

"Yes, it was." It was time to get back to business. "So, things went well?"

"Yes. There were no problems."

"And your assistant ... Moya? Can we rely on him?"

"It was the first test. We will see."

"Good enough then." Elizondo nodded. "When do you expect to return? I will be more comfortable when you are out of the United States."

"I expect to complete the work soon, a few more days, perhaps. My cover identity is secure. There should be no problems."

"Problems do not concern me. I know you will handle everything with your usual efficiency, but the children miss you. Come back to us safely."

"I will."

Elizondo disconnected.

"Our work, it satisfies Bebé?" Moya cast a nervous glance at Garza as the call ended.

"Satisfy is not a word he would use. His only concern is that we complete the assignment."

"Right." Moya nodded. "When do we *complete* the assignment?"

"Soon."

FORTY-SEVEN

That Makes Two of Us

"You know an aide to Senator Sillman? A man named Wilson Bettis?"

Bert Collins, Atlanta Homicide investigator, stood in the office building's lobby near the large plate-glass windows facing Peachtree Street. The reception was better there than in the sub-ground level parking garage.

"I do." Randy Travis was on his way home. "Why?"

"He's dead," Collins responded with no preliminaries. "Looks like a mugging in the parking garage of his office building. Checked with his staff and they said he had a meeting with you the other day. Thought you would want to know. Maybe you could shed a little light on things for us."

"On my way." Travis flipped a U-turn at the next intersection and brought up John Sole on the car's Bluetooth.

"What's up?" Sole said from his car.

"Call from homicide. Bettis is dead."

"Shit. Where?"

"Office building parking garage."

"Meet you there."

Travis arrived first. By the time Sole got to the parking deck where Bettis' body lay beside his car, covered by a blood-stained sheet, Travis was already walking through the crime scene with Bert Collins. Sole caught up and tagged along.

Collins looked up as he arrived and grinned. "Glad you could make it, Sole."

"Hi, Bert. Nice hat," Sole said, nodding at the traditional homicide squad fedora perched atop Collins' head.

"Thanks, John. Want one?" By tradition, every Atlanta homicide detective received a fedora to wear after solving their first murder case.

"I'll pass. Hanging out with dead bodies isn't my thing. Besides," Sole chided, "I like a challenge. You Homicide boys just ask the husband or wife … bingo, case solved."

"Yeah, thank God for domestic disputes," Collins agreed with a wry smile. He nodded at the body under the sheet. "Not this time, though. Not much to go on here."

There wasn't much more to brief either. The crime scene and security cameras told the story. Bettis was walking to his car, about to get in when two men, unidentifiable because of the hoodies, ball caps and gloves they wore, approached from behind, shoved him hard into the car and then shot him. One took his wallet, cell, phone, and watch, then opened his briefcase and dumped it out. The whole thing took thirty seconds.

An exterior camera caught them leaving the building through an alley exit. After that, they disappeared up the street.

"Couple of things don't add up," Collins said as he wrapped up the briefing.

"Such as?" Sole had his own thoughts on why things weren't making sense.

"Video shows he opened the briefcase and dumped it out over the body, but he didn't search it for valuables. It was almost like he was staging the scene to make it look like a mugging."

"But you don't think it was," Sole said.

"I have my doubts." Collis nodded.

"What else?" Travis asked. "You said *a couple of things* didn't make sense. What else?"

"The surveillance video from the lobby and other points of entry. Can't find any record of two men entering. Forget the faces. We're looking for two men of similar size and proportions to each other. Video shows a tall, thin man and another, the shooter, shorter and stockier. There is no video of two such individuals coming in."

"How far back did you go?" Sole asked.

"Two hours."

"Check the entire day's video."

"You think muggers came into the building and hung out all day waiting for someone to rob and murder?" Collins shook his head. "That doesn't make any sense either."

"Maybe not." Sole shrugged. "But when you check the video, don't just search for two men entering together. Keep an eye out for any individuals that match either of the perps' body types and builds."

"That could be a hundred people … a thousand. This is a busy building."

"Yep. No one said the job would be easy," Sole said with mock sympathy. "That's why they call us detectives, Bert. We detect things, like people who don't belong in Senator Sillman's office building."

"You're saying they could have come in earlier … alone at different times."

"I'm saying it's possible."

Collins' eyes narrowed. "Then they waited all day and targeted Bettis. You think we have a hit on our hands? Who would snuff a senator's aide?"

"I don't think anything ... yet. Could be a mugging. Killers tried to make it look that way at least, but things don't add up." Sole looked around the interior of the garage, noting the stairwell door in the far corner, visualizing the approach of the two men behind Bettis as he unlocked his car. He turned back to Collins. "All I'm saying is you might want to check out the possibility that this was a planned hit ... an assassination."

"Assassination! John, you're worrying the shit out of me."

"Good. That makes two of us."

FORTY-EIGHT

On the Go

"Something's up," GBI Agent George Tagland muttered, peering through the binoculars.

He spun the focus ring until the image was clear. Tully Sams leaned against his pickup, smoking a cigarette. That was not unusual. What happened next was.

Three men came out of the small general aviation building at the Brunswick airport. As they came up to Sams, they tossed their bags over the side into the bed, exchanged a few words and climbed into the truck cab.

Tagland watched from the Gulf Aerospace parking lot next door. He picked up his cell phone with his free hand and pressed the speed dial button for his partner, Bob Sewell.

"I think he's heading back ... just leaving the Brunswick airport."

"Roger that," Sewell said.

"He's got company."

"You ID them?"

"No, but there are three of them ... could be the crew."

"I'm standing by," Sewell said. "No activity on the trawler for now."

"Okay, they're leaving now, heading down Glynco Parkway to Highway 405." Tagland started his rental car and pulled from the lot, following Sams' pickup a quarter mile back. "Looks like they're headed back to St. Mary's."

"Want me to let Lance know?"

"Yeah. If this is the crew, they could be leaving soon. Boys in Atlanta will need some prep time to get out there."

"I'm on it."

The call ended. Tagland cruised behind the pickup, blending with traffic to remain hidden then moving out for a better view now and then to make sure Sams continued on to St. Mary's. He did.

By the time he arrived at the bar across from the lot where they had been watching the Sara Jane, Sewell had notified Bill Lance. The DEA and Coast Guard were in the loop now. A Coast Guard cutter patrolled offshore. They had two helos in the air for good measure with instructions to stay well away from the Sara Jane until called in by the surface vessel.

The two GBI agents loaded their fishing gear into a small cabin cruiser they had rented under the pretext of checking out the fishing along the St. Mary's River. As they passed the Sara Jane, tied up at the dock, they waved at Tully Sams and the two crewmen on deck.

"See you found you a boat!" Sams called out as they idled past.

"Yeah," Tagland waved back, holding up a beer to show they were in party mode. "Gonna check out the fishing along the river and backwaters."

"Be careful out there. Easy to get mud-bound if you don't watch yourself."

"Thanks. Will do."

The two GBI agents motored out onto the St. Mary's River and headed for the channel that cut by Cumberland Island before opening out into the Atlantic Ocean. They cruised close to shore, around the small inlets and waterways, keeping an eye on the channel. They didn't have long to wait.

"Here he comes," Sewell pointed.

The Sara Jane was visible, a mile away in the main channel. She made about six knots, just another trawler headed out, with nothing remarkable about her on the surface.

Below the surface, there was a lot that might appear out of the ordinary if not downright suspicious. A crew that arrived that very morning at the Brunswick airport. A refurbished trawler that spent most of its time tied up at the dock. The floundering financial condition of her owner's company. All things considered, a great deal seemed remarkable and out of the ordinary about the Sara Jane.

Tagland picked up his cell phone and punched Bill Lance's number to give the signal that would send the interdiction operation into full speed.

Lance answered. Tagland said one word.

"Go."

They looked like shrimpers this time. That is to say, they wore simple work clothes not so different from any other deckhand. Tully Sams nodded with approval.

Hermie, Paco, and Julio exited the small service building at the Brunswick airport and crossed the lot to the old Ford pickup where their captain waited, leaning against the tailgate, the ubiquitous cigarette dangling from his mouth.

"Where's your boss?" Sams asked as they tossed their small duffels over the sides into the truck bed. "Your *jefe*?" He pronounced it with his best Spanish accent—Hef-fee.

"*¿Qué?*" The three looked at him, smiling, eyes narrowed trying to decipher the meaning of his question.

"Oh." Hermie nodded his comprehension. "*Jefe* ... Esteban Moya ... yes?"

"Right. That Moya fella. He's not coming this trip?"

"No, *Capitán*," Hermie said, shaking his head. "No here ... biz-ee-ness."

"Hmm." Sams regarded the three, wondering how things would work out without Moya as the interpreter.

Hermie understood the concern on Sams' face and patted his chest, motioning at his companions. "We work. We know what to do. You tell. We do. You steer boat. We go."

Sams inhaled a deep last drag on the cigarette, snubbed it out on the bottom of his boot, and tossed the dead butt into the pickup's bed. "I suppose you're right. You fellas know what to do. My job is to get us where your GPS contraption says and then stay out of the way."

"Right." Hermie nodded, grinning, which provoked grins from the others. "You stay out of way. We do."

"All right then. Let's mount up."

The drive back to St. Mary's was uneventful and without the questions this time about the proximity to the naval base at King's Bay. Sams stopped at a Wendy's along the highway into town to pick up lunch from the drive-thru window then headed to the Sara Jane. His three crew members hopped out of the cab, grabbed their duffels from the bed, and boarded the Trawler while he parked the truck in the dirt lot across the street.

After downing the burgers and sodas, they spent the afternoon getting things ready to leave. It was make-work mostly.

Tully Sams kept a spotless boat, leaving little for his temporary crew to do. Hermie and Paco spent most of their time checking equipment that didn't need to be checked and recoiling lines already coiled in the exact spot they had left them after the last trip. The activity kept up appearances, making a show of being a working trawler about to leave port.

A little before noon, a small cabin cruiser slid by in the river channel. The two men on board had approached Sams a few days earlier about going out on the Sara Jane to do some fishing, but he'd set them straight on that account. They waved and shouted a greeting at Sams, lifting their beers. Sams lifted a hand in return and yelled back. Hermie and Paco waved and smiled but remained silent.

As the cruiser passed out into the river channel, Tully muttered, "Damn day fishers."

Throughout the day, Julio stayed below in the galley, checking his GPS equipment and going over the charts. He pointed with a finger to show Sams where they expected to meet the freighter from Lázaro Cárdenas that night. Like the first transfer, this one would be more than thirty miles offshore.

A few locals had raised their eyes at the fact that the Sara Jane had sailed out so far in search of shrimp. There was no need to go so far when there were plenty of whites and browns from the shoreline up to eight miles out.

To satisfy their snooping, Sams spread the word over beers at his local hangouts that Sillman had him heading out farther than the usual eight miles, in search of Royal Red Shrimp. He said that they had migrated down from the north and a trawler could bring in a haul off the Georgia coast if you went out far enough and knew where to look.

Some wished him luck to his face, then shook their heads behind his back, calling the scheme a boondoggle—a waste of time, fuel and money. Most were glad to see old Tully come out of the lonely depression he had sunk into since Sara Jane's death. If he could get back out on the water where he was happiest, there was no reason not to wish him luck, boondoggle or not.

With appearances kept up, the Sara Jane sailed from St. Mary's in the mid-afternoon. Hermie and Paco took up their positions on deck. Julio stayed below in the galley trying to maintain a grip on the contents of his stomach. Tully Sams stood in the deckhouse at the wheel, a smile of pure contentment on his face. There was no place else he would have rather been.

He sounded the trawler's horn a couple of times, just for the hell of it and grinned. Hermie and Paco gave him a thumbs up and grinned back.

God, it was a fine thing to be on the go again.

FORTY-NINE

Both

The third time was the charm. Sole and Travis first tried to contact Senator James Sillman by telephone. He was a sitting senator, and you didn't just burst in on senators without at least going through the proper protocol.

In this case, the protocol was to establish a reason for concern about his safety. So, they called him. He didn't answer.

They called again a few minutes later. Still, no answer.

A reasonable concern for his safety now existed. Someone had murdered Sillman's assistant. Sillman was either out of town, in hiding someplace else, hunkered down in the condo and not taking calls, or had become a victim as well. Sole contacted the building security director, Jimmy Cutshaw.

"Need another favor, Jimmy."

"Getting to be like old times. What do you need this time?"

"Hear about the murder of Senator Sillman's aide, Wilson Bettis?"

"You mean the mugging? Yeah, been on the news all morning. High profile case like that … they'll be talking about it all week."

"We need to talk to Sillman about it."

"You think he's involved?" Cutshaw's voice lowered to a whisper.

"Not sure, but we'd like to talk to him about it and see if he can give us any insight on why someone would want to kill his assistant."

"So you don't think it was a straight mugging," Cutshaw surmised.

"I didn't say that," Sole replied. Cutshaw was no rookie and could put two and two together as well as any cop. "We need to talk to him. Tie up loose ends."

"So tie them up. Talk to him," Cutshaw said.

"We tried. No one is answering the phone. Is he there?"

"Hold on." Cutshaw punched the hold button. He was back a few seconds later. "Checking the building log. Our officers keep track of tenants coming and going." Cutshaw paused, scanning the log. "Yep, he's here. Sillman hasn't been out in a couple of days."

"We will need to get to his door again."

"No problem. Come on over, and I'll get you up there like before."

"One more thing, though."

"What's that?"

"He may not answer the door … probably won't. We need to get in whether or not he opens up."

"Without a warrant?" Cutshaw asked.

"Without a warrant."

"You saying you need to do a wellness check, John? You know that's the only way I can open the door without a warrant. And wellness means there has to be a real concern ... not some pretext ... not with a U.S. senator."

"It's a legit wellness check, Jimmy. Someone killed his assistant, made it look like a mugging. You say Sillman is holed up in his condo and hasn't been out for days, and we know he isn't answering the phone. I'd say that's sufficient reason to check on his well-being."

"And ask a few questions along the way," Cutshaw said.

"That too." Sole nodded.

"We run a tight operation here, John. No one gets in or out without us knowing. No one has been up to his penthouse to do him harm."

"I know, Jimmy. No one is suggesting you don't have things under control. What we don't know is what is going on inside his condo."

"Or what he knows about the murder," Cutshaw, threw in.

"That too," Sole agreed.

"All right. Come on over. I'll get you up to the penthouse. If he doesn't open, I'll get you in, but don't get me fired from this job, John. It would really piss off my wife."

"Got you covered, Jimmy. We'll give you the paperwork to back it up. See you in fifteen."

"You ready?" Sole looked at Travis.

"I was born ready."

James Sillman huddled in the corner of a dark bedroom, away from the windows. He cringed at every footfall in the hallway. Every ring on the telephone sent cold fear through his gut. His heart raced. His breath came in shallow, panting gasps.

The police had contacted Wilson Bettis' assistant, Nancy Stark and questioned her about Bettis' schedule. Who had he met with that day? Was he meeting anyone after work? Was there anyone who might have had hard feelings towards him?

She spent an hour answering their questions. When the Detectives left, she called Sillman.

It took several tries before the phone's chiming made its way through the bourbon haze. Sillman fumbled past the empty bottle of I.W. Harper on the table beside his chair and answered, wondering why Nancy Stark was calling and not Bettis.

"Yes?" he croaked in a whisper, cleared his throat and croaked louder. "Yes?"

"Something terrible … just awful, Senator." Stark was in tears, barely able to speak.

"What?" Sillman sat up straighter in his chair.

"Wilson … Mr. Bettis … he's dead."

The world receded around him, drew back, leaving him floating in the dark. The lights outside the window seemed too distant, like stars a trillion miles away. He was alone in the universe.

"Senator?" Stark said when he made no response.

Sillman's heavy breathing on the line was the only sound.

"Senator Sillman? Are you all right?"

"I … I'm fine …"

"Should I call someone for you, Senator?"

"No … no, don't do that … call no one."

The line went dead in Nancy Stark's hand. Wilson Bettis dead and Senator Sillman losing his mind. It occurred to her that she might want to start looking for another job tomorrow.

Sillman managed to get up from his chair and pull the blinds on the bank of windows. Then he retreated to a spare bedroom. His mind whirled, uncertain about what to do next. The thought came to him that he better check in with Wilson Bettis.

But Bettis was dead, his foggy brain reminded him. A mugging? Could he believe that? A mugger killed Bettis?

He struggled to come up with a plan. Call Bebé Elizondo? His body trembled at the thought, and his hands shook as he pulled the cork from another bottle.

No, the last voice he wanted to hear right now was Elizondo's. The only plan he could devise was to stay huddled in the chair with another bottle of bourbon at his side. He was safe there. The bourbon and the dark made him safe.

The phone rang. He ignored it, not wanting even to check the number to see who called.

It rang again. He ignored it again.

The bourbon helped his mind drift into near unconsciousness. When the doorbell sounded, he almost jumped from the chair. Then there were knocks at the door.

Would Elizondo send someone to knock and ring the doorbell? He wasn't about to go to the door to find out. He pushed himself deeper into the overstuffed chair in the dark corner. Stay quiet. Whoever it is will go away.

A key clicked in the front door lock. Sillman froze, his breathing suspended.

Frantic, his eyes snapped from side to side searching around the room for a place to hide. Even if he had found one, he knew his legs would never lift him from the chair and carry him. His rubber knees would collapse him to the floor, and there would be Alejandro Garza, standing over him, his cold eyes sparkling in the dark like a cat about to pounce on its prey.

Blinding light filled the dark room. Sillman squinted, whimpering in the chair, his head turning from side to side as if that would make the intruder leave.

"Hello, Senator." It was the detective, the one called Sole, standing in the doorway, hand on the light switch, scanning the room to make sure no one else was present. "Are you alone here?"

The whites of Sillman's eyes were like spotlights, unblinking, wide, and terrified.

"Senator, have you been harmed?" Sole persisted.

Seconds passed. Sillman's head drifted side to side in slow motion.

"Good." Sole stepped into the room followed by Travis and Jimmy Cutshaw. "We were concerned for your safety."

The senator's eyes darted from one face to another, trying to comprehend. "You're ..."

"Investigator Sole with Atlanta Major Crimes. We met a few days ago. This is my partner, Investigator Travis." He nodded at Cutshaw. "I believe you know Mr. Cutshaw, the building security director."

"Yes ... he, uh ..." Sillman nodded, attempting to shake off the confusion and the terror that gripped his guts with an iron fist. "I mean, why are you here?"

"As I said, just checking to make sure you are safe," Sole said. "You have heard about the murder of your aide, Wilson Bettis?"

Sillman nodded.

"Did they give you the details?"

"Mugging ... something in the parking lot."

"That's right, a mugging." Sole stepped closer to Sillman, still huddled in the chair. "Seems like you would want to be with your staff at a time like this. I'm sure they are traumatized after what happened to your chief aide."

"Yes ... I, uh ... I was planning to go in later ... meet with them ... make arrangements." Sillman became conscious of his white-knuckled grip on the sides of the chair. He moved his hands to his lap, and then crossed his arms, his fingers tapping his elbows in nervous agitation. "Wilson and I were very close. I am devastated."

"I'm sure you are." Sole nodded. "That's probably why you haven't asked if we caught his killers."

Sillman looked beyond Sole, focusing on the wall behind, avoiding the piercing eyes. "I thought you would tell me if you caught him."

He prayed that the next words out of this pushy detective's mouth were that Alejandro Garza was stashed away in a jail cell, but they weren't.

"Him?"

"Yes, the killer."

"What makes you think there was only one?"

"Well, I ... that is ... you said killer, so I assumed ..."

"Assumed what?" Sole shook his head. "No, I said, killers ... plural. Is there someone you are afraid of, Senator? A particular person who might be the killer?"

"No, nothing like that. No one I know of." Sillman shook his head rapidly. "I must have been mistaken then." He managed to rise from the chair without toppling over on his wobbly legs and ran his hand through his tousled hair. "This has all been quite a shock."

"I imagine it has."

"As you can see, I am quite well." Sillman glimpsed himself in the mirror hanging over the dresser and realized that he did not look well at all. The image staring back at him was red-eyed and gray-faced. The amber stain of spilled bourbon down the front of his shirt was still damp. He pressed on anyway. "There is no need for concern. I will meet with my staff later to see to their needs and make arrangements for Wils ... Mr. Bettis. Thank you for checking, but I have to get ready now."

His work done, Jimmy Cutshaw took the hint from the building's most prestigious tenant. He turned to leave while Sole and Travis stood their ground.

"We'd like to ask you a few questions," Sole said.

"Why?" Sillman forced himself to look into Sole's eyes.

"You may know something ... something you aren't even aware of that could help us find out who killed Wilson Bettis." Sole paused, letting the dread build in Sillman's red-rimmed eyes. "You might even tell us who the 'him' is that you thought we had apprehended." Sole smiled. "Or, who you hoped we had apprehended."

"I assure you I do not." Sillman's Adam's apple worked up and down as he tried to swallow the lump in his throat. "For the last two days, I have been here, working on the drug enforcement legislation. I've only spoken to Wilson on the phone. Who killed him or why they would do such a thing is beyond me." He stepped to the side and moved around Sole and Travis heading for the hallway door. "Now I must ask you to leave."

They followed and stepped out into the hallway. Sillman threw the bolt behind them before they could ask any more questions.

"Well, that was interesting. What do you think?" Travis asked on the elevator. "Guilt or fear."

"Both," Sole said.

FIFTY

Eyes Above

The trip out was more relaxed this time without Esteban Moya's glowering presence and threatening looks. Hermie and Paco were loose and happy to go about their work on deck. Even pale-faced Julio looked a trifle less green around the gills.

Tully Sams gave the Sara Jane her head, pointing her bow to the east with the wheel lock engaged while he leaned back in the helmsman's seat, smoking a cigarette. Hermie and Paco kept watch on deck, bantering with each other like old shipmates, checking gear as if they were indeed out hunting for Royal Red Shrimp in the deeper waters off the coast. Occasionally, they stopped by the deckhouse and spoke in broken English to Tully Sams.

Sometimes they asked questions about this or that piece of gear. Other times, they used hand signs to show the differences between shrimp trawling on the Atlantic coast and working the fisheries of the Pacific banks.

As he watched them move around the swaying deck on

experienced sea legs, Sams allowed himself to imagine they really were headed out to hunt for Royal Red Shrimp. It was a pleasant thought, but it evaporated when Julio came into the deckhouse from the galley.

"Here." Julio gave a sheepish smile and pointed to the coordinates on his GPS device, and then a spot on the chart fastened to the console beside the wheel. "Go here."

Sams noted the position on the chart and made a slight correction to his course. "Okay, it's your charter," he said, mimicking Julio, tapping the chart and making a mark with a pencil. "Here."

Julio disappeared below again. Sams watched him with a smile. Give him a little time and he might make a seaman of him yet.

Sams nudged the throttle forward and made a quick estimate of time and distance to the point marked on the chart. Another twenty-five miles at just over six knots would put them there in about four hours.

Then he would sit back while Hermie and Paco worked the load onto the trawler. Once the bundles were transferred, and they sank the pontoon raft, he'd steer a straight line for the offloading dock up Fancy Bluff Creek. He figured a few more trips like this and Sillman would have his financial problems solved.

Maybe then he would let old Tully out to do some real trawling, even take on Hermie and Paco for real. He knew he could never pay them what they earned working for Moya and his drug bosses, but at least shrimping was honest work, something a man could be proud of.

Twenty-five thousand feet above the Sara Jane, Commander Tom Hunt, the pilot of the Coast Guard HC-144, a Coast Guard Sea Sentry maritime surveillance aircraft, keyed his mic to broadcast over the secure frequency. "CG six-seven-niner-three-zero on station."

"Roger. CG 6-7-9-3-0 on station." The response from the cutter on patrol forty miles off the Georgia coast was immediate.

The six-man crew on board the Sea Sentry settled in for the duration. With a range of two thousand miles, they could cover a lot of open ocean. This mission was different. The target area today did not extend beyond fifty miles offshore.

They had plotted the surveillance grid to cover the area the Sara Jane could reach at maximum speed. The DEA and Coast Guard surmised that if there were drugs on board, they would offload them as soon as possible, somewhere close along the coast. They limited the search area to the distance offshore the trawler could reach and then return from before daylight.

The Sea Sentry cruised at high altitude, mimicking a commercial airliner, using different vectors each time it crisscrossed over the target area. With all eyes on the Sara Jane, they tracked her movements, and those of every other vessel close enough to come in contact with her.

The cutter had already identified the Sara Jane and was staying just below the horizon while its chopper popped up from time to time to check the trawler's course from a distance. The helicopter never approached the trawler and always traveled away from her to disguise its intent.

The surveillance subterfuge worked. When the trawler was thirty miles out, it slowed and started cruising in a circle two miles in diameter. There were no other ships in the area.

"Something's happening," Chief Petty Officer Sonny Thurwell supervised the surveillance crew comprised of the radar and infra-red operator, the navigator, and the flight engineer who served as the visual spotter.

"Report, Sonny."

"The target is circling ... not headed anywhere right now."

"Trawling for shrimp?"

"Negative. I don't think so. Net cranes are lowered, but there's no sign of nets in the water."

"Thanks, Chief. Good work. Check for other targets in the area."

"On it now, Skip."

Hunt switched to the broadcast frequency, calling the cutter below. "Target appears to be in a holding pattern ... circling and waiting." He gave the coordinates.

"Roger that. Do you have any other targets in the area?"

"Checking now. Stand by one." The pilot said, then toggled the intercom back to Chief Thurwell and the spotter team. "Any other targets approaching, Sonny?"

"Could be, Skipper. Stand by."

The Sea Sentry's radar operator handed a set of coordinates and direction of travel to the navigator. It only took a few seconds to plot the container ship's course.

It was not a direct line to the trawler's current position. Instead, it was heading to a point in the ocean a few miles over the horizon from the trawler. If the Sara Jane had continued her previous course, the two vessels would have intersected.

Thurwell keyed his mic. "Possible target, Skip. Container ship ... would be on an intersecting course if the trawler had not stopped to circle below the freighter's horizon."

"ID the ship yet?"

"Working on it."

"Roger.

Commander Hunt relayed the information to the cutter. The freighter's presence proved nothing. It could be heading to a port up the east coast or to a regular transatlantic crossing route. By the same token, the trawler might circle for many reasons—checking gear, testing engines, or because the captain was a crazy fuck who enjoyed riding around in circles on the ocean.

Still, with no other shipping traffic in the area, and the Sara Jane holding its position for no apparent reason, the freighter's course made it the object of intense scrutiny. On board the cutter, DEA's Gene Cusins requested another interdiction ship as a precaution. The Coast Guard was more than happy to comply and dispatched a cutter working out of Savannah with orders to proceed at high speed and take up station east of the intersection point in case the freighter made a run to escape.

Unaware of the eyes overhead and the patrolling cutter below their horizon, Tully Sams and his crew on the Sara Jane spent the afternoon practicing their pidgin English-Spanish and hand signals. Sams figured that if he could give them a command, and they understood, then maybe they wouldn't have to put up with that asshole Moya on board his boat again. He had started to think of Hermie, Paco, and seasick Julio as his personal crew.

The sunset was rapid. In a sky devoid of clouds, the

glowing orange sun descended into the ocean like a torch being extinguished.

The night followed it, falling over them like a cloak, shutting out the rest of the world. Stars in the billions burned fierce and bright in the dark. Sams stepped out of the deckhouse, lit another cigarette, and stretched, arching his back until he was looking up.

The navigation marker lights of an aircraft blinked high overhead. He followed it, noting its course, west towards the coast. Just before disappearing from view, the plane made a wide turn to the south.

Could be an airliner turning toward Jacksonville or Fort Lauderdale, or even Miami, loaded with tourists coming back from Bermuda. From up there, they only saw the blackness below, featureless and empty.

They had no idea what it was like to be down here, part of everything, the living water rising and falling, carrying the Sara Jane on its breast, its heart beating with the thrum of the engines. They missed it all, isolated in a metal tube twenty-five thousand feet in the air.

Commander Hunt banked the HC-144 to the south and flew another five minutes before taking an easterly course. A few minutes later they were back on station crossing the target area, heading northeast.

"What do you have, Chief?" he said into the intercom.

"Trawler is still circling, holding position. Target two, the container ship is approaching what would be the intersection point of their courses … steaming at twenty knots … If they don't change course or speed, they will hit the intersection in two-and-a-half hours."

"Okay. Keep me advised of any changes."

"Aye, Skip."

Hunt craned his head to look out of the cockpit window. The stars were putting on quite a show. He wondered what the night was like below on the trawler.

FIFTY-ONE

One Crazy Fuck

"I don't see how we can do it," Esteban Moya said, peering over the steering wheel of the rental sedan.

Garza had refused to allow him to drive his royal blue Hummer with chrome spinner wheels, which was an annoyance. Subtlety was necessary, Garza reminded him. It was a word that held more nuance than Moya's mind could grasp. Fuck subtlety. He squirmed in the hard, threadbare seat. Subtlety should be more comfortable.

"We will do it." Garza turned his eyes on Moya. "Patience and attention to detail … those are the keys to success. Two qualities that I find lacking here."

"I'm patient," Moya began. "I just don't see why …"

He stopped mid-sentence. You must be truly tired *tonto* —fool, he thought, conscious of Garza watching him. He added, "Sorry. Your ways are new to me. I apologize. I only want to make sure we are successful."

"We will be."

They had been sitting across from Senator Sillman's

high rise since the early morning hours. It was time to plan the next stage of their mission.

"There," Garza said pointing. "That car. Follow it."

"Sillman is not in that car." Moya shook his head. "That is a cop car ... the detectives who were at the building earlier. They are leaving, that's all."

"Everything is connected. That car connects us to Sillman." Garza nodded, eyes focused straight ahead as Moya pulled into traffic and followed the Crown Victoria, staying a block back.

"As you say," Moya said with a shrug, careful to keep the skeptical look from his face.

The detectives' car wound through the streets for several minutes before entering the parking lot of a building Moya knew only too well. His foot pressed harder on the accelerator.

"Careful," Garza ordered. "Do nothing to draw attention to us."

Through sheer will power, Moya forced the muscles in his legs to relax. It was against all of his instincts. For a lifelong criminal, passing by the Atlanta Police Criminal Investigations Division building made about as much sense as walking by a tiger's den with a T-bone steak tied around your neck. It was insane.

Garza turned to watch the car as they drove past the lot. Moya kept his eyes focused on the asphalt ahead, hands clenching the steering wheel, knuckles white. At any moment, he expected a swarm of police cars to come swooping around the corner to arrest them for the murder of Wilson Bettis. Except, he knew they would not arrest Garza. Elizondo's henchman would fight it out with the police, and such a fight could only end in one way. They would go down in a blaze of gunfire, Garza loyal to Bebé to the last, Moya a victim of Garza's blind devotion but dead just the same.

To his complete surprise, they made it to the next corner without being surrounded by police cars. Moya stopped at the traffic signal, eyes fixed straight ahead, not daring to look at Garza who might next order him to drive into the parking lot and pull up beside the detective car.

"Go back to Sillman's building," Garza said, calm and in control.

"Back? But ..."

"We have learned what we needed."

"Mind if I ask what that is?" Moya asked, immediately regretting the sarcasm in his tone, fearful he had gone too far.

Fortunately, the sarcasm was lost on Alejandro Garza who lacked the ability to detect the nuances in words and inflection. He said what he thought and assumed the same of others.

"We have identified the car connected to Sillman," he replied.

"How?" Moya asked. "It's a police car. The kind the detectives drive ... all of them."

"Yes, but only one has this license plate on the back and this car number painted on the rear." Garza held up his hand. He had printed the detective car's tag and unit number in ink on his palm. "Take us back now to the building, and we will watch."

Moya turned at the corner to make his way back to Sillman's high rise. He wondered if Garza was as smart as Bebé thought or just one crazy fuck. Follow the cops to eyeball their license plate close up? Haven't you ever heard of binoculars, *cholo*?

FIFTY-TWO

Ready for the Big Show

The phone chimed as Travis pulled the Crown Vic off Peachtree Street into the parking lot outside APD's Criminal Investigations Division building. John Sole recognized the number and answered.

"What's up?"

"You up for a little trip?" Bill Lance asked.

"Depends. Where to?"

"How about to parts unknown in the middle of the Atlantic?"

"They're headed out?" Sole felt his adrenalin surge.

"They are. The Sara Jane left St. Mary's in the last hour. Our guys saw them pass down the channel. Tully Sams waved at them from the deckhouse. There were two unknown crewmen on the boat. They looked Hispanic."

"Damn right, I'm ready. Where and when."

"Now, as soon as you can get here. Fulton County Airport. We'll chopper to Brunswick then transfer to a Coast Guard bird to take us out to the cutter they have on station offshore. They've already got a fixed-wing aircraft watching from high altitude. Once the air surveillance spots suspicious activity, the plan is for the cutter to come in from over the horizon, sending the assault team and chopper ahead. We'll be on the cutter when they interdict the trawler."

"On the way. Be there in thirty."

The call ended. Travis looked at Sole's grinning face. "Don't tell me," he said, with a disgusted smirk. "You're going out to sea."

"Yep." Sole grinned. "Get me out to Fulton County Airport."

"On the way." Travis made a U-turn and wheeled from the parking lot. He glanced over at Sole, the excited grin still wide on his face. "You don't have to gloat."

"Don't feel bad, partner. If this works out, you'll be making another visit to the Sillman penthouse … this time with a warrant."

"True. That is some consolation."

"Actually, I wish I could be there to see it."

"I'll take pictures for you."

Twenty minutes later, Sole along with Bill Lance and Chuck Rayburn sat inside in a Bell 206 helicopter with a Georgia State Patrol pilot at the controls. Assorted gear, weapons, and communications equipment filled every available space and made the four-seat chopper feel cramped.

The nametag on the pilot's uniform read 'McGuinn.' For ten minutes, McGuinn was all business as he went through the pre-flight checklist. Then he settled the headset over his ears, punched the intercom button, and leaned back grinning over his shoulder at his passengers.

"Let's hope I can get this piece of shit off the ground."

Sole and Lance grinned back.

Chuck Rayburn scowled and muttered, "That's not funny."

McGuinn had the chopper cruising along the runway just above the surface to increase speed as the engines revved up and the rotor gained enough lift to get the maximum capacity load into the air.

Under his breath, he sang an old Mamas and Papas song. "*McGuinn and McGuire couldn't get much higher, but that's what they were aimin' at …*"

The runway disappeared. They skimmed over the grass at the end of the airfield, gaining speed. Trees loomed ahead. McGuinn pulled up on the collective control.

Somehow, they cleared the trees walling in the end of runway. Engines roaring at full power, they rose like a man with a heavy load on his back until they reached two thousand feet. Then, with a momentary dip that had their stomachs in their throats, they leveled out and McGuinn set course for the Brunswick Coast Guard Station two hundred and forty miles away.

Estimated flight time was two-and-a-half hours. They relaxed and settled in for the ride. Chuck Rayburn looked around the small cabin and spoke into the headset mic he wore.

"Only one pilot?"

"Yep, just me," McGuinn answered.

"Who flies this thing if something happens to you?"

"God," McGuinn said in a serious tone. "Hope you're all prayed up for the week."

"Fuck me," Rayburn muttered.

"What's the matter, Chuck?" Bill Lance chided. "Not prayed up, or just afraid of flying?"

"Not much of a praying man," Rayburn replied craning

his head to stare down at the city lights below. "And I'm not afraid of flying. I'm afraid of crashing."

"Okay to use my cell phone?" Sole asked the McGuinn.

"Sure. These aren't the friendly skies." He paused then added for Rayburn's benefit, "In fact, I encourage all my passengers to call home and make their peace with the world ... you know just in case."

Rayburn scowled. The others laughed. Sole punched in Shaye's number on his cell phone.

"Hey, babe what's up?" she asked, without preliminaries. In the background, he heard the kids arguing about something. Shaye lowered the phone and barked at them, "Quiet you two! Your Dad's on the phone." She raised the phone again. "Sorry. So, what's up?"

"Gonna be late. Just wanted you to know."

"How late?"

"Tomorrow ... probably. Might take all day. Something came up. I have to be there."

"What's that noise? Where are you? In a plane?"

"Helicopter, but I can't say any more than that for now. I'll fill you in when I get home."

"All right." Shaye had been down this road before. He would not call her unless there was something important happening—something that carried an element of risk. She added, "Be careful, John. Come home safe."

"Always. No need to worry. I'm just along for the ride. I'll be in the background where it's safe with lots of firepower up front."

"If you say so, but if you're lying, I will beat your ass when you get home."

"I'm sure." He smiled. "Trust me. I'll be fine ... just an onlooker."

"All right, babe. Love you."

"Love you too."

The call ended. Sole looked up to see the grins on the faces of the others.

"What?" he asked.

"That was sweet," Chuck Rayburn chortled.

"Yeah," Bill Lance said, nodding. "Touching."

"You're just jealous." Sole smiled and tucked the cell phone in his pocket. "No one gives a shit what happens to either of you.

"You're right about that." Rayburn nodded soberly, peering through the plexiglass at the ground below.

McGuinn set the State Patrol chopper down on the helo pad at the Brunswick Coast Guard Station on time. Five minutes later, he lifted off for the trip back to Atlanta, his three law enforcement passengers transferred to a Coast Guard chopper tasked to take them out to the cutter, patrolling on station, out of sight of the Sara Jane.

"Another helicopter?" Rayburn's eyes widened as they trotted across the apron to the Coast Guard MH-60 Jayhawk.

"What'd you think?" Lance said, grinning. "Swim out to the cutter?"

"Fuck," Rayburn replied, using the word he had used several dozen times in the last three hours to emphasize his feelings about helicopters.

"What's the matter," the chopper's crew chief asked as he got them aboard and strapped in.

"Nervous flyer." Lance nodded at the Atlanta narc detective, huddling as far away from the open door as possible.

"Understandable," the crew chief said, his face deadpan serious. "This machine is nothing but a flying brick." He shook his head. "No aerodynamics at all. Just that big ass rotor overhead to keep us in the air. If it comes off ... well, it wouldn't be pretty."

Rayburn made a point of trying to ignore the banter about aerodynamics and flying bricks.

The crew chief would not be denied though and continued. "You see there's just this one nut at the top of the whole damned thing."

"A nut?" Rayburn was paying attention now.

The crew chief nodded. "Yep, one nut holds the rotor assembly on top. If that nut comes loose, the rotor goes flying off into space, and we make a big splash in the ocean." He maintained his serious tone, adding, "Funny thing is, you'd think falling into water wouldn't be so bad ... like jumping into a pool from the high dive, but if we fall into that big ocean from five thousand feet, it'll be like hitting concrete. Chopper ... and us ... smashed into a million pieces."

"You done?" Rayburn glared at the Coast Guardsman who was having a grand time entertaining the others at his expense.

"Yeah, I suppose so." The crew chief shrugged. "Anyway, there's nothing to worry about."

"Glad to hear it," Rayburn snapped back.

The chief continued unperturbed. "Yep. I tightened that nut myself ... just to be sure. It's one of my jobs as crew chief on this bird. Want to know what we call it?"

"Call what?" Bill Lance said when Rayburn pretended to ignore the chief.

"Glad you asked," the chief said, grinning. "We call it the Jesus nut because if it comes off, that's what we are all going to be screaming on that long drop to the ocean." He raised his hands, a mock look of terror on his face. "Ohhh .... Jeee ... sssuusss!"

Laughter erupted from the Jayhawk's other crewmen. Even the pilot and copilot chuckled over the headsets. Sole and Lance grinned.

"Fuck," Chuck Rayburn muttered, drawing his knees up and pushing his back hard against the wall.

A moment later, the Jayhawk's engines throttled up, and they jumped into the air. Banking as it gained altitude, they were over the ocean in seconds. The trip to the cutter forty miles offshore took twenty minutes. Sole, Lance, and Rayburn dropped five feet from the hovering chopper to the ship's helipad where the cutter's crew hustled them below as the helicopter roared away.

The silence after the chopper ride made their ears feel as if they were full of cotton. After a minute, they picked up the noises of the cutter—the sea swells breaking against her hull, engine humming through their feet, officers shouting orders.

A crewman escorted them to the bridge where Gene Cusins greeted them. He had been out with the cutter all day, coordinating the interception plan.

"Welcome aboard." Cusins grinned at the three new arrivals, noting Rayburn's gray complexion. "You don't look so good, Chuck."

"Shut up," Rayburn said wrapping a big hand around a steel bulkhead door handle to steady himself.

Sole nodded at the activity on the deck below where crewmen checked weapons and readied the interceptor boats that would deploy from the cutter's rear launch ramp. "Looks busy."

"It is. Everyone getting ready for the big show."

FIFTY-THREE

Little Fish and Big Fish

The Sara Jane crept forward in the dark. Tully Sams leaned out of the deckhouse door, one hand on the wheel, peering into the black. Julio stood beside him, watching the readouts on his GPS device and digital compass. He tapped Sams on the shoulder.

"Here."

Sams turned to look at the display. "Okay."

He shifted the engine into neutral, disengaging the prop while the engine idled. According to Julio the pontoon raft loaded with cocaine was waiting for them at this precise point on the water. Julio's head jerked from side to side in panic, eyes wide, peering into the dark. He began muttering something in Spanish. Sams thought it sounded like a prayer.

The sea was calm, but there was more wind than the night of the first shipment. Drift was to be expected, but Julio was not a seaman. He had no understanding of the effects of wind, tide, and ocean currents on any floating object, even a seven ton floating object. In the time they took to arrive at the drop point, it could have drifted a mile or more.

Sams wondered what penalty Moya, or the one they called Bebé, would impose for losing one of the cocaine rafts. Julio leaned over the side and retched. Hermie said something in terse Spanish to settle their terrified navigator.

"*Calmate. ¡Haz tu trabajo! Encuentra el faro.*" Calm down. Do your job. Find the beacon.

"*Sí claro.*" Yeah, right.

Julio nodded, took a deep breath, and wiped the sweat from his eyes to study the GPS device. It lit his face with a ghostly pale blue radiance that made him look even sicker than usual.

Hermie and Paco scanned the night with handheld lights. They knew Elizondo's team placed an electronic beacon on each raft. Without it, the freighter might as well have dumped a billion dollars of Bebé's cocaine into the deep.

The beacon transmitted its location every thirty seconds. A minute passed, then two. Hermie and Paco stood fore and aft with their flashlights, shining into the dark.

Five minutes into the search, Julio motioned and pointed. Sams made a slight turn of the wheel, adjusting course.

A minute later, Paco called out. "*¡Aquí!*" Here!

Sams inched the trawler forward until Hermie and Paco secured a line to the raft. The load transfer began without a hitch. Sams leaned back in his seat to watch and smoke a cigarette, relaxed and content, riding the swells, surrounded by the black night.

Light exploded in their faces, blinding white so that even with eyes clenched shut, the glare made its way through their eyelids, pinkish red and painful. Sams' muscles jerked reflexively like a man awakened too fast from a deep sleep, his heart pounding in his chest. Hermie and Paco stood erect on the deck, stunned, eyes wide, a look of fear mingled with resignation on their faces. Julio leaned out of the deckhouse and vomited, then ran into the galley retching as he went.

The night had disappeared, vanished in a split second. Men in black battle dress swarmed aboard the Sara Jane. Backlit by the glare they were silhouettes, dark and foreboding.

They moved with practiced agility, jumping from two F470 CRCC, combat rubber raiding craft, bobbing in the water on either side of the trawler. Once the men in black were aboard the Sara Jane, the coxswains of the small boats backed off. A gunner on each trained an M-60 machine gun on the trawler, alert to any sign of resistance. There was none.

Tully Sams recovered and reached for the engine throttle, not sure what he would do, but pushed by the instinct to do something. A large man with DEA stenciled on his back, and a badge sewn on the front of his battle dress, stepped into the deckhouse. He placed a firm hand on Sams' arm.

"You're under arrest."

Two others followed him in and pulled Sams upright and away from the controls. The shrimper's head swiveled on his shoulders, stunned. In thirty seconds, his peaceful night on the big water under a canopy of stars had ended. There would never be another like it for Tully Sams. What remained of his life evaporated like a morning mist blown away by the sea breeze.

Sole Survivor

"Do not resist and no one will be harmed," the large man in black said. "Tell your crew to submit."

There was no need. Sams looked out to the deck. Hermie and Paco stood, offering no resistance, dejected and resigned to what was taking place. The black-clad invaders handcuffed and placed them into separate rubber boats.

Several figures descended from the trawler to the pontoon raft to examine the contents. A flurry of activity followed, the agents speaking in excited hushed tones into portable radios, arms waving and pointing to the contents of the sample bundle they had opened.

One of the DEA men came out of the galley, pushing Julio ahead. "Found this one with this." He held up a satellite phone.

"Who did you call?" Gene Cusins, the DEA agent in charge, said.

Julio stared without speaking. His usual gray seagoing complexion was greener than Sams had seen before.

"He doesn't speak English," Sams said as one of the DEA agents pulled his arms behind him to ratchet shut the handcuffs around his wrists.

"Okay," Cusins said turning to Sams. "Who did he call?"

"Shit," Sams said, recovering a touch of his usual captain's swagger. "Damned if I know. God maybe."

"See if you can get a trace on it." Cusins nodded to the one with the phone.

Two men pushed Sams back against the wall and held him there while the DEA boarding party searched the Sara Jane. On the radar screen beside the wheel, a blip appeared on the horizon five miles from the trawler's radar antenna ten feet above the deck.

The Coast Guard cutter covered the distance in fifteen

minutes. It took up position a hundred yards from the two assault boats, and lowered a dinghy to ferry John Sole, Bill Lance and Chuck Rayburn to the Sara Jane.

Twenty miles away, Commander Tom Hunt in the Sea Sentry, flying high over the action, directed the second cutter to intersect the container ship that made the drop. Boarding a big ship at sea is always a risky proposition. The freighter's crew significantly outnumbered the boarding party, and the possibility of illegal narcotics and men willing to defend against the boarders heightened the interdiction team's caution.

The cutter's skipper radioed the ship and advised the captain to heave to. The freighter's captain ignored the order. A burst of fifty caliber rounds across the bow changed his mind.

Even Bebé Elizondo did not pay enough to risk a fight with an armed U.S. Coast Guard cutter. Besides the *Los Salvajes* cartel boss was sound asleep in his hillside hacienda, not bobbing around on the Atlantic with searchlights in his face. The captain wisely cut his engines and drifted, waiting for the inevitable.

The boarding party, led by a young lieutenant, found most of the freighter's crew asleep. Those who weren't in their bunks were watching a porn movie in the galley. Only the captain, a mate, and one of the cargo crane operators manned the bridge, an unusually scant duty list for a night watch on a big ship.

They secured the crew in their quarters and separated the captain and the other two prime suspects. Then the Coast Guard crew stood a security watch while a civilian pilot and five crewmen with freighter experience came aboard to take the ship into Brunswick.

The DEA agents who boarded with the Coast Guard questioned the crew. Most were bewildered.

The captain couldn't talk fast enough, spewing out everything he knew about the drug smuggling operation. He had a fervent desire to continue to breathe and retain all of his body parts. Prison in a secure U.S. federal penitentiary was preferable to the other option—explaining the failure of their mission to Bebé Elizondo and Alejandro Garza.

At the Sara Jane, a dinghy pulled alongside.

"Thought you'd want to see this," Gene Cusins said as Sole, Lance, and Rayburn clambered aboard the Trawler. "It was your case."

He escorted them to the deckhouse where Tully Sams stood, guarded by two DEA agents. They crammed into the small space, curious to see the old shrimper. He wasn't much to see. Just an old man with a weathered face and rough hands, but the glint in his eyes was defiant. Recovered now that the shock of the DEA's arrival had faded, he returned the stares of the men who crowded around him.

"What's your name?" Cusins asked.

"I reckon you already know that," Sams replied evenly, attempting to lift one of his handcuffed arms to his breast pocket and the pack of cigarettes. He turned his head toward Cusins. "All you big men standing around, I ain't goin' nowheres. I'd like to have a smoke one more time, out here on the water."

Cusins nodded at the agents. "Let him have his smoke."

They removed the cuffs, and Tully Sams pulled the cigarettes from his pocket, shook one out, reached for his lighter on the dashboard beside the wheel, and lit up. His hands were steady, no sign of nerves.

John Sole smiled. The old man had balls. Saltwater in his veins and sand in his voice, he was resigned to what would happen next.

"How long have you been doing this, Tully?" Bill Lance asked.

"This? Oh, I been shrimpin' most of my life, since I was old enough to go out."

"That's not what I mean."

Sole and Lance exchanged smiles. The old man wasn't giving in, even when they had him dead to rights.

"Running cocaine in," Lance clarified. "How long you been doing that?"

"That what's in those bundles?" Sams' eyes widened innocently. He nodded at the raft where they black-clad DEA men still swarmed, securing it for transfer to the cutter. "Just found it bobbin' around out here on the water. No idea it was … what was that you called it? Cocaine?" He shook his head. "Shit that's illegal, ain't it? Damn. If I'd a known that, I'd a steered a different course."

"And your crew?" Cusins asked. "Where'd you pick them up?"

"Hermie and Paco? They're good men. Found 'em in Brunswick just hangin' out. Said they needed work, so I put 'em to work."

"Uh huh." Cusins was smiling now too. You had to respect the old fart. "And the other one? The one with the satellite phone. We will trace the call … find out who was on the other end … maybe your boss, James Sillman."

"Sillman?" Sams nodded. "Yeah, I work for Sillman Shrimp. Out here looking for Royal Red Shrimp ... for a new customer." He shook his head. "But I haven't seen or heard from the senator in quite a while." He smiled. "I'm just a little fish, so to speak."

After that, the atmosphere in the cramped deckhouse was congenial. The questioning ended. There was no reason to press the issue now. They had the trawler, the crew and the captain with a billion dollars of cocaine tied alongside.

Tully Sams smoked his cigarette and then another while the DEA secured the cocaine and tied the raft off to be towed behind the cutter.

Back aboard the cutter, John Sole made a call. It was time to go after the big fish. Travis answered on the first ring.

"We're good to go."

"How much?" Travis asked.

"About five thousand kilos."

"Holy shit!"

"Yeah. Rayburn says street value after being cut and pushed down the pipeline could be close to a billion.

"Jesus." Travis gave a low whistle. "How'd it go down?"

"Uneventful. They surrendered without a fight."

"Perfect." Travis grinned. "You know what that means."

"Yep. Say hello to the senator for me when you cuff him."

Sole almost wished he hadn't won the coin toss. The arrest of a senator, especially one who sent a man like Tully Sams out to do his dirty work, would be more than satisfying.

"Will do."

Travis ended the call and rang the judge they had on standby to sign the arrest warrant they had prepared for James Jadyn Sillman. This time it wouldn't matter if he answered the door or not.

FIFTY-FOUR

Examples

"*Esto es maldito estúpido.*" This is damned stupid. Esteban Moya mumbled as he dozed with his head resting against the window.

With a snort, he jerked himself awake behind the wheel of the rental car. His eyes darted around. Where was he? Then he remembered.

He cast a sideward glance to the right without turning his head. Had he spoken loud enough for Alejandro Garza to hear?

If he had heard, he gave no sign. Garza remained focused on the building they had been watching since ... since when? Moya couldn't remember. He'd been up since the morning of Garza's arrival. His body craved sleep.

Since fleeing the parking garage after Bettis' murder, all they had done was watch the high-rise where Sillman lived. Watching for what? Sillman would never come out, and if he did, it would not be alone. This was *muy estúpido*.

"There," Garza said, pointing.

A car turned from Peachtree Street into the parking

garage of the high-rise. It was a Ford Crown Victoria, same color as the detective car that had been there earlier in the day. Was it even the same day? Moya was no longer sure.

A moment later, another car, same make and model but a different color followed it into the garage. A marked Atlanta Police unit brought up the rear.

"What do you think it means?" Moya ventured.

"Soon," Garza replied.

The phone in Garza's pocket vibrated. He answered at once, without checking the number first. "*Sí.*" His eyes never left the building as he pushed the phone tight against his ear.

Moya tried to hear what was being said. The words were unintelligible, but he could tell that the caller was shouting, delivering the message with machine gun rapidity. Someone was very unhappy. It had to be Elizondo. No one else in their right mind would speak in that manner to Garza.

Seconds passed while the shouting on the other end of the line continued. When it ended, Garza spoke. "Perhaps it would be better to wait, not respond so soon. This is not Mexico. Such action here might have …" For once Garza paused, selecting his words with care. "Might have adverse effects."

The voice on the line rose abruptly so that Moya clearly understood Bebé Elizondo's instructions.

"Do it now! Tonight! They stole my shipment. They will pay!"

Garza offered no further argument. "It will be done." He pocketed the phone, his eyes focused on the building.

Moya waited for some explanation. When none was forthcoming, he spoke. "What is it? Who was that? Elizondo?"

"Who it was, is not your affair. Our assignment has changed."

"What does that mean?"

"They stopped and took a shipment. Your man on the boat managed to get off a message on the satellite phone."

"Who? Who took a shipment?"

"The police … DEA … others. It does not matter. The feeling is that there must be an example. This cannot go unpunished."

"Feeling? Whose feeling?" Moya shook his head. "You said we don't make examples here … that it is different here. Examples are dangerous and accomplish nothing. This is what you told me."

"Our instructions have changed."

"You saw. There are three cop cars with Sillman now … detectives. We go running off wild like that, and we'll be the examples who …"

Garza turned his head. The warning in his eyes was plain. Esteban Moya's words hung in mid-air.

"Tonight," Garza said. "We complete the assignment. You will help."

FIFTY-FIVE

Crime and Punishment

Randy Travis stood in the hallway outside James Sillman's penthouse. One DEA agent, two Major Crimes detectives, and a uniformed officer accompanied him. Everything would be handled by the book, although no one was quite sure what the book said about locking up senators. The consensus was that the arrest of a senator merited sufficient witnesses to document the event, and they were taking no chances.

The building security director, Jimmy Cutshaw, met them with a master key to the condo. At first, they thought the key might be necessary. Travis rang the doorbell followed by three sharp raps on the door to identify themselves and announce their presence.

"Senator Sillman, open the door. This is investigator Travis, Atlanta Police Major Crimes Unit."

There was no response. Travis repeated the process, ringing, knocking, announcing their presence and demanding entry.

Sole Survivor

Cutshaw had the master key in the lock when they heard shuffling behind the door. Shadows moved behind the door's peephole. Someone peered out at them. Then the deadbolt drew back in the lock, and the door swung wide.

Red-eyed, perspiration soaking through his shirt, Sillman shrank back from the officers like a scolded puppy.

"James Jadyn Sillman, we have a warrant for your arrest. You are being charged with trafficking narcotics." Travis added the Miranda Warning before Sillman could respond. *"You have the right to remain silent. Anything you say can be used against you in court. You have the right to talk to a lawyer for advice before we ask you any questions. You have the right to have a lawyer with you during questioning. If you cannot afford a lawyer, one will be appointed for you before any questioning if you wish. If you decide to answer questions now without a lawyer present, you have the right to stop answering at any time."*

Travis paused before asking the required final questions. Everyone present could confirm that he accorded Senator James Sillman all the necessary legal protections during his arrest. "Do you understand these rights as I have explained them to you?"

Sillman nodded and slumped against the wall. Travis thought the look on his face was one of relief.

"Do you have anything you would like to say at this time?"

Sillman stared at him, brow wrinkled in confusion, dazed and disoriented. "Say?" He shook his head. "No nothing to say."

The senator wore only a tee shirt and boxers. The sour odor of whiskey and sweat hung over him. Two detectives held his arms and walked him to the bedroom to put on a fresh shirt and trousers.

In the penthouse living room, Travis noted a Colt Model 1911 .45 caliber pistol on a table beside a leather chair. The chair faced a bank of windows. The window drapes were pulled tight. Except for a dim light in the corner, the room was dark.

Travis retrieved the pistol, removed the clip and ejected the round in the chamber. It appeared the senator had been expecting someone else at the door, someone more threatening than a group of law enforcement officers.

Sillman came from the bedroom between the two detectives. Travis held up the pistol.

"Any other weapons here?" he asked.

"No." Sillman shook his head. "Only that one … it … it was my father's."

"We'll be keeping it for safekeeping," Travis said, placing it in a plastic evidence bag he took from his jacket pocket. "Were you expecting someone else?" he asked holding the bag up before Sillman's eyes.

"No, I was just …" Sillman shrugged, his mouth closing shut as if trying to cut off any words that might escape.

"Sitting here in the dark, windows covered, pistol at your side. Seems like you were ready for trouble."

"I was just … nervous." Sillman muttered, barely audible, choosing his words.

"Nervous? Why?"

"Why?" Sillman shook his head like a man waking from a deep sleep. "I mean … you know … with the murder and all … Wilson Bettis."

"A mugger killed Bettis. Right?" Travis raised his eyebrows in mock curiosity. "You afraid of being mugged here?" He looked around the interior of the penthouse and nodded at Jimmy Cutshaw. "With security all around?"

"I … uh …" Sillman shook his head one more time, a

final reminder to himself to shut the fuck up before he said something he regretted, something Alejandro Garza would make him regret. "Like I said, I have nothing to say to you."

They escorted the senator down to the parking garage. Twenty minutes later, Travis was filling out the book-in sheet and working on his arrest report. It was time to call his partner and share the good news.

Sole answered immediately with a question. "Get him?"

"Got him," Travis said nodding. "The good senator is cooling his heels in an interview room."

"Still wish I could have been there to see the look on Sillman's face. Say anything?"

"Nope. Not verbally at least, but I don't think I've ever seen a man as terrified as the senator. He was relieved that it wasn't someone else at the door."

"I'll bet he was. Still working on who is behind this, but it is big. We're talking major cartel … Pablo Escobar, Medellin Cartel size operation, maybe bigger. Whoever they are, they have the reach to snuff a senator given the time and opportunity."

"Good thing we showed up before they got to him then."

"Yeah, but be careful. They are probably still looking for him. I don't think these people will let it go. They'll want their pound of flesh."

"Will do. What's next on your end?"

"Headed into Brunswick to offload the cocaine and prisoners. DEA is working with local sheriffs to cordon off and pick up whoever was receiving the drugs on this end. It's a big area along the coast, but only a few roads in. They're looking for any vans or trucks out on the marsh roads."

"Sounds like things are winding down. The excitement around here is about over."

"Yeah. I'll be back tomorrow."

"Sounds good. I'm headed home as soon as I get Sillman booked."

The call ended. Travis continued his report.

Sole dialed home. It was late, already past midnight, but Shaye would expect him to call.

"Hi, babe," she said after the first ring.

"Hey. Just wanted to let you know we're wrapping things up. I'll be home before the kids are off to school."

"Good. I miss your cold ass snuggled up here," she said, yawning.

"I miss your hot ass.

"I'll bet you do," she chuckled.

"Love you. Talk to you soon."

"Love you too," she said drifting back to sleep.

He ended the call and stepped out onto the deck of the cutter. Tully Sams stood at the bow smoking, one hand cuffed to a railing in case he decided to take his chances overboard.

Sole knew he wasn't the type. Sams would take the medicine for what he'd done, which in his mind probably was not much and not really wrong. If it meant prison, so be it.

Sole had to respect the old shrimper, even felt sympathy for him. From Tully Sams' perspective, he had just been doing his job, taking a shrimp trawler out for his boss. If some asshole wanted to load drugs on board so other assholes could fry their brains with them, who was he to object as long as he got to go out on the big water and do what he was best at?

Through all of the scurrying activity surrounding him and armed men boarding his boat, Tully Sams remained apart from it, above it all, a simple man with a simple view of the world.

Unlike Sillman, he would not be caught huddling in a penthouse condo waiting for retribution. He accepted his part. Others might call it a crime. He wouldn't argue the point. He would meet the punishment for it head-on.

FIFTY-SIX

Ground Zero

"Follow them."

"No disrespect, but are you certain that is wise?"

Garza turned in the seat to look at Esteban Moya and repeated his command. "Follow."

"Yes." Moya replied, nodding. "As you say."

Hijo de puta loca—crazy son of a bitch. This asshole was going to get them killed or arrested, or both.

Moya waited for the motorcade of police vehicles to pull from the parking garage below Sillman's building then pulled the rental car onto Peachtree Rd. to follow. His eyes darted from the rearview mirror to the cars in line ahead and back to the mirror. It was a fucking parade. He let off the accelerator and let them pull farther ahead.

"Move closer," Garza said.

"But …" Moya started to object, then thought better of it. "Certainly. As you wish."

He accelerated until they were only a couple of car lengths behind the rear police vehicle, a marked Atlanta patrol unit. At any moment, he expected the car's blue lights to light up and swerve to pull them over.

The large number of police vehicles arriving at Sillman's building after the seizure of the cocaine from the Sara Jane could mean only one thing. James Sillman was under arrest and headed to jail.

The police cars filed into the Criminal Investigations division parking lot. As before, Moya continued past, went around the corner and then came back to park along the curb at the end of the block.

Sleep deprivation was catching up with him. His head bobbed and swayed as he tried to watch the police parking lot through the haze of fatigue.

Alejandro Garza had no such problem. He seemed impervious to human frailties like fatigue. He was a machine.

An hour passed, then another. Moya tried to work up the courage to say something. Perhaps they should come back tomorrow or even the day after, rested and alert. Police might not be expecting us then, and it might be easier.

His mouth opened to speak the words. He eyed Garza, sitting ramrod straight in the seat beside him. His throat constricted.

"There." Garza nodded at the police parking lot. One of the Crown Victoria's was pulling out. "Follow that one."

Moya's mouth closed, and he breathed a sigh of relief. *Gracias a Dios*—thank God.

"You sure that's the right car?" Moya asked starting the engine. He waited for the Crown Victoria to pull from the lot and turn right at the end of the street.

"Get closer."

"Closer?" *Esta mierda de nuevo!*—this shit again, Moya mouthed to himself. "You sure?"

"Closer," Garza said, eyes fixed on the detective car.

"Right, closer."

Moya eased the rental car up behind the Crown Victoria as the acid flared in his gut. He wanted to shout. What the fuck are we doing!

Garza looked at him and nodded, becoming aware of his anxiety for the first time. "Calm yourself."

"I'm trying." Moya said. "It's just that ..."

"That you have never followed the police before?"

"Yes, it seems crazy." Moya added hastily. "Not that *you* are crazy, or that I am afraid." He nodded. "You know I will do as you instruct."

"Yes, you will." Garza nodded. "You worry too much. Think of the police as hunters, a coyote after a jackrabbit. They focus on the jackrabbits, the ones they follow. They do not expect to be the jackrabbit, to be followed. If we are careful, we are safe."

Moya did not feel very safe, but decided it was best to acknowledge Garza's lesson and let it go. "Thank you for explaining."

At the next red signal, they rolled up on the detective car's bumper. Garza looked at his palm and compared the inked numbers there to the license plate and car number. He nodded.

"It's the car."

"Okay, it's the car. Now what?"

"Let him get ahead. Now that we know which car it is, we can follow at a distance."

"Right." Moya nodded. At a distance sounded good, the more distance, the better.

The Crown Victoria made its way through the light traffic to the interstate and took I-75 northbound. After several miles, it exited onto a surface street in northwest Atlanta.

The detective car cruised slowly. The driver seemed as fatigued as Moya. After a few blocks, it pulled into the lot of an all-night convenience store. Randy Travis exited the car, stretched and walked inside.

"Evening, Billy," he said to the short round man behind the counter.

"You mean, morning, don't you?" Billy the night clerk smiled.

Travis glanced up at the clock over the cash register. It showed just after two in the morning.

He nodded. "Right, morning. I lost track."

"Big case?" Billy was a police groupie and kept a police scanner on behind the counter at night. He nodded at it now. "Nothing over the net."

"You won't hear anything on the police bands." Travis shook his head. "Not on this one."

"Big then," Billy pressed, hoping to get a little more information from Travis, the detective who came in for milk and donuts at the end of every shift, morning or night.

"Time will tell." Travis smiled.

"Close-lipped as always," Billy grumbled.

"Goes with the job. You should know that by now." Travis leaned over the counter. "But I'll give you a hint."

"Yeah?" Billy leaned forward, excited, looking around to make sure they were alone, and lowering his voice to a whisper. "What is it?"

"Watch the news tomorrow," Travis said and turned to the back of the store.

"That's it? Watch the news. How am I supposed to know what case it is from that?"

"Oh, you'll know," Travis called over his shoulder.

He walked back to the cooler, yawning all the way, and pulled out a quart of milk, then snagged a bag of powdered doughnuts from a shelf on his way back to the register.

"How do you do it?" Billy shook his head as he rang up the sale. "Eat all that sugar before you go to sleep. I'd be up for two days."

"Nope." Travis shook his head. "Hypermetabolism. I burn it up quick ... sleep like a baby."

"Hyper ... meta ... what?"

"Metabolism. My body works at a higher rate ... burns a lot of energy."

"That doesn't sound healthy."

"It's not. That's why the doughnuts. Gotta give it something to burn."

Billy bagged the donuts and milk and slid the paper sack across the counter to Travis. "Here ya go ..."

Billy looked up, eyes wide. There was a rushing sound, and the door behind Travis chimed as it was flung open. A gunshot's sharp crack reverberated in the small space. A small, red hole appeared in Billy's forehead, freezing the wide-eyed stare on his face as he collapsed to the floor.

Hand at his waist, reaching for his service pistol, Travis whirled to find two men in ski masks pointing guns at his face from a distance of four or five feet.

One, taller than the other shouted. "*¡Hazlo!*"

Travis didn't speak Spanish, but the meaning was clear. Do it!

As he brought the Glock up, two nine-millimeter slugs punched through his sternum. One bored through the right atrium of his heart. The other cut the aorta.

The taller man stepped forward, lowered his pistol, and pulled the trigger. The bullet crashed through the detective's skull, embedding itself in the linoleum floor.

"Get the cash," Garza said.

Moya pulled his eyes from the body of the detective and climbed over the counter, to empty the cash register till. A video monitor beneath the counter showed images of the store interior and the gas pump outside. The blood pooling around the detective on the floor looked black on the screen.

"Should I find the video recorder?" He looked at Garza.

"No. This was a robbery. Let them see the recording to prove it." Garza nodded at Travis' body. "Get his wallet and cell phone."

Moya came back over the counter and stood over the detective. Killing was one thing, but disturbing the bodies after was something else. It was *sacrilegio*—sacrilege. Besides, there was blood everywhere, and he didn't want to ruin his shoes.

He hesitated. Garza stared.

Moya knelt, trying to avoid the blood on the floor. He retrieved the wallet from the detective's back pocket but had to hunt for the cell phone, rolling the body on its side. He pulled it from the front pants pocket with two fingers and held it up for Garza to see.

"Good." Garza nodded. "Now we go."

Outside they ran to the rear of the store where they'd left the rental car. After driving a block, they pulled off the ski masks.

"Where to? Back to Sillman's building?"

Esteban Moya wanted to get as far from Alejandro Garza as he could. He knew that wasn't in the cards. They had just murdered a cop. He clung to the wheel to disguise the trembling in his hands.

Fuck! A cop! Dead and he killed him, or at least helped.

Moya was no stranger to murder, but shooting down a

police officer was far different from slitting the throat of a rat informant. He stared ahead wondering what else Garza had in store for them. How long it would be before other detectives tracked him down and threw him in prison for the rest of his life, or killed him outright, claiming that he resisted arrest. He decided he would not resist when they came for him, but he was not sure that would matter.

Until they pulled up to the rear of the convenience store, Moya did not understand what plan Garza had devised. He simply told him to put on the ski mask, have his gun in his hand and do exactly as instructed.

The stakeout of the senator's building had implied one thing. Sillman was their target, but killing a cop exposed them to a new world of dangers. This wasn't Mexico! Garza had said it himself. The police here did not work with the cartels.

For Moya, the police represented the enemy, but they were also sacred and untouchable. Extreme anger or stupidity might result in the murder of a cop, but the price for such rash action was always high, too high for Moya's taste.

He realized this was what Garza had talked to Elizondo about on the phone, why he had started to question their assignment. Garza understood the risk as well, but the loss of the shipment enraged Elizondo beyond reason. He ordered them to kill the cop. End of story. Bebé ordered it, and Garza would get it done.

Fuck! Moya's brain screamed the word. He killed a cop! Fuck!

A ton of shit was about to fall on their heads. Moya knew his head and his dumb ass that would be at ground zero when it fell.

FIFTY-SEVEN

Howl

Captain Clarence Pointer's number vibrated and popped up on the Sole's phone. "What's up, Cap?"

"Where are you, Sole?"

"Just getting on the chopper to head back to Atlanta."

"Get here quick." Pointer's voice sounded strained, the words clipped off and short.

"What's wrong? Snag with Sillman? I figured he might not go quietly. Doesn't matter though." The door swung shut on the State Patrol helicopter, and Sole put a hand to his ear to block out the noise of the engines starting. "Relax. We got him. That boatload of cocaine will trump any legal maneuvering his lawyers might try."

"It's not Sillman. It's your partner."

"Travis? What's wrong with Travis?"

Pointer paused before saying the words. "He's dead."

"He's ..." Stunned, Sole's voice trailed off. Several seconds passed before he spoke, his voice hard now. He wanted details without the bullshit. "What happened ... exactly as it went down?"

"Looks like bad luck. Stopped at a convenience store on the way home after locking up Sillman. Got caught up in a robbery. Looks like they walked in on him, took him by surprise. It's all on the store video. Shot Travis and the store clerk. Travis went for his service weapon but not in time. One perp fired twice ... hit him in the chest ... it was probably fatal but didn't matter. The second walked over and put one in his head. Travis never had a chance."

"Any ID on the perps?"

"Negative. Usual ... ski masks, dark clothes, gloves. They didn't want to be recognized."

"I'll be there in a couple of hours." Sole ended the call and looked at the pilot. "Get this bird in the air."

Esteban Moya cleared his throat and asked, "So ... back to the Sillman building, right?"

"Quiet." Garza studied the phone they'd taken from the dead detective.

He scrolled through the screens for a few minutes then took out his own and typed a number from the recent call list on the detective's phone into a reverse number search website. A minute later, he entered a credit card number. It took another minute for the report to load onto the screen.

"Go to this address." He turned the phone for Moya to see the location the reverse number search showed.

"Why? What's there?"

"Go."

Moya did not repeat the question. The drive to the northeast suburban neighborhood took twenty minutes.

Lights off, Moya let the rental car slow to a stop a block away from the address. Garza was out of the car, moving like a cat through the darkness before Moya had cut the engine. He followed, heart pounding so hard in his chest he thought it might wake the people sleeping behind the closed windows of the homes lining the street.

Garza stopped in front of one house, looked at the number on his phone and nodded. "Here."

He followed Garza, feet swishing through the dewy front yard grass. It was a bad dream that just kept getting worse, and Moya was trapped in it.

Garza scanned every window they passed. At the back door, he stooped and examined it from top to bottom, trying the knob to make sure it wasn't unlocked. Then he reached into a pocket and retrieved a key.

"You have a key?" Moya whispered, incredulous.

"A special key."

It took less than a minute. Garza forced the bump key's pointed triangular teeth and deep grooves all the way into the lock then dragged it out, bumping it up and down to disengage the locking pins as he turned the lock.

Moya was astounded when the lock turned in the cylinder. Garza eased the door open a half inch, feeling with his fingers and a pocket knife around the edges for entry alarm sensors. Satisfied there were none, he pushed the door open and stepped inside.

Shit. Moya had hoped that alarm sirens would sound and send them running back to the rental car. Garza motioned him to follow, and he stepped over the threshold knowing that his world was about to change again.

Bill Lance gave Sole a ride from the State Patrol landing pad at the Fulton County Airport. When they arrived at the convenience store, the parking lot and building swarmed with investigators and evidence technicians.

Captain Pointer met them outside. "You might not want to go in," he warned Sole. "I know how close you and Travis are. It's not a good idea, John."

Sole motioned to the store's interior where a sheet covered a form lying on the floor in front of the counter. "I want to see."

"Yeah, I figured you would anyway," Pointer said, resigned. "I'll show you, but you're not working this one."

"Show me."

Inside, Pointer walked him through the crime scene and what the investigators had pieced together so far. It wasn't much.

Kneeling beside the body of his partner, Sole pulled the sheet back from his face. It was expressionless. Not at peace, not at rest, not angry. Just dead. The neat, nine-millimeter hole in the side of his forehead was offset by a gaping, half-dollar-sized chunk of skull blown out of the back of his head.

Sole's fist clenched the sheet. He sucked air in long deep breaths, fighting back the anger. Pointer and Lance and the other investigators in the building waited, letting him process what had happened.

"You say he walked in on the robbery?" Sole raised his eyes to Pointer.

"They walked in on him." Pointer nodded at the counter. "Looks like he was buying donuts and milk. They came in behind, and ... well, you see what happened."

"I see." Sole nodded. "The clerk?"

"Behind the counter on the floor. They shot him first ... took out Travis as he turned going for his weapon."

"Empty the till?"

"Everything," Pointer said. "Took Travis' wallet too."

"Take the clerk's wallet?"

"No. That is strange. Maybe they didn't have time." Pointer shook his head slowly. His eyes narrowed in concern. "Travis' phone is missing too but not the clerk's. Do you think they targeted Travis and made it look like a robbery to cover their tracks?"

Sole was on his feet, calling to Bill Lance as he ran to the car. "Take me to my house!"

Behind him, Captain Pointer was on the radio, ordering units dispatched to the Sole residence in northeast Atlanta.

Three marked police units lined the curb as Bill Lance pulled into the driveway. A uniform patrol sergeant came from inside to stop Sole in the yard. He put his hands out and tried to prevent him from entering.

"You shouldn't go inside."

Sole pushed him aside and ran into the house.

"How bad?" Bill Lance asked running with the sergeant to follow Sole.

"Bad." The sergeant shook his head. "Bad as I ever saw."

They caught up with him in the back hallway.

"Noooo!"

It was a howl, primal and agonized. Its unfathomable grief echoed through the house, carrying the terrible pain out into the night.

FIFTY-EIGHT

Promotion

Enough was enough. Esteban Moya drove through the early morning Atlanta traffic with one desire in his heart—to get away from the monster seated beside him.

"Where to now?" he asked, working hard to keep the exasperation out of his voice.

"Ortega's office," Garza said.

"He won't be there this early."

Garza pulled out his phone and punched a number on speed dial. Someone answered it immediately. "It's done. Meet us," Garza said without any other preliminaries.

He shoved the phone back into his pocket, looked at Moya and said, "He'll be there."

Yeah, he'll be there, Moya thought. El Toro was probably shitting himself about now, but he would be there as ordered.

At least the night's work was done. Garza would deliver whatever final message Bebé Elizondo had for them. Then, they could put him on a plane back to Mexico, and Esteban

Moya could try to forget everything he'd seen and done in the last forty-eight hours.

It wouldn't be easy. Killing Bettis was one thing. He was stupid and arrogant. The death of the cop was rash. Revenge was one thing, but killing cops in America would only lead to more trouble.

As for the regrets he had about the murder of the store clerk, he wisely kept them to himself. The clerk was collateral damage. Wasn't that what the military called it when innocents got their asses blown away because they were too close to the shit? The clerk's ass was definitely blown away —collateral damage.

Then there was the house—more collateral damage. The wife and children killed because they were there and for no other reason. Moya watched horrified as Garza slit the throats of the children, first the daughter then the son. He was not squeamish, but murdering children in their sleep had taken him deeper than he had ever been into the darkness of the life he had chosen.

Some small noise must have awakened the wife because she met them in the hallway, a pistol in her hand, but Garza was too quick. She crumpled to the floor the blood pooling around her dark hair, two holes in her pretty head, never knowing the fate of her children. Moya told himself it was kinder for her to go that way.

They went through the house looking for the asshole detective who had caused all the problems with Sillman. He was the one they wanted, the one who should be dead. Moya told himself that If the detective had been there, his wife and kids would be alive, but he knew it wasn't true. They would all be dead. That was Garza's plan.

But it hadn't worked out. High and mighty Alejandro Garza fucked up on that one, although Moya had no intention of saying so. They took the time to rummage through belongings, take a few things to make the murders look like part of a home invasion, but Moya had no belief the ruse would fool anyone.

The police were not stupid, and this was not Mexico. They would piece the puzzle together soon and realize that all the murders were related. Then they would come after the killers with everything they had. He and Ortega would be dodging the police, trying to stay out of jail while Garza drank tequila and ate frijoles, or whatever the hell they ate in Mexico, protected by the *Policía Estatal*.

The whole thing was bullshit, but there was nothing to do about it now. They had to get Garza on that plane and away from them before he caused more damage.

He pulled into the parking lot at *Taqueria Ortega* and drove to the rear. As Garza had promised, they found Bautista Ortega's car by the back door. Inside, El Toro sat in his usual position behind his desk in the tiny office.

"How did it go?" Ortega looked up and smiled, a bead of sweat trickling down the side of his face. He placed his damp palms down flat on the top of his desk as if to steady himself.

"We're almost done," Garza replied, taking a seat in a chair across from the desk.

"Good." Ortega forced his best smile across his face. It was a poor effort. He glanced at Moya. "And I trust my man, Esteban, has been of good use to you."

"He has." Garza nodded.

"Excellent." A look of relief spread across Ortega's face, and his shoulders relaxed. "I always want to be of service to Bebé ... and you, of course."

"Of course." Garza's eyes glittered with an almost mirthful twinkle that was out of character.

Sole Survivor

"So, what is next?" Ortega forced the smile wider. "You mentioned the mission is nearly completed. What else remains to make matters satisfactory for Bebé?"

"There is one thing."

It happened so smoothly, so quickly, it was as if Garza reached for a pack of cigarettes in his pocket. The pistol appeared in his hand, pointing into Ortega's face from a distance of four feet. It jumped in his hand, barking loudly five times.

Ortega was dead before the first bullet that crashed through his skull had embedded itself in the wall behind. Garza emptied the remaining rounds from the gun into his face, making a point. Ortega was finished. He had failed Bebé Elizondo, and failure has a steep price.

Garza turned to Moya, frozen in the chair beside him, mouth agape eyes wide. His head moved side to side, his mouth opening and closing like a fish out of water, gasping for air. He was next. His words came in a squeak. "No … no …"

"Relax." Garza lowered the pistol and returned it to his pocket. "Bebé has promoted you."

"Promo …" Moya blinked, trying to keep from collapsing and falling out of the chair.

"Yes, promoted. You have performed well. Bebé is pleased."

"I … I'm thankful that …" Moya shook his head to clear away the terror.

"I am leaving today. You will clean up this mess," Garza continued, jerking his head at the gore that had been El Toro's face. "Then you have another assignment."

"Another?" Moya paled.

"Yes. There are two others, but Bebé has instructed me to return to Mexico. You will see to these others."

"Me? But I am not expert in these things."

"You will handle them." Garza's tone made it final.

"I will do my best," Moya said. There was no point in arguing. He would handle them or Garza would be back with another assignment that included him.

"After," Garza continued. "Business will return to normal, and you will be Bebé's representative here." He paused and looked into Moya's eyes. "You want this promotion, do you not?"

"Yes, of course. Absolutely." Hell no, he did not want the promotion, his mind screamed while his head bobbed up and down emphatically. "Please thank Bebé for me

"Good. Now here is what you must do next."

FIFTY-NINE

There Were No Ghosts

The first funeral was quiet.

In keeping with Jewish tradition, they buried Shaina Ruth Berman Sole and her children within two days after their murders. Captain Pointer stepped in for Sole and had a word with the Medical Examiner to expedite the recovery of evidence from the bodies. Everyone knew how they had died. Prolonging things would not make the hunt for their killers any easier and would only add to the family's grief.

Saul Berman's rabbi arranged the service at their synagogue. As with all Jewish funerals, the emphasis was on simplicity. Rich or poor, all Jews are buried in the same way. Wealth and position in life have no influence on the standing of a Jew who leaves this world. In death comes equality.

Sole was invited to stand in the Minyan, the group of males that recite the mourner's Qaddish and other prayers. He declined, remaining seated during the service, his shoulders shaking in silence as he wept.

Saul Berman stood with the others, supported on either

side by two friends. At one point he was about to collapse, and they seated him in a chair while the prayers continued.

The three bodies were interred side by side. There was no marker. Jewish tradition dictated that headstones would be placed on the graves after a year of mourning.

At the Berman home, friends came to pay their respects throughout the afternoon. Saul and Naomi sat nodding, receiving the visitors, numb to what they said.

John Sole remained alone on the back porch. Captain Pointer and other detectives and officers he had known for years attended the service, then came to pay their respects to him on the porch.

Blank-eyed, he stared at each as they spoke their words of condolence. Why were they here? The words meant nothing. They changed nothing. They only reminded him of why they were there, and he wept more.

When the last mourners departed, and they sat alone in the Berman home, Sole came into the house to sit across from them. Face wet with his tears, he spoke.

"It's my fault." He forced the words out in a hoarse whisper.

Naomi shook her head. Saul Berman regarded his son-in-law with a puzzled look as if he had spoken in a foreign language.

"Your fault?" Saul said. He shook his head. "No. Don't say that."

"If I had been there ..." Sole clenched his eyes shut for a moment to stop the tears, then relented and let them pour down his face. "If I had been there ..."

"John, no. Don't do that. Stop blaming ..." Saul began.

"No! If I had never been a police officer ..." Sole shook his head.

If I had never married Shaye, he thought, or had children. Or better, if I had never come back from Iraq or had just gone to prison for stealing that car, none of this would have happened. They would be alive. The fierce look in his eyes reflected the rage he felt for himself.

"It is my fault, and I am sorry for what I have done to your daughter and grandchildren. I don't have the words to say how sorry." He was weeping now, tears falling to the floor. "Forgive me. Please forgive me."

Saul Berman rose and placed a hand on his shoulder. "There is nothing to forgive. You have been a son to us. This loss, the grief and pain, is something we all share."

"I don't understand why this happened," Naomi said, her eyes looking deep into his. "But I know that you did not do it. There is evil in the world. I've seen it. It is real. The person who took them from us is evil." She shook her head. "You are not evil, John. You are not responsible for what has happened to our family."

Sole looked into their eyes, wanting to accept their words, but the truth burned in his heart. He was responsible. Someone else may have held the knife and gun, but it was his arrogance, his failure, that had caused their deaths.

He had to be there when they took the cartel's boatload of cocaine. Why? Because his ego demanded it? It was a game. He even tossed a coin with Travis for the privilege. He played the game with fire and put everyone at risk—everyone except himself. Shaye and the children had paid the price for his foolish arrogance.

"Stay with us tonight," Saul said.

"No." Sole shook his head, rising from the chair. "I've caused too much pain here."

Walking out into the night, he took the first steps into his exile.

The second funeral was not quiet.

They buried Detective Charles Randall Travis with full police honors. The family held the services at the Baptist Church he attended as a youth. Every seat was filled. When there was no more space for family and friends, police officers present gave up their seats to stand and line the walls in blue. John Sole sat with Travis' mother.

After the prayers, the sermon, the eulogies, the final hymn and Amen, they took Travis' body to the cemetery. More than a hundred police and private vehicles escorted the hearse.

The honor guard waited for them. Men dressed in blue wearing white gloves served as the final pallbearers to accompany the body to the gravesite. After a few more words by the pastor, a three-volley rifle salute echoed off the gravestones. The department bugler played taps. An American flag was folded and handed to Mrs. Travis by Captain Pointer along with the sympathy and thanks of the department and the grateful citizens of Georgia.

It was over. In the space of a week, John Sole had buried his wife and children, and now his partner and friend. Travis had become another victim of his arrogance.

He hugged Mrs. Travis, declining the offer to come by her home for supper that evening. With a final kiss on her forehead, he left, promising to call and knowing he wouldn't.

The house was quiet. It had never occurred to him before how quiet it was, how quiet death could be.

With his back against the wall, he slumped to the floor in the hallway where Shaye had fallen, attempting to protect their family. He listened, not believing in ghosts, but wanting to believe, desperate to feel their presence, to be haunted by them, to hear the soft whispers of their memories around him. The ghosts remained silent.

No tears fell now. He had cried all of his tears. Only the grief-filled emptiness of life without Shaye and the children remained—a life that extended excruciatingly into the future until it ended one day, or someone ended it for him.

He sat like that for the rest of the night, dozing a few minutes, then waking with a start to stare around, wondering where he was and why. Then he remembered, and the pain pierced again, a flaming sword twisting and turning in his heart.

He listened to the sounds of the house. A small noise there could have been Bobby in his room turning in his bed. A rustle down the hall might be Samantha getting ready for school. The sighing of the wind outside was Shaye, calling to him, waiting in their bed for him to come to her.

They were just noises. There were no ghosts, to visit and bring solace.

The morning broke, and a gray light filtered into the house. He rose and left through the front door for the last time, locking it behind him, taking only his memories.

SIXTY

Lines and Sides

"You can't hide, you know. They will find you here."

Luis Acero froze. The gruff voice of the man who seated himself on the stool beside him was unforgettable.

The bartender wandered over and looked at the man without speaking.

"Gimme a beer."

"What kind?" The bartender threw a bar towel over his shoulder, annoyed that he was forced to speak to the newcomer.

"The kind with alcohol. You pick it."

The bartender grunted and pulled a longneck from the well with a fat red hand. He thumped a **PBR** down and shuffled away.

"How ya doin' Luis?" Sole lifted the bottle, turned it up, and downed half.

"You …" Acero's mouth hung open.

"Yeah, me." Sole nodded and turned the bottle up again finished it off and thumped the bottle on the counter to get the bartender's attention. "Another."

"How did ..."

"How'd I find you?" Sole swiveled on the stool to face Acero. "That's what I do, Luis ... find criminals." He smiled. "Like you."

"Fuck you." Luis picked up the glass in front of him, trying to hide the tremble in his hand. He raised it for the bartender who ambled over, poured a shot of Jack in the glass, put another beer in front of Sole, and returned to the end of the bar where an episode of Oprah blared from the wall-mounted television.

"You some badass detective," Luis said after taking a large gulp of whiskey. "You so badass, your partner's dead, and your ..." He clamped his mouth shut, afraid he had gone too far with this man.

Sole nodded and absorbed the insult because it was true. It was the same thing he told himself a thousand times a day since the funerals.

"Fair enough," he said, turning the beer bottle up again. "Thing is, Luis. You have a problem."

"Yeah? What?"

"They will figure out who the rat is, if they haven't already, and they will come after you. They will find you. That's why you're hiding out isn't it?"

"Just keepin' low for a while."

"Bullshit. We both know that's not true." Sole shrugged. "Thing is, there is no place you can hide, nowhere to run where they won't find you. I found you. If I can find you, they will too. It's just a matter of time."

"The fuck you think I am ... stupid? Yeah, they after me. That's why I ..."

"What?" Sole smiled. "I gotta say, honestly, Luis, you're not very good at it. Left that shitty apartment, found another dive, staying off the street, drinking ..." Sole looked around the bar's shabby interior. "Drinking in a shithole like this." He shook his head. "That doesn't make you safe."

"Fuck you. I ain't got to listen to you no more."

"True enough. You don't, and for the record, I won't tell anyone where you are." Sole nodded and sipped his beer. "But do you think they don't have eyes? You think the word isn't out along with a big reward to the one who finds you and points a finger in your direction?"

Sole shook his head. "You definitely have a problem." He motioned with the bottle to the door and the street beyond. "They're out there, eager to be the one to cash in, and you don't know who they are. Every pair of eyes you pass might be the one who tells them they spotted you." Sole nodded at the bartender. "Maybe it's him."

Luis, head swiveled to eye the bartender, leaning his belly on the bar top watching Oprah.

"Or, it could be the drunk sitting at the end of the bar who was here when you came in and then left without speaking." Sole smiled. "See what I mean. It could be anyone. Who you can trust? That's the big question. Who?"

"You sayin' I should trust you?" Luis smirked. "You the reason I can't show my face."

"I'm saying I'm the only one you can trust. I can help you, and you can help me."

"What the fuck kind of help you want from me?" Luis turned to face him. "And what makes you think I would help you. Helping you is dangerous ... people end up dead helping you." He shook his head. "Not me. I ain't gonna end up dead to help no fucking cop."

"You'll be dead, anyway. Seems the only chance you have is to help me get to them first." He smiled again. "You might say I'm your salvation."

"What the fuck you talkin' about? Salvation. That's just

more of your bullshit. You sayin' arresting them is gonna keep them off my ass." Luis shook his head. "No way. There's too many of them. They just send someone else. What you say might be true enough. I might be a dead man walkin', but I ain't in no hurry to make it happen quicker."

"Arrest?" Sole shook his head. "I didn't use that word."

"What's that mean?" Luis' eyes narrowed. "You mean …" He shook his head. "You full of shit, that's what you are … playin' me like always."

"Am I? They murdered my wife and children … killed my friend. What would you do in my position? Arrest them?"

"So what you gonna do?"

"Does it matter?" Sole shrugged. "I'll make it so they won't be after you. They'll be looking for me." He nodded. "They'll come for me, and I'll be waiting."

Luis stared down, turning the glass on the bar between his nervous fingers. Minutes passed as he considered Sole's proposal.

They would come for him, probably were already looking for him. The asshole detective was right. It didn't matter where he went; they would find him.

"What you want to hear?" Luis asked without looking up.

"Who did it?"

"Who you think?"

"I want to hear it. Who was there at the store where they killed my partner? Who was in my house when …" His words trailed off.

"Word on the street is Moya did it … him and some bad dude from Mexico."

"How certain is the word on the street?"

"Real certain. Heard about it before I decided it was best to lay low. He's in charge now."

"What do you mean? In charge?"

"Ortega's gone."

"Gone where?"

"Who the fuck knows, man? Gone … chopped up in a hundred pieces and dumped in the Chattahoochee. When they say gone, that's what they mean."

"So Ortega's gone, and Moya took over."

"Right. That means he was part of it. They were cleaning up the garbage. Ortega … the white dude, Bettis … your partner … you, except you weren't there." He nodded. "But Moya was there."

"Who was behind it? Who gave him the order?"

"Who you think? That cartel in Mexico. They don't play around. That's why they sent their man. Some big player. Everyone shittin' themselves when he showed up."

Sole sat without speaking, staring at the wall across the bar. Then, swallowing the last of the beer, he reached in his pocket and laid a roll of cash on the bar.

"Take this. Should be enough for a bus ticket and a room in another city for a couple of weeks."

Luis touched the roll and looked up, confused. "Why you doin' this?"

"Let's just say, we're connected now, you and me." Sole stood. "You still have the phone?"

"Yeah."

"Keep it turned on. Stay where I can reach you. I'll contact you when it's safe to come back."

"Shit. Ain't never gonna be safe. Like you say, they ain't nowhere to go that they won't find me."

Sole was gone, the door to the bar swinging open and closing again before Luis finished speaking.

The visitation room at the United States Penitentiary on McDonough Boulevard in Atlanta was used by families and lawyers to meet with inmates. Sole had flashed his badge and said he needed to confirm some details in an inmate's statement.

The door opened and a corrections officer brought the old man in. Sole nodded, and the cuffs were removed. The officer closed the door and left them alone.

"How are they treating you, Mr. Sams?"

"Not bad." The old man reached for his shirt pocket. "Call me Tully. Mind if I smoke?"

Sole shook his head and leaned back watching the old shrimper. He was handling things well. "You don't seem too bothered about being locked up."

Sams shrugged. "Nothing to do about it. They got me dead to rights. Besides …" He took a long drag on his cigarette, turned his head up and exhaled a plume of smoke toward the ceiling. "I'm too old to worry about what they will do with my ass. It's just me now. My wife, Sara Jane, passed on from the breast cancer a while back. Figure whatever happens it can't be worse than trying to get on without her." He smiled. "Might even speed things up so I can see her old face again."

Sams paused looking up, musing. "Do you suppose her face will be old like mine, or is she gonna be changed … young like she was when we first married." He slammed a hand down on the table. "Damn she was a fine pretty woman."

"I can't say," Sole said. "I suppose you'll be the same, old or young, whichever it is. You'll be together though, and that's something."

"You're damn right." Sams' eyes narrowed. "You're the one aren't you? The one that was out there with the Coast Guard when they picked up my boat. Saw it on the news. Another cop, your partner, they killed him and then your …" He shook his head. "Sorry. That's a terrible thing that happened." Sams looked into Sole's eyes. "I wouldn't never been a party to that if I'd known what they were like … what they would do."

"I don't blame you, Tully."

"Good." A look of relief flooded over the old man's face. "So what can I do for you?"

"Just a few questions."

"Shoot."

"Who was Sillman working with?"

"Don't know exactly. Mexicans … a cartel he called them … lots of money though. Spared no expense in fixing up the Sara Jane."

"He never mentioned a name?"

"No." Sams shook his head and then nodded. "But I do remember one of the crew they gave me, he mentioned a name when I asked who they worked for. They come from the fishery out on the Pacific down around Mexico."

"What was the name?"

"It was funny … not really a name. They called him Baby."

"Baby?"

"Yeah, but they didn't say it like that. More like Bay-bay."

"Any last name?"

"No, none I caught. Just Bay-bay."

"And the crewmen he supplied. They were real seamen?"

"Yeah. Hermie and Paco at least ... a pleasure to have on board. The other two not so much."

"Other two? I thought there was only one other when we stopped your boat."

"There was that night. Julio was the one in the galley with all the GPS gear. The first trip out though, there was another. He ramrodded things, but he didn't show the second time out."

"What was his name?"

"Something or other Moya?"

"Moya?" Sole's back straightened in the plastic chair. "Esteban Moya?"

"Yeah, that's it," Sams said nodding.

"So you're saying that this Moya was there the first trip out, but on the second, the night we picked you up, he was not."

"Right. That mean something?" Sams asked.

"It might," Sole replied, standing. "I think that about wraps things up." He turned for the door to call the guards then stopped and faced the old man. "I hope things work out for you, Tully. You got pulled into a bad deal. I'll put a good word in for you, but I'm not sure that will mean much."

"I appreciate it." Tully Sams shrugged. "Like I said, either way, maybe things will get me back to my Sara Jane sooner."

"I hope so for your sake." Sole had come to understand the endless, empty pain of loss and loneliness. "Take care of yourself, Tully."

James Jadyn Sillman was not so philosophical about his imprisonment. He was in tears when they escorted him into the room.

Sillman no longer had penthouse views of the Atlanta skyline. Like Tully Sams, he was spending most of his time in a six-foot by nine-foot solitary confinement cell.

His attorney was with him when he walked into the small, gray block-walled room. Shackled hand and foot, he took a seat at the metal table in the center of the room.

The correction officer removed the handcuffs, nodded at Sole and left the room. Sillman rubbed his wrists before lifting his head to stare red-eyed at Sole.

His attorney spoke first. "We have accepted this meeting as a courtesy, Detective, but as we said, Senator Sillman has nothing to add to his previous statements."

"Fair enough." Sole leaned back in the metal chair, looking at the top of Sillman's slumped head, waiting for him to raise his eyes.

A minute passed before Sillman gathered the courage to meet Sole's gaze. "I ... I know you."

"Yes, Senator, that's right. We met twice in your penthouse."

"I'm sorry about what happened to your ..."

The lawyer leaned forward and whispered into Sillman's ear then turned and spoke to Sole. "Senator Sillman is sorry to meet you like this. He has been wrongly accused and plans to vindicate himself fully at trial."

"I have no doubt he will try ... or you will." Sole smiled. "Either way, I'm not here for an apology. I'm here to offer assistance ... the chance for the senator to help himself."

"How so?" the attorney's fox-like eyes narrowed.

"I need information. I believe the senator has it."

"What sort of information?"

"For the sake of argument, counselor, let's stipulate that as far as this conversation is concerned, your client had no intent to break the law." Sole shrugged. "Someone tricked him ... fooled him into loading cocaine onto one of his boats."

"The senator is not a fool, and your implication is offensive, but ..." The lawyer nodded. "But, for the sake of this conversation, as you say, let's say someone loaded cocaine onto one of his trawlers. He has many such vessels. Shrimp harvesting is his business. So if someone loaded cocaine onto one of his boats ... without his knowledge ... what is it you want him to help you with?"

"Simple. Tell me who."

"Who?"

"Yes. Who ... *tricked* ... the senator and loaded cocaine onto his boat?"

"As I said, if it happened, it happened with no foreknowledge by the senator."

"Right." Sole leaned forward, elbows on the small steel table until his face was inches from the lawyer's. "Let's stop playing games, counselor. The senator can tell me who loaded the cocaine onto his boat ... without his knowledge, of course."

"Yes, well ..." The lawyer pursed his lips and leaned away from the detective. "And what would you do with that information ... if the senator had a name to give you?"

"Use it to find that person."

"And then?"

"I would put in a good word with the DA and Federal prosecutor... tell them it is possible, at least, they duped the senator, that he was unaware of the scope of what was happening on his trawler." Sole shrugged. "It might not exonerate him, but being duped into a crime is far different from planning and executing one." Sole smiled before adding, "Definitely different from planning a crime to save the family business from bankruptcy and secure millions for himself."

He sent the message. They had the senator dead to rights, thanks to the work Travis and Bill Lance had done. An annoyed look in the lawyer's eyes told him the message was received, and Sillman's legal team understood their client was in deep legal shit.

"A moment, please while I confer with my client." The attorney turned to the senator, leaning in to whisper.

Sillman gave him no time to confer. Fear oozed from his pores. He shook his head and whispered in a croaking terror-filled whisper. "No."

The lawyer leaned closer and whispered again.

"No," Sillman repeated, shaking his head side to side sending tears coursing down his cheeks. "No. You don't understand what they'll do."

"Fine." Sole rose and nodded at the door where the corrections officer watched through the glass pane. "You think you're safe here as long as you keep your mouth shut." Sole shook his head as he walked to the door. "You're not."

The steel door clanged shut. Senator Sillman sat sobbing at the table.

It was a day to make the rounds, and he had one more stop to make things official.

Clarence Pointer looked up as Sole walked into his office. "Hello, John. I didn't expect to see you back so soon."

"I'm not." Sole took a seat across from the Major Crimes Unit commander.

"No?" Pointer lowered the case file in his hands and peered at Sole over his glasses. "Seems like you've been back all day. Got word you checked in on Sams and Sillman."

"I did." Sole nodded.

"And?" Pointer wanted a more specific explanation.

"And they didn't say much," Sole said.

"Understandable." Pointer nodded, but he would not be pushed off so easily. "So, what *did* they say?"

"Sams talked about seeing his wife again in the near future."

"He really thinks he'll be out that soon?"

"No, he's planning on dying in prison … the sooner, the better to hear him talk. His wife, Sara Jane, passed away from cancer a while back."

"Oh, sorry." Pointer's brow wrinkled in curiosity. "Sara Jane? Wasn't that the name of …"

"Yeah. He named the trawler after his wife. The cocaine, the money, meant nothing to him. It was about carrying on without his wife. Being out on the water helped him do that."

Pointer nodded. "And Sillman?"

"He was lawyered up … not talking."

"Doesn't sound like you learned anything new."

"Like I said. Not much." But enough, he thought.

Sole did not mention his meeting with Luis Acero.

"Okay. Well, you've made your report. I appreciate it. Now take some time off. You're not ready to come back. You've had a terrible loss." Pointer frowned, embarrassed, knowing that no one understood better than John Sole the loss he had suffered. "I mean, just take the time to heal, John. Let the pain subside awhile. We'll cover things here."

"That's the reason I came to see you, Cap." Sole removed his service weapon and badge from his waist and laid them on Pointer's desk. "I am taking some time off. I won't be back."

"That's not what I meant." Pointer leaned back in his chair. "You sure about this, John? You're a cop, a damned fine one. Don't do something that will ruin your life."

"Too late for that, Cap. It's already done."

Pointer's eyes narrowed, wrinkling his brow. "You're not going to do something ... dangerous, are you?"

"I'll be fine," Sole replied meeting Pointer's gaze.

"That's not what I asked." Pointer sighed and leaned forward. "John, we walk a line. We stay on the right side of it. You can't cross that line. Remember the side you're on."

"I don't see lines anymore, Cap." Sole stood and turned to the door. "I don't have a side."

"John, let me set up some counseling for you ... get you some help to deal with things."

"I'll be fine."

John Sole turned and left the building and the life that had been his for almost two decades. He did not look back.

SIXTY-ONE

Sole Survivor

The key rattled in the lock. Esteban Moya turned the bolt, pulled open the rear steel security door at *Taqueria Ortega* and entered. The shop had been closed for several hours, floors mopped, food prepped for the next day and employees gone home.

There had been little discussion about his takeover of the business. The employees knew such talk was unhealthy. Besides, Moya had given them all a pay increase as a sign of goodwill, saying that El Toro had been underpaying them for years. The staff smiled and thanked the new *patrón*, grateful to have someone looking out for their best interests.

As for the legal transfer of the business, Elizondo provided documents with Ortega's signature. Although Ortega never signed the papers, no one questioned the perfect counterfeits. Signed and notarized by an attorney, they transferred ownership to Moya with no inheritance or distribution provided for Ortega's family.

That matter settled, Moya settled in to become the suspected but unproven drug lord of Atlanta with tendril-like operations extending throughout the Southeast and up the east coast. Calm settled in over the city's drug trade as he prepared to complete the assignment Garza had given him.

There were two others on the list to be eliminated. Like it or not, Moya knew he had to take care of it. Bebé's patience would end at some point, and he did not want his name added to the list.

Luis Acero was in hiding, and the detective had disappeared from the police department and not returned to the house where they had murdered his family. Moya had his people scouring the city to find them, but the waiting was making him a nervous wreck.

Moya flipped the light switch to the right of the door. The bright overhead fluorescents made him squint as he walked to the small office that was now his. He pushed the door open and froze.

Maria Valdes, the night manager who had closed that evening and would have been the last to leave, sat behind his desk. Eyes wide, hands and mouth bound with duct tape, she stared at Moya.

Her eyes cut to the left. Moya turned to follow her stare, then crumpled to the floor. His head throbbed. Lightning flashed through his brain. The blue steel of the pistol had opened a gash over his right eye.

Stunned, he squinted up through the blood flowing into his eyes and mumbled, "What …"

The man standing over him wore black gloves and a ski mask. He knelt and put a knee on his chest, wrapping Moya's feet and hands together with the same roll of duct tape he had used on Maria.

As Moya lay helpless on the floor, the man in the ski mask lifted Maria from the chair, hefting her over his shoulder. She whimpered through the duct tape as he carried her helpless through the back of the building to a storage closet.

After lowering her to the floor in the closet, he raised a single finger to his lips telling her to remain silent.

"*Silencio. No te haré daño. Quédate aquí. No hagas sonido.*" Silence. I won't hurt you. Stay here. Make no sound.

Maria Valdes nodded, eyes wide but slightly less frightened. The door closed, leaving her in the dark.

She listened to his footsteps recede toward the office and forced herself to remain silent. The gringo spoke with an accent, but his voice was not threatening. Perhaps, he spoke honestly and would not harm her. His words and voice sounded truthful, but who could ever tell. She prayed to the Virgin of Guadalupe to save her.

The man in the ski mask returned to the office to find Esteban Moya trying to scramble along the floor like an inchworm, working his way toward the door. He laughed and stood in the doorway, blocking his path. Moya stopped, rolled on his back, and looked up at his captor. He panted from the exertion of squirming along the floor.

"Who the fuck you think you are? Do you know who I am?"

"I do." The man nodded, his eyes alive and intent behind the black ski mask.

"You're a dead man!" Moya sputtered.

"Eventually," the masked man said in a matter-of-fact tone.

He reached down and jerked the bound man up by the shoulders. Moya kicked as the man dragged him to the chair behind the desk, and shoved him down into it. He pulled the front of Moya's shirt up, wiping his face with it to clear the blood from his eyes.

Turning away, he pulled the ski mask from his head and

sat in a chair across from the desk. It was the chair Garza had occupied on the night of Ortega's murder.

Moya's eyes widened. "You!"

"Me," John Sole agreed, nodding.

"You ... you'll go to prison for this!"

"That's a possibility, but don't worry about me." Sole smiled. "You should worry about what is going to happen to you."

"What? You think you can frighten me with your threats like that woman." Moya grimaced in defiance, shaking his head, his damp hair swinging across his forehead. "That's not so easy. I'm no wetback. You can't force me to say anything. It's the law!"

"Is that a fact?" Sole pointed the pistol at Moya.

"Bullshit! You're a cop ... just trying to scare the shit out of me!"

"Is it working?"

"Fuck no. Who you think you're dealing ..."

The pistol roared. Moya grunted and sank back into the leather chair.

Then he shrieked. "You shot me! You fucking shot me!" He looked down at the blood streaming down his left arm. "I'll have you in prison for that!"

"Had to get your attention." Sole's voice was mild as if they were chatting about the weather. "Do I have it?"

"Fuck you!"

"I'll take that as a yes." Sole lowered the pistol. "Who was there?"

"Where?"

Sole raised the pistol, pointing it at Moya's right arm. "That night."

"Which night?"

There was no escape now for Moya. Luis Acero had

pointed the finger at him as one of the killers, and Tully Sams confirmed Moya was not on the Sara Jane as expected the night of the murders.

The pistol roared again. Moya shrieked louder. More blood dripped to the floor.

"You're fucking crazy, man!"

"Don't play games, Esteban. You won't like the outcome. I'll just keep putting holes in your body parts." He lowered the pistol, pointing it at Moya's groin. "All the parts until you beg me to stop and start talking."

Moya was breathing hard now, his face twisted in pain. "I need help … medical attention … goddamit, it hurts!"

"Soon. Tell me what I want to know."

"I don't …" Moya shook his head then stopped as Sole raised the pistol again.

"You do. You have the name. You weren't out on the trawler, or I would have arrested you then. You were there, in my home. You murdered my wife and children and my partner."

Sole locked the pain and memories deep inside where they wouldn't be dirtied by what he was doing. He replaced them with something else, deadly and determined.

"All right." Moya nodded sweat streaming down his face. "Yes, I was there, but I didn't do anything. You got to believe that. I just …"

"Stood there while someone cut my children's throats?"

"Okay … okay." Moya spit the words out rapid fire. "I get it. This looks bad, but …"

"Looks bad!" Sole hissed, fire in his eyes.

"You don't understand. There wasn't anything I could do," Moya whimpered through the pain. "He would have killed me."

"Who?" Sole thundered.

"If I tell you, they will kill me ... my family ... everyone."

"And if you don't, what do you think I will do?"

Moya stared down the barrel of the pistol, the black hole of the bore ready to spit fire and send a bullet crashing through the bridge of his nose. "Okay," He clenched his eyes shut, his face twisted with the pain and loss of blood. "His name is Garza ... Alejandro Garza."

"Who sent him?"

"The Cartel ... *Los Salvajes.*"

"Who? Who sent him from the cartel?"

"A man ... they call him Bebé Elizondo."

"Good." Sole nodded. "Where are they?"

"Shit! How the fuck do I know? Mexico somewhere. They don't give their address to someone like me. I do what I'm told, that's all."

"Okay, Mexico somewhere." Sole nodded. "I believe you."

He lifted the pistol. His eyes told Moya what would come next.

"You said you would get me help!"

"I am." Sole aimed at the spot just above Moya's nose.

"You shouldn't be here!" Moya snarled, a trapped animal, lashing out when it realizes there is no hope. "You should have been there ... dead with the others! Now, look at me! Look what you've done." He looked down at his mangled, bloody body, his voice rising to a shriek. "You were supposed to die with them. You shouldn't have survived! You should be dead!"

"Yes, I survived." Sole shook his head. "You won't."

He squeezed the pistol's trigger. As promised, Esteban Moya's suffering ended.

Outside, he stood for a moment looking up at the night

sky. A shooting star streaked past the crescent moon. A sultry breeze ruffled his hair, carrying the fragrance of a nearby magnolia in bloom. He was oblivious.

John Sole had passed through a door and closed it firmly behind him. Life was forever changed. He was no longer a police officer, no longer a father, no longer a husband, no longer a son. He was alone, the sole survivor of that other life.

SIXTY-TWO

Relief

Maria Valdes sat in the dark, sobbing and repeating her prayers. Her muscles twitched, straining against the tape binding her every time the thunder of a gunshot reverberated through the closet door.

She prayed that it would end. Then it did. There was a final roar, and a minute later she heard the rear door open and close. She prayed the unknown man in the ski mask was gone.

When employees arrived and began preparations for the day's menu, they heard sounds from the back storage closet. They were as startled as Maria was relieved when they released her from the closet and called the police. The discovery of Esteban Moya's body, still bound with duct tape and seated in the chair behind the desk sent several scurrying away before the police arrived. There would be questions, and answering questions was dangerous.

Maria remained and told the story of the masked man who had bound her and locked her up before putting a bullet hole through the head of the new owner of *Taqueria*

Ortega. The detectives who responded to the scene conferred with each other and agreed that Esteban Moya's death was most likely part of an ongoing feud between rival crime factions—a feud that, in their minds, resulted in the disappearance and probable death of Bautista Ortega.

The killer left no evidence behind, and they had little expectation of ever solving the murder. The weeks passed, and the investigation went to the back burner as detectives moved on to other more pressing cases, involving more sympathetic victims.

You never knew. One day a break in another case might point at a suspect in the murder, or it might never be solved and end up in the cold case file. The general consensus among the detectives was that Esteban Moya's death was more relief than a concern.

SIXTY-THREE

Unfinished Business

"It is good to have you home." Bebé Elizondo embraced Alejandro Garza the way he might a long-lost brother as he stepped through the front door of the hacienda. "We have missed you."

Garza nodded. "It is good to be home."

"All went well? Our problems resolved ... the message sent to the gringos?" Bebé motioned his lieutenant to a seat in his office.

"In part," Garza replied truthfully.

"How so?"

"One was not present. We could not complete the assignment as you directed."

Elizondo's eyes narrowed, unaccustomed to failure from Garza. "Explain," he said, his tone harsher than Garza had experienced in the past.

"The detective ... his name is John Sole. He was not home. We had no choice but to eliminate the other targets in the house, but he still lives. I have given orders to Moya to eliminate him as soon as he returns."

"Can we trust Moya to carry out your instructions?" Elizondo asked, sitting back in his chair to consider the report.

"Yes. He wants to please you more than anything else."

"I'm sure he does." Elizondo smiled. "And no doubt, you emphasized the importance of pleasing me."

"I did." Garza nodded, completing his report as always, concise and direct.

He refrained from reminding Elizondo that he had tried to warn him about the dangers of acting in haste without consideration of the consequences. American law enforcement would not be intimidated, and most could not be bought. A student of history, Garza was reminded of the words Japanese Admiral Yamamoto uttered after the sneak attack on Pearl Harbor.

"I fear all we have done is to awaken a sleeping giant and fill him with a terrible resolve."

Garza wondered about the sleeping giant they may have awakened. Like Yamamoto, he understood that once committed to such actions, there could be no going back.

Unconcerned with sleeping giants, Bebé made plans for continued shipments into the United States. Alternate methods would take his products into the North American narcotics market.

There seemed no end to the stream of proposals. Each claimed they had a better way to get the shipments to the north, eager for a share of the enormous profits.

Two weeks had passed when Garza came to the hacienda for lunch with Elizondo. They sat in the dining room alone, the children at school, Sofia and her kitchen staff withdrawing to allow the men to discuss business in private.

"I have news," Garza said without preamble.

"Yes?" Bebé smiled as he rolled a tortilla to dip into the fragrant *sopa* Sofia had prepared for them. "Speak."

"Moya is dead."

Elizondo's hand halted midway to his mouth with the tortilla. Then he shrugged. Death was part of their business. "That is unfortunate. Do we have another to replace him?"

"There is always another," Garza said. "The problem is that his work remains unfinished."

"Unfinished? You mean …"

"Yes. The detective was not killed. John Sole lives. The other, *la rata*, is in hiding."

"Very fortunate for this detective, but temporary. As for the rat, it is only a matter of time before he is found." Elizondo dropped the tortilla and folded his hands on the table, considering this news. "Do we know who killed Moya? This cannot go unanswered."

"No." Garza shook his head. "There is no word, and our contacts tell us the police have no leads."

"All right. Have our people identify the killer. When they do …" Elizondo shrugged. "Do what must be done."

"Yes." Garza nodded.

Elizondo noted Garza's expression. "I know you did not agree with me about taking action, making a point to the Americans."

"I did not," Garza said.

"Yet, you perform your assignments to perfection and without question. I am fortunate to have one as loyal as you at my side." Elizondo thought for a moment. "You may have been correct, my friend. I allowed my emotions to overcome my reason. That is never a good thing. Not in our business."

Out of respect, Garza made no response. Bebé apologized in his own way.

"So, what do you recommend now? Elizondo continued.

"Nothing."

"Nothing? Because you are displeased?"

"Not at all." Garza gave a slight shake of his head. "You ask what we should do about Moya's death and the detective. I say we should do nothing. Continue making your arrangements for shipments to the north. Conduct business as usual."

"And you?" Bebé asked.

"I will watch. When the time is right, I will handle our unfinished business."

SIXTY-FOUR

Only Justice

They hung suspended before him. Shaye, Samantha, Bobby, Travis. Images in his mind, so clear, so real, sometimes it seemed he could reach out and touch them. But they were just images, memories burned into the neurons in his brain, nothing more.

He swiveled on the bar stool. The images followed. He lifted the glass from the bar's sticky surface and drank the cleansing, burning liquid. The images remained but not so clear. He sipped again and again, until they blurred.

Drinking them away, made him feel guilty. He sipped again, and the guilt melted away too. The alcohol settled like a glowing ember in the center of his chest, searing away the memories, turning them to ash for a while.

He was moving again now, restless. Moving was best.

He roamed through small towns and big cities, country roads and barren desert. Nameless towns and blank faces were his world. He was one with the teeming humanity that surrounded him, losing his identity but finding his reason to continue.

John Sole became another face in the crowd, an everyman and a no-man all in one, anonymous and alone. Inside, an invisible fire burned, scorching away his former life until only the flames remained, searing hot and dangerous.

He understood now. The lines between good and evil Captain Pointer spoke of didn't exist, not really. Good and evil tumbled through the world together like leaves tossed on a cold wind. They blew through lives randomly. Avoiding them was like trying to avoid the wind. It was everywhere.

You could take shelter for a time, but as soon as you stepped out, the wind would smack you in the face. If it was a good wind, you were lucky. If it was an evil one … well, those were the breaks. No, there were no lines. There was only justice.

For John Sole it was even simpler than that. One day, he would find them, or they would find him.

Next in the Sole Justice series

vinci-books.com/roadtojustice

John Sole's quest for vengeance leads him to a small Texas border town that hides a vicious secret.

The former cop's hunt for the cartel that murdered his family brings him to Creosote, where he meets Isabella, a café owner. When Isabella's son rescues a captive girl, Sole must confront a dark underworld.

Turn the page for a free preview…

Road to Justice: Chapter One

THE LIGHT WAS GONE

He was going to be a rich man. A broad grin spread across his face as the cantina door slammed shut behind him. The music and din from inside faded. The grin remained. Visions of the US dollars that would soon fill his pockets fluttered around in his alcohol-fogged brain.

He stumbled a little in the dark, making his way toward the curb, feeling the desperate urge to take a piss. He looked up and down the narrow street. It was empty.

"Not here, in front of the cantina, you *tonto*," he mumbled to himself, lifting a finger to his head and tapping it to remind himself that good manners required him to at least move away a few feet.

With his hands at his crotch working down his trouser zipper, he shuffled stiff-legged to a point about ten feet down the street from the cantina entrance. A final look around to ensure no one was watching, and he exposed himself, letting loose a stream that splashed happily in the gutter. Mario Acosta sighed and smiled, a happy man.

Shaking out the last few drops, he zipped up and arched

his back with a pleasing shiver he always got after a good piss. Then he wiped his hands on the sides of his pants and turned to stagger toward his car parked in a side alley halfway down the block.

He passed the stuccoed wall of a residence, and the fragrance of gardenias hit him in the face. The sickly sweet odor on top of the tequila made the bile rise a little in his throat, and he hurried past the house. Pissing in the street was one thing, but puking out your guts was something else. He was no little girl whose stomach was turned by a few shots of tequila.

Of course, *a few* was a relative term, and Mario had lost count hours ago. He had been drinking at Rosita's, his favorite cantina in Torreón since noon. It was now past eleven in the evening.

He stumbled along the pavement, squinting with one eye shut at a single street light. There, he thought. There in that bright light, just in the alley is where I left my car. Not so far, is it? First, move one leg and then the other.

Like a man on stilts, Mario wobbled and walked, two steps, then three then, *mierda*—shit, a step backward and to the side. He put a hand out to steady himself against a building. For a moment, he considered resting his back against the wall and sliding down to the pavement to relax a little, maybe take a short nap.

No. He shook his head. No. Get to your car. You can sleep there until you feel better. If you sleep here on the street, *los policías*—the cops—will find you.

Yes, but they probably won't arrest you, he thought, reasoning with himself. That would make too much work for them.

True, but it was more likely they would take turns

pissing on you as you slept. That would be sport for them, not work.

Mind made up, Mario continued his slow, unsteady progress toward the street lamp and his car in the adjacent alley.

"Too much tequila," he mumbled and laughed. "But why not? I am going to be rich! I deserve a night to party. No working in a grimy factory making car parts for American Chevrolets like *mi papa*."

Not Mario Acosta. No, Mario Acosta had found a way to become rich, and by the grace of God and the Virgin Mary, he was going to be un *hombre rico como un puto rey!*—rich as a fucking king!

He grinned and pushed himself forward. Almost there, a few more steps and then…

Mario stopped just outside the circle of light thrown by the street lamp and breathed in the warm night air. With great deliberation, he lifted his right leg and planted his foot in the light. He stood for a moment, relishing his victory at navigating all the way down the street without falling and breaking his neck.

He turned to the alley. Sure enough, there was his car, a cheap Japanese model ten years old. That would change, he thought. Soon a better one that always starts and with tires that don't go flat from driving over stones in the road.

With a hand extended, he leaned toward the car until his fingers made contact with the warm metal. Ah, success. He rubbed his hand back and forth over the dusty surface as he searched with the other for the keys in his pocket.

There, they are. He pulled the leather key fob out and held the jingling bits of metal, sparkling in front of his eyes, squinting at them in the light from the streetlamp.

"There you are," he giggled.

A rush of feet over the pavement behind him caught his attention. He turned in time to glimpse three figures in dark clothes run into the circle of light and toward him. Something heavy and hard, struck him in the temple, sending blinding white pain through his eyes. Then the light was gone.

Road to Justice: Chapter Two

MEANEST SON OF A BITCH AROUND

The rifle shot cracked like a bullwhip in the hot, dry air. Across the green ribbon of water, a half-dozen people scurried around on the bank searching for what scant cover there was. There wasn't much along this part of the Mexico-United States border.

A woman waved a hand from behind a low, dense pile of brush. Her voice carried plainly across the river. "*¡Por favor! No dispares ¡Hay niños aquí!*"

"What she say?" Ralph 'Lucky' Martin levered another .30-30 round into the Winchester Model 94, western-style carbine and squinted through the scope, sighting on the pile of brush.

"Didn't get it all, but I heard *niños*. That means kids. They got some young'uns with 'em, I suppose." Stu Pearce stood up on the toes of his boots to peer across the hundred yards of water. "I don't see 'em, but there's a lot of rustlin' about in the brush."

"Fuck, I didn't hear no shit about no kids. Maybe she

was trying to say she got beenos ... you know, *frijoles* for super." Martin gave a mean, short laugh.

Kneeling with one knee on the ground and the other supporting his elbow, he settled the butt of the Winchester into his shoulder. With a quick turn of his head, he shot a stream of tobacco juice from his brown-stained lips. It sailed in a long arc into the dust as he turned back to the scope and rested his finger on the trigger.

"Hold on, Lucky!" Pearce stepped closer and looked down at Martin. "I heard her say *niños* ... children. We ain't supposed to be shootin' children. Shit, we ain't supposed to be shootin' no one."

"I ain't shot no one ... yet." Martin looked up, and the same nasty smile was on his face. "Besides, who's gonna tell? You?"

"Boss says hold 'em on the other side of the river. That's all." Pearce shook his head. "No bloodshed and no killin'. Just make 'em cross like they's supposed to ... where they's supposed to."

The woman who had called out took advantage of the interlude to change position. She scrambled along the ground towards a mesquite that would offer more protection than the pile of brush and river grass along the bank.

"Fuck!" Martin jumped to his feet.

He let loose a shot that kicked up dirt about a yard from her feet as she scurried towards the tree tugging two small children by the hands. They were toddlers and couldn't keep up. By necessity, the woman dragged them over the stony ground through the briars and brush as they wailed in pain from scratches and bruises.

"Dammit, Lucky!" Pearce shouted. "Range is too far for that cheap-ass scope of yours. Hold your fire, or you're liable to be off and hit one."

He'd seen Martin like this before. When his blood was up there was no calming him down short of killing him, and Stu Pearce was not going to try that.

"Who gives a fuck?" Martin shouted back.

He jacked another round into the chamber and fired at the mesquite. The smack of the bullet into the trunk was audible on the U.S. side of the river.

A man stood up from the brush and waved his hands. "Hey, *gringos*!" He jerked his forearm up in the universal obscenity. "Fuck you, *gringos*! *Vete a la mierda Tu madre es una puta!*" He jumped up and down to draw Martin's attention away from the woman trying to conceal herself and her two children behind the small tree. "Fuck you, man! Your mother is a whore!"

It worked. Lucky Martin levered round after round into the Winchester, firing them off in rapid succession.

"Son of a bitch," he muttered as he tracked the man scrambling along the river bank on his hands and knees away from the mesquite.

Some of the rounds hit the water along the shore, raising little geysers that sprayed down on the man. Others thudded into the surrounding mud.

A howl of pain echoed across the water. The man rolled over on his back, his hands holding a bloody knee as he rocked back and forth in pain.

"*Hijo de puta!* You son of a bitch!" he shouted then turned on his side to stare at the rifle pointed at his face from three hundred feet away.

"Goddammit, Lucky!" Pearce shouted. "You hit him! How we gonna explain that to the boss?"

"Ain't gonna be nothin' to explain when I finish them off."

"Be sensible," Pearce tried to reason. "Somebody will report it. Word will get out."

"Won't be no one to report it."

"You mean ..." Pearce shook his head. "No, Lucky. You can't do that. I don't want no part of murderin'."

"Then stay the fuck away, and you won't have no part in it." Eyes on fire with rage, he turned to Pearce. "Don't get in my way, Stu."

The man on the ground shouted something toward the pile of brush. Two more children popped up, these older, nine or ten, Pearce figured. They ran headlong to the mesquite where they huddled down beside their mother and siblings. The narrow tree could not hide the squirming mass of bodies that sought cover there from the Winchester's bullets. It was only a matter of time.

Pearce tried one more time. "Lucky, you can't do this. I know your blood is up, but later, when things calm down, there'll be hell to pay, and you'll be wishin' you hadn't."

Martin swiveled, bringing the rifle to bear on Pearce from a distance of three feet. Hands stretched out, palms up, Pearce shook his head and backed away. "Take it easy, Lucky!"

"Warned you once, Pearce. I won't say it again. Get in my way, and I'll put one in you and tell the boss them Mexes over there did it, and I had to take care of them for it." He sneered. "I'll bet there won't be no problem then ... me defending one of his men and all. Probably give me a bonus for it."

Pearce wished he hadn't left his rifle in the truck. He wouldn't have used it except in self-defense, but right now, he was defenseless. He backed up another ten feet, watching the muzzle of the rifle and Martin's finger on the trigger.

The argument was over. Lucky Martin had won, as he

always did. It was one of the reasons he had earned his nickname.

Thick and stocky of build Martin was a bully at heart. Most people gave him a wide berth, but that wasn't why they called him Lucky. In truth, although he was far from being the smartest man around, he still managed to win at things, whether it was cards, betting on horses or claiming the prettiest, youngest whore for himself over in Creosote. He always managed to come out on top.

Today he won the debate with Stu Pearce. What started as some mean spirited, but harmless, plunking with the rifle to scare them was about to turn into a blood bath. Pearce knew that Lucky wasn't really all that lucky. He was just the meanest son of a bitch around, and most people gave him a wide berth, for safety's sake.

Lucky turned back to the man still lying across the river, holding his leg. Their eyes met across the distance. The man was unflinching, awaiting his fate.

"That's right," Martin whispered, resting his cheek on the butt stock. "You hold still for just a minute."

The man did. It was the only means he had left to protect his family.

Lucky Martin raised his nose for a second checking the wind. There was none.

At a range of a little over a hundred yards, there was no need to adjust the scope's elevation for the angle. He let the crosshairs rest on the center of the man's face.

Through the scope, he could see the man's eyes, intent, watching, waiting. He nodded. Martin jerked his eyes away from the scope.

"What the fuck does that mean?"

"What?" Stu Pearce asked, hopeful that Lucky had changed his mind.

"Motherfucker nodded at me like I need his permission to put a round through his head."

"He's just trying to protect the woman and little ones."

"Yeah, well it's too late for that."

Martin settled the rifle back on his shoulder. "You think I need your fucking permission," He shouted across the water. "I don't! You're a dead man!" Eyes squinting through the scope, his finger touched the trigger.

Road to Justice: Chapter Three

CREOSOTE

She walked down the center of the gravel road that passed through town. The gravel was firm there, packed down by the trucks and cars passing over it and made for easier walking.

The red glitter polish on her toenails flashed in the sunlight with each step. The polish was the reason she wore sandals with thin leather soles. On most days, she would have been barefoot.

The soles of her feet were tough enough to walk along the road without protection. She'd grown up here, had walked these roads and surrounding scrub country since she was old enough to stand on two feet. But the polish was new, just applied after her shower this morning, and she wanted to protect it, at least for a day or two.

Isabella Palmeras had lived in the tiny backwater place called Creosote, Texas all of her life. Calling it a town would have been too grandiose. The collection of dusty block buildings and frame houses that made up the community did not even appear as a dot on maps.

Creosote was a gathering place more than anything else, a stopping place where people looked around and took stock before continuing on. Some worked their way farther west to the Rio Grande and Mexico beyond. Others saw nothing here but scrub and dust and moved on to Laredo to the north or Brownsville to the south.

A few stayed. When they did, it was because Creosote was what they were looking for. There was no newspaper, no law enforcement, at least not within twenty miles, no town council, or mayor. No website or Wikipedia entry would show up for anyone searching the place online. For all practical purposes, Creosote was nowhere.

Over the last century and a half, the ones who did stay arrived without fanfare. Mostly, they just showed up one day, stumbling across the place as they made their way across the vast South Texas plains. If ever there were an accidental assemblage of persons congregated in one place for no apparent reason, it was the community of Creosote.

As in most out of the way places, order was arrived at through mutual agreement. That doesn't mean that everyone got along. They didn't.

There were disagreements, and when no satisfactory solution to disputes could be arrived at, the issue was frequently settled by force. In the old days, Creosote had seen its share of gun battles in the street. These were not the fast draw duels pictured in Hollywood movies. They were dirty, messy affairs, with blood being shed at close quarters in an unspeakably brutal fashion.

That is not to say that Creosote was lawless. There was law of a sort. There had always been some local Texas lord who ruled over things, serving as judge, jury, and executioner when necessary. These days Tom Krieg and his partner Raul Zabala sat enthroned as the lords of the prairie, enforcing their own form of justice.

Dressed in denim shorts and a flowered cotton halter top, Isabella swung her long brown legs through the morning air, relishing the sun on her bare shoulders. A breeze blew in off the plains carrying with it the scent of sage and the acrid taste of the dry dust that was everywhere. She sucked it in savoring the smells and tastes like a person sampling a favorite wine.

The quarter-mile walk from her small frame home at one end of town to the place where she worked took only a few minutes. The business had no name. There was no need for one. Everyone knew what it was and who owned it.

Isabella's grandfather started it after he came back from the war in 1945. If someone had to say where they were going, they would just say, "To the café."

Like her grandfather, Isabella served two meals a day for those interested. These consisted of a breakfast of eggs, bacon, black beans, and tortillas and an afternoon meal of hamburgers. The evening was reserved strictly for drinking. It was seven AM, and she walked down the center of the road to prepare the morning meal for the hungry and those just looking for something to fill their guts and ease their hangovers.

She stopped on the concrete block in front that served as a step, turned the knob, and pushed the door open. There were no locks. They wouldn't have done any good anyway. If someone wanted to get in, they could, but no one ever had. By mutual agreement among Creosote's residents, the café was Isabella's and not to be touched or disturbed in any fashion on pain of having your ass beaten by the rest of the inhabitants.

A noise on the morning breeze caught her attention. She turned her eyes out toward the open plains.

Vehicles approached. No doubt Krieg or Zabala or some of their men. Plumes of dust billowed high behind three fast-moving trucks, hanging in the air for a minute before dissipating in the breeze.

A frown crossed her face. "Wonder what they're in such a hurry for?" she muttered.

She glanced across the road to another low-walled block building. Oh, that.

Mazey's whore house was already open, the door flung wide in welcome to the approaching customers. The girls could be seen moving about inside cleaning things up from the previous night's festivities. Mazey herself sat in a rocker on the ground outside the front door. She lifted a hand and waved.

"Mornin' Isabella."

"Mornin' Mazey. Looks like you got business coming."

"Yep." Mazey nodded. "For both of us, I expect."

Like Isabella, Mazey Higgins had lived in Creosote all of her life. Older than Isabella by twenty years, she had seen the boom days when drill crews had come through looking for oil. They had stayed for a while then moved on. Many of the shacks and buildings in town had been left by the drill crews, taken over by various residents and newcomers as needed.

"Guess I better, get some food going inside. Talk to you later, Mazey."

"Yeah, me too. Gotta make sure the girls got things in order." Mazey lifted her sturdy bulk from the rocker, pulled her bathrobe tighter around her, and shuffled inside in her slippers. She called over her shoulder, "Have a nice day, Isabella."

The sound of a compressor and air wrench vibrated through the air. Isabella walked around to the shed at the side of the café and peered through the open door.

"Sandy, come help with breakfast. Looks like a crowd coming."

A blond boy of eighteen poked his head above the engine cowling of a four-wheeler. "Be there in a minute, Mom. Just got to put this back together for Mr. Westerfield. He said he'd pay me thirty bucks to get her running."

Sherman 'Sherm' Westerfield lived in the backcountry about five miles out of Creosote. He had become a sort of grandfather figure to Sandy, always finding some small job for him so that he could pay him for it. For some reason, he had developed a soft spot for the boy. People thought it was because old Sherm's own boy had died in Afghanistan some years back. Whatever the reason, Isabella suspected that he would just dole out money to the boy if she weren't around to make sure he earned it.

"Did you get it running?"

"What do you think?" Sandy grinned.

Isabella smiled. Her son had a gift for tinkering with engines, continually pulling things apart to see how they ran, and reassembling them, so they ran even better.

"Alright, then. Put it back together. I expect Sherm will be in this morning for breakfast." She looked across the plain at the approaching dust cloud kicked up by the trucks. "They sure as hell are hauling ass. I better get moving."

She turned toward the café door, calling over her shoulder. "I could use a hand cleaning up after breakfast."

"Yes, Ma'am. I have to take this old buggy out for a spin first and make sure it runs."

"Take it for a spin, but don't get lost for the day."

"Yes, Ma'am."

Sandy disappeared behind the engine cowling. Isabella went into the café and began breaking eggs into a bowl. Across the road, Mazey had the girls cleaning themselves up for the approaching clientele.

Other residents slept off their hangovers or sipped their morning coffee on the cinder block stoops of their dusty shacks. Life continued in its typically slow fashion on the little patch of Texas dirt known as Creosote.

Grab your copy...
vinci-books.com/roadtojustice

About the Author

Glenn Trust is the author of the bestselling *Hunters, Sole Justice, and Journey Series* of mystery/thriller/suspense novels. He has also written standalone works, including *Dying Embers, Mojave Sun,* and short stories.

There are no superheroes or knights in shining armor in his stories. According to Trust, knights are for fairy tales. His books are gritty and based in the real world, with characters who face their frailties while dealing with their roles in the story. The heroes are average people doing the best they can.

The villains, as real villains often do, look like us. Trust's monsters hide behind the smiling faces that pass us on the street. They look like us, and this makes them more frightening.

He is a Georgia native but has lived in most regions of the country at one time or another. Varied experiences, from construction worker to police officer, corporate executive to city manager, color and provide insight into the characters he creates. His stories are known for detailed plots, solid research, and realism.

Today, he writes full-time and lives quietly with his wife and two dogs, Gunner and Charlie.